Panic seized him...

David was surrounded by jabbering women. Someone gave the *skaggy* a knife. She quickly cut the laces on the deerskin around his ribs and removed it. There was a gasp from the onlookers. Most of his body was well tanned, but it was white where the binding had been.

The *skaggy* touched the pale flesh over his ribs. It was as if she thought there might be some magic in keeping part of himself so white. She placed the knife between her teeth and touched him with both hands. Then she stepped back and stared at his privates. She raised a hand and made a grabbing motion in the air. She took the knife from her mouth with the other hand and made a cutting motion. The pantomime was clear enough. Behind her an old crone cackled.

Call The Beast Thy Brother

WILLIAM O. TURNER

CHARTER BOOKS, NEW YORK

All of the characters in this book are fictitious and
any resemblance to actual persons, living or dead,
is purely coincidental.

CALL THE BEAST THY BROTHER

A Charter Book / published by arrangement with
Doubleday & Company, Inc.

PRINTING HISTORY
Doubleday edition published 1973
Berkley Medallion edition / November 1977
Charter edition / August 1986

ISBN: 0-441-09031-1

Charter Books are published by The Berkley Publishing Group,
200 Madison Avenue, New York, New York 10016.
PRINTED IN THE UNITED STATES OF AMERICA

Chapter 1

He knelt on the bluff in wet brush and watched the *Maria Kane* weigh anchor. She had a deckload of logs and squared timbers, and he guessed she would put in at Port Townsend tonight. She would want daylight and tomorrow's ebb before undertaking the long gusty passage down the Strait of Juan de Fuca to Cape Flattery and the Pacific.

She raised a jib, which brought her about, then her foresail. She slid out of the misty little bay into the choppy narrows. Spreading canvas, she swung defiantly close to the north point of the bay and swept out of sight.

He rose, staring after her, and at this moment the world seemed an internal thing. There was no substance to anything except what his senses gave it. He studied the hazy islands across the narrows, the empty bay, the Indian shacks on the beach; all were captive within the gray sky-boundary of himself. The feeling frightened him. He had been too long in the woods, too long in the February rain, too long without a meal. Laughing at himself, he turned into the trees at his back.

He knew this piece of woods well now, after four days of hiding in it. He worked leisurely through the tangled brush at the edge of it, holding his arms high to keep them dry. After a few yards the brush thinned and

1

there was only the soft duff under the big trees. They were firs mostly and an occasional giant cedar. Then there was the maple he had climbed when he heard the search party coming. He paused under it now, thinking how he had hugged the trunk and prayed that no one would look up. Yes, prayed. His father would appreciate that, if he ever got the chance to tell the old man the story.

The mate had been in charge of the party, and it had carried rifles. Jumping ship had seemed a small enough infidelity until he saw the rifles. He had grasped the monstrousness of it then, from the captain's point of view. He could almost hear the little rooster clucking orders. Take him whole and able if you can, Mister, and we'll stripe him when we get him aboard. But we can't have this sort of thing, you know, so take him at any cost, even if you have to shoot him.

No one had looked up. But the next day the Nisquallies had come, puffing the cigars with which the captain had hired them. He had seen none of them in the woods before, but they came straight to the maple tree as if they were certain he would be there. They were armed with clubs but they had made it plain that they were gentle by nature and preferred *mahkook* to violence. He had bought them off with the coin in his pocket. Most of it was copper, which was fortunate, because they valued that more than silver or gold. One of them had tried to demonstrate that it could be brightened with earth and spittle. Another insisted that urine was better, and he had demonstrated, too.

He had left them piddling and polishing. They made no attempt to follow him. That night he had gone down to the beach and eaten a handful of seaweed. It had

2

made him briefly ill, and afterward he was hungrier than ever.

The woods were less than a mile wide, a strip along the shore that widened out to merge with endless timberland to the north and northeast. East and southward lay the Nisqually prairie, a great uneven expanse of brush and grass that stretched off toward the distant Cascades and the great snow-peak looming out of them. He came out of the trees in view of the palisaded fort on a creek bank half a mile away. This was Fort Nisqually. It housed a Hudson's Bay post whose function was to provide food for other posts on the West Coast. The company claimed title to thousands of acres of the prairie, on which it grazed great numbers of sheep and cattle and grew potatoes and wheat.

He asked Indian herders the location of the mission, or he tried to. He knew scarcely a dozen words of Chinook, the trade jargon of the Northwest Coast, and they spoke no English. They understood the word *Jesus*, though, and he gathered from their gestures that the mission lay southeast, probably straight upcreek. He set off in that direction, avoiding the fort. Hudson's Bay people might not be hospitable to ship jumpers.

A smeared sun was trying to break through the overcast, but there was a brisk wind on the prairie. His wet shirt and undershirt caught the chill from the wind and held it against his skin. His duck trousers chafed him. It seemed as if he walked miles along the bluffs above the creek before three big log buildings came into view, solid structures on a slope above a branch in the creek. A long, two-story building had three stone chimneys and was obviously living quarters. Behind it stood a big log barn with fenced pasture behind it. The third building stood off by itself a bit. Its little belltower marked it as a church.

He pointed for the living quarters, trying to remember the pastor's name, as he had been trying off and on for four days. He had never met the man, but there had been a good deal of talk about him in eastern church circles when he had gone to found a mission on the shore of Puget Sound. Talk and fund-raising. That had been three or four years ago. Meanwhile the Whitman massacre had overshadowed all other missionary news and crowded this man's name out of memory.

He knocked on the door, possessed again by the feeling that everything existed within himself. After a long wait, the door was opened by a squat Indian girl in a shapeless green gingham dress. At that instant the name came to him.

"I want to see Dr. Cargo," he said.

She regarded him shyly and doubtfully, and he didn't blame her. He was hatless, his denim shirt was still wet enough to cling to his skin, there was a quarter inch of stubble on his face. She gave him a slow nod and closed the door.

He waited two or three shivering minutes and was about to knock again when the door was opened by a tall, scowling man in a dark suit and shoestring tie.

"Yes?"

"Dr. Cargo?" It could be no one else.

"Yes?"

"I'm off the *Maria Kane*. I've been——"

"She's sailed?"

"Yes, sir."

"You jumped ship?"

"In a manner of speaking. The captain broke his

4

word to me. You see, we'd agreed—''

''I dare say you have a story calculated to tear my heart out, and I haven't time to hear it just now. Go around to the back. I'll tell the girl to feed you.''

''I could use a change of clothes, too.''

Dr. Alexander Cargo drew himself up, eyebrows raised. He was an imposing man in a rather hawkish way, with glaring eyes and a large nose. ''We've nothing to spare. You can sit by the kitchen fire for a few minutes and dry out if you like.''

''I'm a Methodist.'' It wasn't easy to grin at this man without feeling insolent. ''Does that help?''

Dr. Cargo had started to close the door. He jerked it open again, his scowl tempered by an underlying glint of curiosity.

''Really? Say the Apostles' Creed for me.''

''I believe in God, the Father Almighty, Maker of heaven and earth, and in Jesus Christ, his only son–''

''Good heavens, you do know it.'' There was a sudden friendly laugh. ''Come in, come in. You're probably a fast-talking blackguard. You'll probably steal my watch, but at least you've been to Sunday school. Captain Hammet broke his word, you say?''

''It's a long story, but he did.''

They went through a hallway into a parlor. There were braided rugs on the floor and a fire in the fireplace. There was only one window, paned with greased paper, and most of the light came from the fire. The furniture was homemade, solid and comfortable-looking.

A woman came in from another room, halting suddenly when she saw a visitor. She was young, dark, slender. She wore a dark silk dress with white collar and cuffs. It gave her an aspect of both primness and stylishness.

"We have a beached sailor," Dr. Cargo said. "May I present Nail."

"Nail. David Nail."

"Mr. Nail, my wife. Captain Hammet broke his word to Mr. Nail. Can you imagine that? Don't you think we might stake a mistreated Christian seaman to some dry clothes and perhaps some bacon and hot-cakes?"

The correct ministerial words honed by an underlying suspicion, David Nail thought. Ministers should never be sarcastic. It made pouting children of them.

"I'll speak to Neena," Mrs. Cargo said.

She went back the way she had come. David moved to the fireplace and put his back to its warm caress.

"Nail," Dr. Cargo said. "N-a-i-l?"

"Yes." It was coming now.

"Not a common name. There's Dr. Samu—"

"Neither is Cargo." He couldn't resist interrupting, dragging it out.

"There's a Dr. Samuel Nail at the First Church in New York, of course."

"My father."

"Your f—!" Dr. Cargo let surprise prevent him from pronouncing the word. He froze for a moment in speechless incredibility. "Good heavens! Well, we'll have to take care of you, won't we? This is a pleasure. Good heavens!"

David found a poker and jabbed at the fire; then he put his back to it again. It was convenient to have a father whose name would assure hospitality from prac-tically any Protestant minister anywhere, but there was something uncomfortable about it, too. Explanations were in order, but he was damned if he was going to be in a hurry to make them.

"You're very kind," he said.

Mrs. Cargo came in with a pair of sailcloth jeans and an atrociously striped red-and-white shirt over her arm.

"Dorothy, this is Dr. Samuel Nail's son. Can you imagine? Dr. Nail of the First Church."

She raised her eyebrows and gave the visitor a new appraisal. She cocked her head at him and produced a look that was warm, curious, welcoming.

"Yes, I've heard Dr. Nail several times." She smiled now. "My family is Presbyterian but my mother was Methodist before she married. In fact, she's a great admirer of Dr. Nail."

Her husband took the clothing she had brought and held it at arm's length. "These won't do at all. Don't you think my blue suit might fit him? It's a bit natty for a man of the cloth and I've hardly worn it." He held up the striped shirt, holding it by the shoulders. "Good heavens! Makes me want to come to attention and salute. It's what we call a trade shirt. The louder they are, the better the Indians like 'em."

Dr. Cargo flung the clothing back to his wife and took David by the arm. "Come. We'll see what we can find."

David moved reluctantly away from the fire, his clothes steaming. As he left the room, he looked back at the woman and met her eyes. They were big and black in the dim, dancing light. She smiled gently, swallowing at the same time as if some surge of emotion must be kept inside her. It was the kind of smile a woman gives a sick child when she is going to leave him for a little while.

7

They climbed a staircase and went down a narrow hall to the doctor's bedroom. He delved into a closet and came out with a gray-blue suit with a long-tailed coat. He laid it on the bed and extracted underwear, socks, shirt, collar, and a shoestring tie from bureau drawers.

"I don't need all this, Doctor. Just a shirt and a pair of trousers to wear until my stuff dries out."

"Put 'em on." Dr. Cargo had a way of making elaborate gestures as he spoke. "Bring your wet ones down and we'll have the girl wash and iron 'em. You'll stay with us, of course."

"I thought I'd go overland to Oregon City."

"On foot? It's a hundred and fifty miles of the roughest trail imaginable. Put on the clothes. We'll talk about your plans later. I'll see you downstairs."

Alone, he stripped and sponged off with icy water from a stone pitcher. He got his razor from a pocket of his wet trousers, gave himself a scratchy shave, and got dressed.

He kept remembering the woman's smile. She's no older than I am, he thought—well, not more than a year or two. Twenty-six at the most. He must be around thirty-five. She's probably just bursting with Christian love and charity for Everybody. Like Mother, like all ministers' wives. As soon as they get married they do their damnedest to be saints.

They did very well, too, he thought, most of them, most of the time. The protests, the little vanities, the sharp words got buried very deep indeed. So deep that on rare occasions they burst out unpredictably. He remembered Mother. He remembered the time she had tongue-lashed a peddler whose only offense was to catch her at a busy moment. She had whipped out at him with a torrent

8

of ugliness that had frightened all three children so badly that they had run into the kitchen. . . . And the servants. It had been hard to keep servants more than a few months. And the children. Even when he was small it had seemed to him that some of the sudden bitter scoldings he got were really meant for his father. At other times and just as suddenly there had been saccharine love words, lavish endearments. . . .

The starched collar and shoestring tie were an uncomfortable elegance, but the doctor seemed to expect him to put them on and he did. He found his hosts waiting for him in the parlor. Alexander Cargo leaped to his feet. They had moved a small table close to the fire and, with a sweeping gesture, he pulled out the chair that had been placed at it. The man's high-spirited hospitality puzzled David. He didn't know whether to take it seriously or for the mockery it sometimes seemed.

"I'm not cold any longer, Doctor. Fact is, I'm burning up."

"Good heavens, David. You haven't a fever?"

"I probably have." He and the doctor got on either side of the table and lifted it back from the fire. "I don't think it's an illness. When you've been outdoors for several days in cold weather, your temperature is apt to come up when you come inside, you know."

The Indian girl in the sacklike green dress appeared with a tray. Mrs. Cargo took it from her and set it on the table. As David sat down, she laid a hand on his forehead.

"You do have a fever," she said.

There were hotcakes in front of him and several pieces of bacon, thick and crisp with bulging eyes of fat. "I'm not going to be sick—I'm much too hungry. I expect I'm going to be very drowsy in a little while. If I can get a spot of sleep, I'll be fine."

"I'm going to put you to bed and doctor you." She was pouring him a cup of coffee. "I'm a very good doctor."

"It occurs to me that David might have studied medicine himself," her husband said, pulling up a chair. "I'll have a cup of that, I think."

"One year," David said. He poured sorghum over the hotcakes and forked a wedge into his mouth. "Then I gave in to Father and switched to divinity school. Then I switched to law."

"This was at—?"

"Harvard, Wesleyan, William and Mary."

"Good heavens. Where did you graduate?"

"I didn't."

Dr. Cargo poured honey-thick cream into his coffee and passed the pitcher to David. "I understand the difficulties of a young man waiting for his call. There are so many opportunities."

There are so many whores and so much liquor, David thought. He wanted to say it aloud, and he almost did. He wanted to shock them, to make it plain that he rejected churchy primness. But the words weren't entirely true; whores and liquor hadn't really been the problem. Moreover, he had the feeling that he would seem merely brash in a youthful way and not shock them at all. Ministers and their wives did not shock easily.

"You were going to tell us about Captain Hammet," the doctor said.

"I gather you know him."

10

"I sold him his load of timber. He came here for dinner one night. Dorothy was quite taken with him."

Dorothy Cargo had poured herself a cup of coffee and had sat down a little apart from the table. "I'm always taken with captains," she said.

"I don't understand about the timber," David said. "You sold it to him?"

"I have a timber claim and a water-power mill. There's no reason why a missionary shouldn't make a little money on the side, is there? I have a man in charge, of course, so the enterprise takes little of my time. There's a huge demand for timber in California, what with the gold rush and all."

David found himself wolfing the food. They watched him in silence, and he suddenly felt the need to talk.

"Maybe it was an exaggeration to say the captain broke his word to me. But he did mislead me. You see, I came around the Horn on the *Gemini*, as a passenger. I found myself stranded in Sacramento. I—well, I lost most of my money in a card game. I didn't have enough for passage to Portland, so I offered to work my way on the *Maria Kane*. He said the ship was bound for Oregon, and I assumed that meant Portland or Vancouver. He said he was short-handed but he thought he could replace me at Portland. I swear he said Portland. If he couldn't, I would have to stay on for the trip back to Sacramento. Well, it turned out we came straight up to Port Townsend. We unloaded some fruit and freight there and I found a beached sailor who agreed to take my berth. The captain wouldn't accept him. Claimed he knew the man and that he was unreliable. So when we put in here, I jumped."

Alexander Cargo nodded, eyebrows raised, lips pursed.

"He never intended to put in at Portland. I know that now," David said. "And there's another thing. He had a man flogged. Maybe he had it coming—he went to sleep on watch—but it didn't endear the captain to me."

"That's preposterous!" Dorothy Cargo said. "If Captain Hammet shows up here again, I won't have him in this house. I mean it, Alex."

"Ah, my dear," the doctor purred. "Going to sleep on watch is a grave matter. The captain was within his rights."

Rights, David thought. Rules. Ministers were dedicated to a confusion of rights and rules.

"Ten lashes with a broad strap," he said. "The bos'n was decent enough to lay it on flat, and the man wasn't cut to speak of. They left him tied to the foremast for most of a watch. That was the worst part."

"More humiliating than anything else, I should think. Why do you want to get to Portland?"

"I'm headed for Oregon City."

"You plan to settle there?"

"I don't think so."

"Friends there?"

"No. I just want to see it."

"Good heavens, why?"

"Just a whim. People have left the East and gone there and are starting from scratch to build exactly what they left behind them. I guess I want to ask them why."

"I don't understand."

David laughed. "My father says I suffer from a bad case of aimlessness."

"Is Oregon City meant to be a cure? Or an indulgence?"

"Heavens, Alex." Dorothy Cargo rose and set her cup and saucer on the table. She drew her chair closer and sat down again. "Haven't you heard of a young man traveling just to see the world?"

"Oh, a voyage of adventure. Quite fashionable right now."

"This may sound dreary," David said, "but I've grown up in a life tailored to fit my parents, my teachers, even my brother and sister, but it doesn't seem to fit me. I want to find one that does."

"What does your father say to that?"

"Paul—that's my brother—graduated from Wesleyan and went into the ministry. Father had his heart set on my doing that, too. If I'd gone into law or medicine or business, I think he might have understood. But I haven't done any of those either. He's decided that there's something seriously wrong with me. Oh, he doesn't say so bluntly—he settles for 'aimlessness.' "

"You're probably right about the ministry," Alexander Cargo said. "If you don't feel the call, it's better not to go into it."

There was a smugness to his tone that brought an ever-so-slight reaction from his wife. A small shifting of her eyes, perhaps an interruption in the rhythm of her breathing—David was sure of nothing except that she was annoyed. The doctor smiled and made a gesture calculated to dismiss the subject.

"Good heavens, discussion of a call must be one of the things you're running away from. This—ah, new life that you're looking for. Why not start right here?

13

There's fine money to be made in timber."

"I hadn't thought about that."

"Stay with us a while. Rest up. We'll talk about it later."

"You're very kind."

"That's settled then." Alexander Cargo drew a huge watch from his pocket and scowled at it. "Good heavens, the morning's nearly gone. I've got to get to Chebaulip for a Puyallup funeral. I shall protest, but they'll undoubtedly put the deceased to rest in a tree."

He bounced to his feet and left the room. David drained his cup. Dorothy Cargo was on her feet to refill it.

"No, thanks. I mustn't eat too much all at once. I've been starving for four days."

"That's preposterous. Why did you wait for the ship to sail before you came to us?"

"I couldn't ask you to hide me."

"Alex would have worked something out with the captain."

"I couldn't have known that."

"He'd have got you off. I'd have insisted on it." There were two or three ounces of the thick cream left in the pitcher. She poured it into his cup and he drank it.

Alex came down the stairs at the end of the room. He wore a riding coat that hung to his ankles and a broad-brimmed black hat cocked at a rakish tilt. The coat hung open to reveal a pair of parrot-bill pistols strapped to his waist. He kissed his wife and shook hands with David. As he left, he snatched up a double-barreled rifle that stood beside the door.

"He always goes armed to the teeth," Dorothy said wearily.

14

"My father likes guns, too. He loves to hunt. It doesn't seem to go with the ministry somehow."

"I agree," she said. She laughed. "Alex is a terrible shot. Are you ready for your nap? I'll show you your room."

They went upstairs to a long narrow room at the end of the building. The Indian girl was smoothing the counterpane on a huge bed. A fire was laid in a fireplace at one end of the room.

"*Kloshe*," Dorothy said to the girl, nodding approval of the bed. She pointed to a water pitcher and motioned toward the door. "Get fresh water. *Kloshe chuck*."

The girl took the pitcher and left the room.

"Neena refuses to learn English," Dorothy said. "She doesn't even understand Chinook very well. I'm trying to learn Nisqually, but it's difficult. Alex speaks it well. He's good at languages."

She sat on the bed, bouncing gently to demonstrate its buoyancy. "It has rope springs and two feather ticks. It ought to be comfortable."

"Once I hit it, I'll be gone for the rest of the day."

"Shall I light the fire?"

"Lord no. I'm warmer than ever."

She rose and laid a hand on his forehead again. "You're sweating. That's a good sign."

She left the room and came back at once with a nightshirt, which she laid on a chair. Neena returned with the pitcher of water. Then they left him alone.

There were too many covers on the bed. He stripped back the counterpane and some of the blankets under it. Then he undressed and got into bed naked. There was a knock on the door, and Dorothy appeared with a

15

chamber pot, which she placed into a commode near the bed. Most women would have sent the maid with that, he thought. Her glance brushed the nightshirt that he had left on the chair.

"I promised to doctor you. What shall I do?"

"I'll try to think of something."

He thought that the faintest hint of a smile touched her eyes. She went to the foot of the bed to fuss with the covers he had laid back, arranging them so he could pull them up easily if he wanted them. She came back to stand over him. Her eyes ran the length of his body. She touched his thigh through the covers, just above the knee. The pressure of her fingers was barely perceptible.

"You're nothing but skin and bones. We'll have to fatten you up."

She stepped back and gave him her motherly look. Her eyes were dancing, glistening. And she was gone.

He stared at the beams of the ceiling for a time after the door closed. He tried to recapture the feeling of the world existing within himself. The world and all its creatures. He could not. He wriggled into the unbelievable comfort of the bed and closed his eyes.

Chapter 2

He woke to the scrape and rattle of the door, blinked at sliding shadows as Alexander Cargo set a lamp on the washstand. He started to get out of bed and stopped, conscious of his nakedness. Ebulliently, the doctor chided him for sleeping the whole day. He offered a choice of supper on a tray or in the dining room. David said he felt fine and chose the latter.

He dressed quickly, cursing the collar and tie. Downstairs, he found there was another guest for dinner, a man he had seen aboard the *Maria Kane* when she started loading, before he had jumped ship. Even before introductions, he realized that this must be the man in charge of the timber business.

He was muscular, top-heavy, around thirty years old. He looked uncomfortable in a faded brown suit with trousers tucked into boots, coat tight in the shoulders and short in the sleeves. He gave no indication that he recognized David, saying "Glad to meet you," without smiling. His handshake was dry and calloused. His name was Will Triplet.

Dorothy warned them they were to have "a typical backwoods dinner," but there was gleaming silverware on a linen tablecloth. Neena brought plates of beans, baked potatoes, venison steaks. Alex offered a one-sentence blessing. He explained in his chiding manner that he cut it short out of deference to Will, who was an atheist.

"Stop that right now," Dorothy said. She turned to David. "They argue about religion. They argue endlessly."

"Truth of the matter is we both worship Mammon," Will Triplet said. "Alex won't admit it, but I will."

Good heavens, I refuse to starve on a missionary's pay," Alex said. "That's hardly being greedy, is it? I leave it up to you, David. What do you say?"

"My father would agree with you."

Father was one of the few well-paid ministers in America. Mother had come into a comfortable inheritance besides. Alex would probably know that.

"What's more," Alex said, "a good part of the money I make from timber will go into this mission."

"That will soothe your conscience," Will Triplet said. There was no twinkle in his eye, no tone of good-natured banter in his voice. Yet the argument seemed to be an amiable one. "Me, I've got no conscience to soothe. Make it while you can, I say, and enjoy it. When you're dead, you're dead."

"If I believed that," Alex said, "I'd be as greedy as you are."

Will Triplet produced a short, forced, rather unpleasant laugh. "You're the greediest man I know. Besides everything else, you're greedy for God's approval. That's what I can't stand about you."

"What you can't stand about me is that I believe God's approval exists. That gives me something you can't have, something to live for."

"Something to be a hypocrite for."

"Anybody who sets his sights high and falls short can be accused of hypocrisy. Isn't that so, David?"

18

David said he supposed it was. Making it a point to smile broadly, he added, "It seems to me that atheists and orthodox are often much alike. They have to accept it all or reject it all. Their minds work exactly the same."

"Good!" Dorothy said. "David wins the argument. Now let's talk about something else. Business, weather, anything."

Will waved his fork in a gesture of surrender. After a brief silence, Alex said he had picked out a site for a new timber claim. It was on an island twenty miles north, he said.

"Why so far away?" David said. "There's timber everywhere."

"You need a creek, a good anchorage, and an Indian village close enough to furnish labor. I plan to set up a steam-powered mill. I've ordered the machinery. I'm hoping it will get here by summer. It's coming by ship, of course."

"I've never set up a steam operation," Will said. "I dare say I can do it easily enough, though."

"I'd you like to set it up *and* operate the new mill. David can take over here."

"Me?" David said. "How did I get into this?"

Alex shrugged elaborately. "I'm assuming you'll accept the offer I'm going to make. We'll go into details later, but I'll tell you now that I'm counting on you to file on the new site. I've pre-empted all I'm allowed, you see. I'll put up the money, of course. And if you want out, I'll buy your title from you. You can't lose, you see. How does that sound?"

"Fine, I guess. You've caught me by surprise."

"Why not closer to the fort?" Will said. He had

heavy eyebrows that met above the bridge of his nose and added darkness to his frown. "Why not Fox Island?"

"There are already people there."

"A few settlers—farmers."

"Settlers bring more settlers."

Will Triplet snorted. "It'll be fifty years before there's serious settlement of this country."

"Five," Alex said. "I predict that in five years we'll have a wagon road over the Cascades that will bring settlers in here directly without their having to go down the Columbia and then come north. They'll come by the hundred then, the thousand. There'll be sawmills everywhere. By that time I want to have the best locations, the best machinery. I want to be big enough to set prices, buy up competitors—"

"If you're right," David said when he got a chance, "if the Puget Sound country is on the verge of an influx of settlers, what's going to happen to your Indians?"

Alex put on a sad expression and made a gesture of helplessness. "It will be difficult, difficult. We'll get white vices, white diseases, and white greed in wholesale doses. I'm trying to prepare my little group, of course. I hope they'll become truly Christian and adapt quickly to civilization. There'll be more missionaries along soon, I hope. There'll be schools for the children, Christian schools—"

"Christian," Will Triplet said. "The magic word."

"The people here on the Sound are gentle and peaceful," Dorothy said. "They are also infuriating sometimes. They're children. They'll adjust only when they have to."

There was an edge of impatience to her voice. David

looked into the beautiful face and saw a hardness there that he didn't like. A beautiful woman is always a disappointment, he thought. They've always been spoiled.

Will Triplet was nodding in agreement with her. "These shore Indians are the laziest people on earth," he said. "You should try to get an honest day's work out of 'em as I have to do. A worthless people, I say."

"They're children," Dorothy said again. "If settlement comes, they'll have to grow up, that's all."

"Maybe they'll go to war," David said.

"The upriver horse Nisquallies might," Will said, "but the shore people wouldn't know how. They're scared of the very word. Last summer we were shut down for a month just because there were rumors of Haida canoes fifty miles north. The Nisquallies moved off the beaches and went inland."

"Haida canoes?" David said.

"Haida. Mention the name to a shore Indian and you'll see fear in his eyes. They come down here on slave raids from away up in Canada."

"The Queen Charlotte Islands," Alex said. "Seven hundred miles north of here—almost to Alaska."

"These jaspers are really fierce," Will went on. "I saw a Haida raiding party once, three canoes cruising past Port Townsend unconcerned as you please. The largest must have been seventy foot long. Had more than thirty warriors in it. Bright red, the canoes were, and carved and painted with monsters. The sight was frightening, I admit. But if the shore people here would organize and put up a fight, there'd be an end to the raids."

After coffee, they went into the parlor. Will Triplet

produced a clay pipe, which he filled from a pouch and lighted with an ember. A bit later he said good night, lighting up again as he stepped through the door. Dorothy excused herself then, and Alex explained his proposition in detail.

"You'll run the present mill as a partner. You'll get a full share of the profit. Will needn't know that. I treat him fairly, but he is not a partner. Last year the profit was around six thousand dollars. We ought to do even better in the future. You can live here with us. To be fair to the board of missions, I'll charge you ten dollars a month for room and board.

"As I mentioned, you'll pre-empt the new land that I want for my steam mill. It's a full section, and the price will be eight hundred dollars. I'll put up the money, which you needn't pay back. But you must give me the right to cut timber on the land. You must also give me an option on it in case you want out of the deal. I'll pay you four hundred dollars for it. So you can't lose. We'll put all this in writing, of course, so there'll be no misunderstanding."

David said nothing. It seemed indeed that he couldn't lose. If he chose, he could file on the land, make a quick four hundred dollars, and get out. But it would be foolish not to stay at least for a year or two and share in that six-thousand-dollar profit. Yet he didn't feel at ease with Alexander Cargo. The man was too impetuous. And for some reason that he was not at all clear about, David didn't much like Will Triplet.

"You agree?" Alex said eagerly. "Can I count on you?"

"Why not have Will Triplet take out the new claim for you?"

"He's not eligible. He's a British citizen."

"And you'll make me a full partner? I should think you'd want someone who knew something about cutting and milling timber."

"I want an intelligent person whom I can trust. I understand the potential of this country. I intend to cash in on it. But most of my time must go to the mission. Will will be occupied at the new mill. So if you'll take over the present one, I'll be glad to share its profit with you. There'll be other opportunities later. You can get rich, David, really rich, and in a short time."

David squinted into the fire, nodding his acceptance without voicing it yet.

"If you lack enthusiasm right now, that's understandable," Alex said. "You've been through a trying time, and I've thrown this at you suddenly. When you've had a chance to—"

"I'll accept on the following conditions," David said. "We're partners, not employer and employee. I'll need advice from you and Triplet, a lot of advice, but I won't take nagging. I'll run my mill—and my life—my way."

Their eyes met. Alex seemed doubtful, disappointed. After a thoughtful moment, he laughed.

"Conditions accepted. If it doesn't work out, so be it. So it's agreed. We're partners." He leaped to his feet and extended his hand. David took it without getting up from his chair.

"We'll have a look at the new stand of timber tomorrow," Alex said. "Then we'll go on to Port Townsend and get the pre-emption papers on their way. There's no land office there, but there's a man who handles such matters. We'll travel by canoe, of course, and we'll start early."

"How long a trip is it?"

"With a good crew, three days for the round trip. Maybe four."

"Suppose I don't feel up to it?"

"Then, of course—" Alex's face fell. "I assumed you had recovered."

"I'm merely trying to make a point. You've got to get over the notion that you can make plans for me and that I'll get caught up in your enthusiasm and go along with them. You're not my boss, remember?"

"You *are* touchy. The trouble is that I must be back for services Sunday. Tomorrow is Wednesday. If we leave then, I can make it even if the trip takes four days. So it's either tomorrow or wait till Monday. You see, it's been a monumental task to get the Indians to count the days and come to meeting on the Sabbath. Some of the back-country people and the Puyallups come fifteen miles or more to attend service. If I should disappoint them, they might not come again."

"We'll leave tomorrow," David said.

He grinned. Alex gave him a curious look. They both laughed.

They were up long before the late-winter dawn, break-fasting on coffee and hotcakes prepared by Alex. Neither Dorothy nor Neena was in evidence. They carried their gear, packed in blanket rolls and a pair of saddlebags, to the barn. Here they found an Indian named Luke saddling horses by lantern light. He was half Klickitat, Alex said, and very good with horses. He shared a lean-to behind the barn with Neena and her husband.

In the first feeble light of day, they rode the three miles to the mill. Here, Will Triplet was tinkering with machinery, waiting for his crew to show up. They left the horses with him and walked down to the beach and the Indian village. Two of the structures were permanent—long, low houses large enough to provide crowded quarters for a dozen persons. They were sunk into the ground and rose about four feet above it. Sides and roof were of cedar slabs. The other shelters were huts built of poles with woven grass mats over them.

Alex stopped in front of one of the large houses. He shouted "Ho" several times. When he got an answer from inside, he shouted his name and followed that with a stream of Nisqually. The dirty deerskin-door curtain was pushed aside and an Indian man came out, followed by several others. They and Alex held a lengthy discussion, with a good deal of pointing to the north and northwest. After a while the Indians went back into the house.

Alex expelled a noisy sigh. "It's settled. We get a canoe and a four-man crew for three blankets. They'll get us halfway there and refuse to go farther until I add to the fee. Oh, they're rascals. The trip is likely to cost me six or eight blankets before we're through. Trade blankets, of course. They cost me seventy-five cents apiece."

It turned out that five Nisquallies accompanied them, the fifth an old man who did no work but was entitled to go along because he was head of the family. He sat in the place of honor at the center of the canoe, a blanket over his shoulders, and stared with faded eyes at forest-capped points and islands as the craft slid through the narrows. David and Alex perched behind

25

him on a slender thwart that promised to become quickly uncomfortable.

The crew erected a mast and rolled out a sail woven of reeds. When they passed a great jutting rock that Alex identified as Point Defiance, a strong crosswind hit them. They immediately struck the sail and took to paddling. As the morning wore on, it became clear that they weren't expert in the use of a sail. It saved them work when the wind was exactly right; otherwise they paddled. It went up and came down a half dozen times during the morning. When it was up, they laughed and talked. When they paddled, they chanted songs.

It was not yet noon when they beached on a large island. The Indians built a fire and got out baskets of dried salmon and some sticky stuff David couldn't identify. Alex had brought sandwiches, and he gave one to each Indian. In return, the baskets were passed to him and David.

"Eat a little of it so as not to hurt their feelings," Alex said. "A mouthful or two won't hurt you."

The salmon wasn't bad. But one taste of the sticky stuff, which turned out to be dried blackberries soaked in fish oil, was enough. Four Indians who lived on the island came along the beach with a huge basket of oysters. Alex was known to them, and they joined the group. They shared the oysters, which were laid on the coals of the fire until they popped open and were then sloughed down.

After lunch, accompanied by the locals, Alex and David climbed a steep path and were on the new timber claim Alex had picked out. They paced it off, a four-mile walk. They blazed trees to mark its boundaries, and Alex kept track of the count by notching a stick every hundred paces.

By this time it was the middle of the afternoon. They shoved off again, passed the northern tip of the island, and were in a broad channel eight or ten miles wide. They made good time the rest of the day. When the sun set, sliding into a bank of dark clouds above the snow-capped mountains on the Olympic Peninsula, the crew swung the canoe toward shore. Alex wanted to travel for another hour or two, but they turned nervous eyes on him and shook their heads.

"It's the old man who's the real captain," he said disgustedly. "He says there are bad water spirits around here that come out at night."

They camped on the shore of a small bay near the mouth of a creek. The Indians turned the canoe upside down; then they cut poles and laid them against it. They covered the poles with branches and mats and had a low shelter in which to sleep.

They built a fire, and Alex got a pot of coffee brewing. The Indians boiled water in cooking baskets by adding heated stones. They stirred in dried salmon to make a pasty soup and that, along with a left-over sandwich or two, was supper.

Alex had provided David with a handwritten Chinook vocabulary of about three hundred words. David had begun to memorize it and he found now that he could participate in the camp conversation in an elementary way. The Indians were at first fascinated that, stumped for a word, he could look it up on the list. After he'd repeated the procedure a few times, it struck them funny and they laughed heartily. He joined in, clowning a bit by deliberately making mistakes and correcting them by consulting the sheaf of papers.

Alex insisted on saying evening prayers. He had everyone kneel·(except the old man, who had fallen asleep), clasped his hands, turned his eyes heavenward. He prayed in Chinook, rolling his voice out across the bay, and finished with the Lord's Prayer in Nisqually.

The old man woke up long enough to crawl into the shelter, choosing a place at its center. The others followed. David and Alex bedded down at one end. David muttered that they would be lucky if they didn't pick up *inapoos*, the Chinook word for lice.

"You did well tonight," Alex said. "They like you. You'll make a good mill boss, better than Triplet."

"We're supposed to be ten thousand years more advanced. When you laugh with them, you feel that isn't true."

They woke to dreary daylight and drizzly rain. They ate a cold breakfast and were quickly on their way. After a while the drizzle stopped. Patches of blue sky appeared. The wind swung around to the south. They raised the reed sail and plunged swiftly through choppy waters. They passed south of Marrowstone Island, curled around the end of another island, and were in a narrow passage along the eastern shore of the Olympic Peninsula. Early in the afternoon they sighted a log blockhouse rising out of a stockade. Port Townsend lay just to the north of this.

There was a pier, a warehouse built on piles, a log customs building. Behind these lay the town, if you could call it that, a few log houses scattered along a road that paralleled the shore.

There were two large craft in port, a schooner tied up at the pier and a ship anchored off it. The latter had a deckload of timber. David took a hard look at her. As they drew closer, Alex stared, too.

"The *Maria Kane*"

"The *Maria Kane*," David confirmed. "She's still here."

Chapter 3

They landed on the beach near the pier and were descended upon by a covey of Indian boys who, in spite of the chilly weather, wore nothing but shirts.

It was the same every place in the world where ships put in, David thought. You were greeted by a swarm of ragamuffins eager to beg, steal, guide, pimp for their sisters, carry your bag, or polish your boots. This bunch clustered around him and Alex, jabbering in Chinook mixed with a few English phrases they had picked up, mostly obscene.

They kept demanding *chikamin*, money. One of them snatched at the pistols Alex wore under his coat. Alex cuffed him and sent him sprawling. The boy got up with murder in his eye and picked up a rock. David thought for a moment that they might be in an ugly situation, but Alex designated the boy and another to carry their gear and all was forgiven.

Leaving the crew with instructions to be on hand at daybreak, they climbed a bank to the muddy, rut-scribbled street. Buildings were few and were scattered half a mile along the shore. Most were small log cabins, but a hundred yards from the pier two large structures stood side by side, built of lumber and painted red. Alex knocked on the door of the first and was greeted by a large woman who seemed glad to see him. He paid off the Indian boys and sent them scurrying with the word "*Klatawa*" and a wave of his hand. The woman showed them to a dark, chilly room furnished with two cots and a washstand. They left their gear here and went to the building next door.

The first floor was one large room with a bar tucked into a corner near the door. The rest of the space was taken up by a clutter of merchandise, varied, untidy, odoriferous. There were barrels of flour, potatoes, salted fish, stacks of pelts, jugs of sorghum, shelves of dry goods with bacon slabs hanging in front of them. There was a meat counter and a tobacco counter and a hardware counter with a hatchet sticking into it.

Two sailors were at the bar. To David's relief, neither was from the *Maria Kane*. A sharp-faced woman stood behind the bar, drinking with the sailors. She nodded at Alex, threw back her head, and yelled "Murchison!" at the top of her voice. There was a muffled answer from the floor above, the scrape of a chair, the sound of boots. A plump man with bushy gray sideburns came down the stairs and greeted Alex with a handshake. Alex introduced David, explaining that Mr. Murchison would see to the filing of his timber claim.

They sat down at a round table against the back wall. Murchison read the description of the claim, got pen and ink from a nearby shelf, and said he foresaw no difficulty about the matter. He promised to get the papers on the first ship headed for one of the Columbia River ports. Alex produced a deerskin poke from which he extracted a stack of double eagles to cover the pre-emption price. Murchison wrote out a receipt and suggested a dram of brandy to close the deal. To David's surprise, Alex agreed.

Murchison waddled to the bar for a bottle of French cognac and three two-ounce whisky glasses. He filled the glasses to the brim and downed his at a gulp. Alex did the same. David had expected to sip but he sloughed his down, too, enjoying the scalding fragrance of the drink and the spreading warmth that followed.

They drank the second slowly. Alex talked about the sawmill equipment he had ordered. I mustn't be unloaded at Port Townsend, he told Murchison. The ship was to go to Nisqually and pick up Alex, who would direct it to a beach near David's claim, where it could land the machinery.

There was sudden activity at the door as four seamen trudged in, carrying rifles. David laid his arms on the table and buried his face as if he were drunk. He was too late.

"There's Nail, Mr. Perrin! Damn me, sir, it's him. The one as jumped last week, sir, when we was loading logs. Sitting big as life with the town marshal till he seen us and now he's hiding his face."

Boots rumbled toward them. David didn't move. Murchison—besides being trader, saloonkeeper, and land office representative—must also be town marshal. Therein lay at least a small hope.

Someone had him by the hair, pulling his head back. He shot to his feet, flinging out an arm that knocked the man hard against the wall. It was the mate of the *Maria Kane*, Mr. Perrin.

Alex was also on his feet, catching Perrin as he caromed off the wall, spinning him into one of the seamen. He then planted himself between David and the four of them, throwing open his coat to expose the

33

brace of pistols at his waist. He stood glaring, arms akimbo, fingers inches from pistol butts.

"Stand where you are, gentlemen. If Captain Hammet has complaint against this man, tell him to come and see me. Now back to your ship. Out of here! Do as you're told."

Mr. Perrin was a square-built man with yam-colored hair and burning eyes. He took a deep breath and made an unsuccessful effort to keep anger out of his voice.

"Dr. Cargo. I didn't recognize you. There's a misunderstanding here. This man jumped the *Maria Kane*. He got away with it and all of a sudden jumping is the fashion. We lost two more as soon as we put in here. We got one back this morning but it looks like the other took to the mountains. Nail started it, we want him and, Doctor, we're going to take him."

"Do as you're told, Mr. Perrin. Take my message to Captain Hammet."

The men behind the mate had spread out to surround the table, rifles ready. Murchison got to his feet.

"Yes, Mr. Perrin," Murchison said. "Consult your captain. Under the circumstances, I insist on it."

"Damn the circumstances," Perrin said. "A ship's master has authority over his company and you know it. It's a town marshal's duty to cooperate."

"Maybe it would be best if Dr. Cargo went aboard with you instead of bringing the captain ashore," Murchison said. "In the meantime I'll be responsible for Mr. Nail's availability."

"I'm taking Nail aboard." Perrin gestured with his rifle. "Lay hold of him there."

Alex had let his coat fall over his pistols; now he flung it open again. It seemed unlikely that, facing four

34

rifles, he really intended to draw, but David was never sure. A seaman, a man David knew as Goldie, flung up his rifle and fired.

The explosion was thunderous in the low-ceilinged room. Alex staggered backward in a cloud of black-powder smoke, clutching at his right shoulder. There was an instant of awe, of utter silence, with dust trickling down from the ceiling. Alex tried to draw a pistol with his left hand. David caught him from behind just as he went limp.

They peeled off blood-soaked clothing, cut away his undershirt. Blood oozed from a wound high in his chest, two inches from the armpit. Terror touched Alex's face.

"The artery—"

David wadded up Alex's shirt and pressed it hard against the wound. "I don't think the artery's damaged. Blood's flowing, not spurting."

The seamen who had been at the bar and the woman barkeep had come over. She had a bung starter in hand. "I'll get the doctor," she said. She hurried out of the building.

They lifted Alex onto the big tabletop. David wadded part of the shirt against the wound and bound it tightly.

"The bullet didn't go through," he said. "It's in there somewhere."

"I aimed high," Goldie said. "I didn't want to do the man in. But he was going to draw. You all saw that."

"He was going to bluster," Perrin said. "He's a blustering damn fool, and what happened is his own fault. Well, he's not going to die. We'll take Nail and be on our way."

He reached for his rifle, which lay on the table beside Alex, but Murchison beat him to it. He pointed it at Perrin's chest. The two seamen who still had loaded guns immediately swung them to cover Murchison. He tried to ignore them, but his voice had a quake in it.

"The man who fired the shot is under arrest. So are you, Mr. Perrin. You other two go get your captain."

Perrin looked into the muzzle of the rifle very soberly and then grinned. "A standoff, Marshal. Pull that trigger and my men will pull theirs."

"Then we'll go to hell together, Mr. Perrin."

The words were brave, the voice wasn't. Still grinning, moving deliberately, Perrin reached for one of the pistols at Alex's waist. David sprang forward and caught his wrist. Perrin struck him backhanded, staggering him. By the time he got his balance, Perrin was pointing the pistol at him, thumbing back the hammer. At that moment the doctor arrived.

"Goodness sake! What is this?" He was a small man with a pointed beard. He wore a black frock coat that seemed to have been thrown on hurriedly over work clothes. "Put up those guns. Give me room. Idiots playing with guns—"

He bustled into the middle of them, set his bag on the table, and bent over Alex. Perrin touched the muzzle of the pistol to David's cheek.

"You'll come along now," he said. "One more bit of treachery out of you and it's a bullet in your skull."

The sharp-faced woman had returned with the doctor. She was still carrying the bung starter. She raised it behind Perrin and brought it down hard on top of his head. He dropped the pistol and collapsed in a heap.

"Stop it!" the doctor said. His voice rose to a mighty

roar. "Goodness sake! Merciful heaven! How in the name of Jesus H. Particular Christ can I treat a patient in the middle of a brawl?"

"Don't blaspheme," Alex said weakly.

"Shut up," the doctor said. "This is no time to be sanctigoddamnmonious."

Perrin's men hovered over him. David slipped the other pistol from Alex's belt. He stepped behind one of the sailors, put the pistol to his head, and quietly relieved him of his rifle. The other rifle lay on the floor near Perrin as its owner tried to revive him. David picked it up.

When the doctor had Alex temporarily patched up, he brought Perrin around with smelling salts. Subdued, Perrin submitted to being locked up in a storeroom with Goldie. The other two sailors went back to the *Maria Kane* for the captain.

Alex walked wobbily between David and the doctor to their room next door. Murchison snatched up the brandy bottle and followed.

When they had Alex in bed, the doctor suggested Alex take a good pull at the bottle. He took two or three. The doctor dipped the end of a probe into a bottle of carbolic acid and went to work. After a good deal of digging that set Alex to moaning and turned him deathly pale, he announced that the bullet was lodged in cartilage between the scapula and the top of the rib cage. He went in with forceps and drew it.

Nothing vital had been hit, he said, but the wound was deep and ragged. There would be a period of fever and weakness. Alex couldn't be moved for at least a week.

"Poppycock," Alex said feebly. "I've got to be

back at the mission for services Sunday."

"You try it and the services will be for you," the doctor said. "Over your coffin. I guarantee it."

"A little flesh wound," Alex said. "We'll leave in the morning as we planned."

It was agreed that David had best keep out of sight when Captain Hammet arrived. When the woman who ran the boarding house appeared and announced that the captain was on his way up the street, David followed her to an empty room and waited. In a few minutes Murchison came in and said the matter had been settled. Charges against Perrin and Goldie had been dropped and the men released in return for David's freedom.

Alex was paler than ever. The doctor was still with him. He had him bundled in blankets and was trying to get some hot soup into him. When Alex saw David, he managed a scowl. He spoke weakly, stuttering as if on the verge of a chill.

"Captain Hammet swears that you knew from the beginning he wasn't going into the Columbia this trip. And he says there was no agreement to put you ashore if he could find a replacement."

"He's a liar," David said.

"He also says you have an aversion to anything resembling work."

"Be damned to him," David said. He was about to say more, but the doctor caught his eye and gave a little shake of his head. David went over to his own cot and sat down on it.

"Hammet wants to do business with us in the future," Alex said. "Otherwise I'd never have got you off. I suppose he considers us obligated to him now."

"You're the one who got shot," Murchison pointed out.

"In England there's a new school of naturalists that holds that man is a species of ape," the doctor said. "Today I can believe it."

David spent a hectic night, waking whenever Alex moaned, getting up a half a dozen times to tend to nursing chores. Toward morning he fell into heavy sleep and didn't wake until after daylight. The doctor was in the room, changing Alex's bandage. Alex looked half dead. He revived feebly when he saw David.

"I'll be better tomorrow," he groaned. "We'll leave then. Before daylight. Make the trip in one day. Tell the crew."

David walked to the beach, seeing with relief that the *Maria Kane* had sailed. The Nisquallies were waiting around the canoe. They seemed to have heard what happened to Alex. At least they understood at once when David explained in halting Chinook that they wouldn't travel today. One of them said that the delay would cost another blanket, but David ignored him.

He spent most of the day in Murchison's store, letting the doctor and the landlady take care of Alex. He sat at the table against the back wall, smoked a cigar, wrote a letter home, studied the Chinook vocabulary. Late in the day, the doctor came in and joined him. David ordered a bottle of cognac, to be put on Alex's bill. Murchison dipped into the pickle barrel, and the three of them put in a pleasant hour of sipping and munching.

Doc, it turned out, had plans for getting rich as a cooper and fish packer. He had his wife and three

Indians busy manufacturing barrels that were piling up behind his shop by the hundreds. When the salmon runs started, he would fill the barrels with salted fish and ship them to California. Medicine was his real love, of course; after his second brandy, he declared that a talent for it was to be regarded as a sacred trust. The need to make a living out of his practice was a profanity he hoped to remove.

"What are you doing out here?" he asked David suddenly. "What are you looking for? Money? Adventure? A chance to grow up with a new country?"

"I guess I'm looking for something to look for."

"Go home. Go back to school and study medicine."

"I suppose I could learn coopering on the side," David said.

Murchison laughed. Doc was not amused. "Damn it," he said. "It's immoral to make money off the suffering of human beings."

David went to bed late, waking with a start when Alex called his name. The first thick gray of daylight showed at the window. Alex was sitting on the bed, turning up the lamp.

"We've got to get started. Help me get dressed."

"No." David got up and stood over him. "You're damned good and sick. We're not going to try it."

"I've got to—" Alex tried to stand and was immediately dizzy. David steadied him as he sank down on the bed. "Good heavens, I can't, can I? Even if you got me back, I'd be too ill to conduct services. Dorothy can't do it. Or won't. She leads the singing. She's good at that. David, you've got to do it."

"I couldn't conduct a service, Alex."

"That's it—you're going to have to do it. Make the

crew get you back tonight. You'll have to push. Promise them ten blankets if you have to, but do it. Push, push, push."

"Alex—"

"Listen carefully. The niceties of what you believe or don't believe don't matter a hang. They come fifteen, twenty miles. Give them some kind of service. Tell them stories. Bible stories. Dorothy will help when she sees you're determined. Luke will help, too. He speaks a little English."

Alex closed his eyes, gasping, shivering a little.

"All right, Alex. God knows, I owe you. I'll get back and put on your little show. This once, Alex. Only once."

Chapter 4

Will Triplet had been watching for them and he met them on the beach, carrying a lantern and puffing on his pipe. He heard the news about Alex grimly at first. Then, when David had given him some of the details, he laughed.

"Maybe it'll teach the old Christer a little humility," he said. "He's got it into his head that God is on his side and he can do anything."

At the mill, he wrote out an order on the Hudson's Bay Company for ten blankets, payable to bearer. Tomorrow the crew would take it to Fort Nisqually and collect.

"They rooked you good," he said to David. "I get six days' work out of 'em for one blanket. You'll spoil the blighters."

"I suppose I'll learn to cheat them as well as you do," David said. He was in no mood for criticism. "But I'm damned if I'll brag about it."

He rode slowly through the short dark stretch of forest and urged his horse to an easy lope when he reached the prairie. He dismounted at the barn, swung open the door, found a lantern, and lighted it. The Indian called Luke came in the back door of the barn and took over the care of the horse. David explained that Alex would not be back for a few days and that they must have services without him.

"He says you'll help. You know some Bible stories you can tell your people?"

"Big whale eat Jonah. Get sick tum-tum. Spit him up. Daniel go into bear's house. Don't get hurt."

"Bear's house?"

"Sure. *Siam*. Big grizzly."

David smiled. Since the Indians weren't familiar with lions, Alex had substituted a grizzly. "You know stories about Jesus?"

"Son of *Saghalee Tyee*. Loves all the *tillicums*. Hates the devil, that son-of-a-bitch."

"You'll do fine," David said.

He found Dorothy reading in the mellow warmth of the parlor. There was a faint stale odor in the room that somehow disturbed him. He said quickly that Alex had had an accident, that he was all right but wouldn't be able to travel for a few days. She didn't seem particularly alarmed. By the time he had given her a full account, she was wearing a curious little smile.

"I promised him I'd conduct services," David said. "You're supposed to help. You and Luke."

"I've taught them two hymns: the 'Doxology' and 'Onward, Christian Soliders.' We'll sing them both—over and over again if necessary."

She dug up Bible stories and prayers Alex had translated into Chinook and Nisqually. David selected some of those in Chinook. She brought in ginger cookies and milk.

"You're going to preach a sermon?" she said.

"A short one. In Chinook."

"I got the impression you're—well, sort of a skeptic."

"I suppose I am."

44

"So am I, David. I never discuss such things with Alex, of course. When I don't agree with him, he gets furious."

"I suppose he would."

"He preaches to me sometimes. He simply rants. David, he's such a hypocrite."

"I don't know. I don't understand ministers."

"I'm worse than a hypocrite," she went on. "I'm a complete fake."

He thought of his mother. He wondered if she had ever in her life thought of herself as a fake. He decided she had not.

"This is a time of decision for me, David. A terrible time. Alex is mad. You must know that."

"Sometimes I think all preachers are mad," he said lightly. "My father, my brother, all of them."

"Alex couldn't hold a parish back in the States. That's why he became a missionary."

She waited for his reaction. He met her eyes, held them a moment, then looked away. He could think of nothing to say.

"I was brought up in a rather religious family," she said. "Comfortably, fashionably religious. I had a lot of beaux. When Alex came along, he managed to conceal his failures, and Mother thought he was a great catch. I did too, I suppose.

"I was twenty when we were married. He was twenty-nine. We moved to a parish upstate. The congregation liked his violent preaching, but they couldn't take his arrogance. You can tell people in a sermon that they're on the road to hell and they'll love it. But you can't tell a board member that during an argument about church business."

"Alex did that?" He wanted to smile.

"He has no tact, no judgment, no restraint. I married a monster, David. A great mad, strutting monster."

He had a crazy impulse to ask her if Alex was a monster in bed. He had a feeling that she wouldn't be much offended, either, that she would laugh and give him some kind of answer. He was likely to be the one who would be embarrassed, he decided.

"We went from one little back-country church to another, never staying long. We lived on nothing. Then Alex heard that the Board of Missions had plans for a mission on Puget Sound. I don't know how he managed it, but he talked them into putting him in charge of it. He can be very persuasive when he wants to."

"You never had children?"

"A son. He died when he was three months old."

"I'm sorry," David said.

"I'm glad to be childless right now," she said stiffly. "Children would complicate a situation that's terribly painful already. I can't stand much more, David. I'm not devout. I keep busy, but I have no special affinity for the work. I—well, I'm dodging the issue, aren't I? The truth is I can't stand much more of Alex."

"That's too bad," he said.

"He's impossible. He's convinced God is on his side. He thinks he can do nothing wrong."

Will Triplet had said almost the same thing just a little while ago. In almost exactly the same words. David was again aware of the stale odor in the room. Tobacco. Pipe smoke.

Will had been here recently and he had been here for some time. What if he had? It was no reason to jump to

46

conclusions. If the meeting was clandestine, he had been damned careless to smoke his pipe. But the same appraisal of Alex, the same words—Had Will said them to her, or she to him?

Dorothy sighed and then suddenly gave him her motherly look. "Forgive me, David. I shouldn't talk to you like this. I simply had to spill over to someone. It's the spilling that's important, not what I've said. That can be forgotten. I'm sure you understand that."

"Of course. I just wish I could say something helpful."

"You're very kind to listen. Heaven knows I have no one else I can confide in."

"What about Will Triplet?" he said, watching her closely. She looked away and then looked straight at him.

"Why should I confide in Will?"

"Seems possible."

"Maybe so," she said, frowning. "Maybe I should talk to Will."

She was lying, he thought. Not by bearing false witness but in the way women lie by not bearing true witness. She had already talked to Will.

"I keep thinking of what my father would tell you," he said. "But that's no good."

"What would he say?"

"Pray about it."

"Of course." She got to her feet and picked up a lamp. "That's exactly what Alex would say. It's scandalously late and I'm going to bed."

They went upstairs together, each carrying a lamp. She went with him to his room and looked in to see if everything was in order. He set his lamp on the

47

washstand. If she puts hers down, it's an invitation, he thought. She did not. She paused in the doorway to say, "Thanks for listening, David. Sleep tight."

It was cold in the room. He undressed and put on a nightshirt that was laid out on the bed. He was bone tired. He blew the lamp and settled into the embrace of the feather ticks. He lay still, listening, hoping against all reason that she would come back. He puzzled about the smell of stale tobacco in the parlor. The room had a good dose of it.

He was jealous, he realized. That was infuriating because he wasn't sure if he even liked her very well.

Sunday school was announced by Luke's ringing a ship's bell in the belltower. Thirty-odd families gathered in the dim, log-walled sanctuary. Owing to the prevalence of polygamy, this toted up to around two hundred souls, about half of them children. There were a score of infants on cradleboards. Older children straddled the benches that served as pews, risking splinters in bare bottoms. Adults sat in expectant silence, blankets over their shoulders.

David climbed to the pulpit and had his moment of inadequacy. Why are they here? he asked himself. What do they expect of me? He raised his arms in a great sweeping gesture of blessing and said in Chinook that God welcomed His people to His house. It immediately bothered him that he had taken it upon himself to speak for God, even to say welcome; he had meant to avoid that sort of presumption. He said a few words about the Golden Rule, with Luke translating. Luke told his stories, producing smiles and chuckles, and taking up a good deal of time. Dorothy led the singing of "Onward, Christian Soldiers." David read the Lord's Prayer in Chinook. Many knew it by heart and joined in.

A few more arrived for the main service, including some whites and halfbreeds from Fort Nisqually. And, surprisingly, Will Triplet.

Thanks largely to Luke, it went smoothly enough. He told more Bible stories and did a little preaching on his own. Painfully aware of the difficulty of expressing even a suggestion of the abstract in Chinook, David delivered the short sermon he had scribbled the night before.

"We don't know where the world came from. We don't know where people came from. The Nisqually people have stories about the beginning of things. My people have such stories, too. The stories of both people are good. Sometimes they help us to understand a little bit. Still, we do not understand very much. So we say God made the world—"

After the service he stood in front of the church in a trifling rain and shook the hands of those who offered them. Will Triplet slapped him on the back.

"Most agnostic sermon I ever heard," Will said.

"That should please you."

"You're a conscientious man. You tried not to tell them anything you didn't believe yourself. You tried. But that Luke—he's a bullshitter if I ever heard one."

David bit back the irritation he felt at this man so eager to pronounce judgment. He said, "I couldn't have got along without Luke."

Will chuckled. "No, you couldn't. You'll never be a success as a preacher, Nail. I mean that as a high compliment."

49

Dorothy joined them. She had gone to the house and put on a long blue cape.

"One of Will's crew has a sick baby," she said. "I'm going to take a look at it."

Luke came running up with her horse. Will boosted her into the sidesaddle. David watched them ride off, Will gigging his big gelding unnecessarily to show off his horsemanship. David wondered if there really was a sick baby.

He strolled behind the church, where the Indians were gathering. There was a shelter of sorts here, a sixty-foot-long roof set on posts. Adults gathered under it and began making fires in a row along its edge. Children scouted up wood or played games without regard for the misty rain.

He asked which families had come long distances and made it a point to speak to them, thinking that this was what Alex might do. They accepted him with friendliness, yet he was ill at ease. We are enemies, he thought. They just don't know it yet. If I were truly their friend, I'd tell them that we white creatures have a passion for preaching about Jesus but we are really thieves at heart. We'll come in numbers soon and herd them onto reservations, preaching the Golden Rule all the while. I can already feel the hatred they'll have for us then.

He went to the house feeling drained. He stretched out on his bed, telling himself the evening service would be easier. He dozed off and was wakened by Neena. She had fixed dinner for him. Evidently, Dorothy had told her to do so.

Dorothy was not back for vesper service. Luke undertook to lead the singing and did it surprisingly well. When it was over, David went directly to the house. Neena wasn't around. He lighted a lamp in the parlor and sank into a chair. He sat staring into the lifeless fireplace. He pushed aside the dissatisfaction that stirred in him. I gave it an honest try, he thought. Now it's over. Forget it.

Dorothy came in through the kitchen, flushed, eyes dancing. She swept off her long blue cape with a flourish.

"How'd it go?"

"All right," he said. "How's the sick baby?"

"He'll live, thank heavens. Ministering to the sick is a risky business, you know. If they die, you're apt to be blamed."

There was no baby, he thought. She spent the afternoon at Triplet's cabin. He said, "And if they live?"

"Then you're a great doctor. Sometimes. Sometimes the medicine men hate you."

"Is that all it means—your own popularity?"

"David, what an ugly thing to say!"

"Sorry. I guess I'm in an ugly mood."

"I asked for it, I suppose. You get a little hard in this business. You cover up the sad, tender feelings. Especially when you've lost a baby of your own."

"I'm sorry," he said again.

There was a throbbing in the air, a drumming sound and a wild, rhythmic chant, rising and fading. He got up and went to the door. The fires behind the church had been built up.

"I thought they had gone home," he said.

"They're gambling. Alex tries to discourage it. If you go out and speak to them, they'll leave. They'll go to the village a mile up the river and gamble there."

51

"Let's go out and have a look."

The rain had stopped. A breeze spun through the darkness, whipping the fires. David and Dorothy were joined by Luke. They worked through the crowd toward men seated in two parallel lines, facing each other with a fire between them. A man at the center of one line moved his hands over each other in a swift, intricate juggling ritual. The others on his team beat on logs and chanted.

This was the local version of *slahal*, Dorothy said, the bone game. The man at the center of the line had a small carved bone that he transferred from hand to hand. When he stopped the juggling motions, a player on the other side had to guess which hand the bone was in. If the guess was right, the guessers won one of the losers' ten tally sticks. If wrong, they gave up a tally stick. The game went on until one side had all the sticks.

"One team is made up of Puyallups," Dorothy said, "the other of Nisquallies."

"What are the stakes?"

"Each player makes a separate bet with a player on the other side. They play for blankets, canoes, sometimes slaves."

"Slaves?"

"Some of the rich ones own slaves. Does that surprise you?"

"Why don't they run off? They could just go into the forest and be free."

"Most of them were born into slavery, I think. They accept it; it's their place in life. Besides, their heads weren't flattened when they were babies. They'd be immediately recognized as slaves almost anywhere around the Sound."

The Puyallup team made a correct guess. A tally stick was tossed across the fire to them. It was their turn with the bone. They began their own chant, their own lucky song.

"One Sunday Alex preached three sermons against gambling," Dorothy said. "That night there were two games going at once."

David thought of his father, remembering how angry he had been when the ladies' aid society wanted to hold a raffle.

The bone juggler's hands froze before him in two clenched fists. The Nisqually guesser made his guess and was wrong. The Puyallups took up their chant with triumph in their voices. Some of the Nisquallies turned sour faces in David's direction. There was muttering among them. Luke tugged at David's sleeve.

"You stand on Puyallup side. Bring luck. Better you stand in middle."

David laughed and pointed to Dorothy to give her credit for the luck. They moved so they were an equal distance from each team.

"Why don't you break it up?" Dorothy said suddenly. "Make them move to the village."

"Is that what Alex would do?"

"Yes, he would. Don't you see? They're trying you."

"Gambling is part of their way of life. Let them do it."

"That's exactly the point, isn't it? We're trying to teach them our ways, aren't we? I may be a fake as a preacher's wife, but a church is a sanctuary, a refuge from the shabbiness of the world. It's wrong for them to gamble here."

"I'll bet you a dollar on the Puyallups," he said.

"That would amount to complete surrender, wouldn't it? It would be letting them dominate us."

"That's the gist of it, isn't it?"

"What is?"

"Who dominates whom."

"It's part of it."

"Vanity," he said. " 'All is vanity and a striving after wind.' "

She laughed emptily. "I'm going back to the house."

He let her go, wondering if she was angry with him. The Nisquallies won a tally stick and began chanting with new enthusiasm. He counted the sticks stuck into the ground in front of the teams. Seven on the Nisqually side, thirteen on the Puyallup.

His curiosity was aroused by an old man shuffling up and down behind the line of Nisqually gamblers, followed by a teen-age girl. He had noticed the pair before, chiefly because the girl—by white standards, at least—was the most attractive female here. In contrast to the other women, who were inclined to be short and pear-shaped, she was slender, lean-hipped, long-legged. She wore a knee-length skirt of shredded cedar bark and a short deerskin cape that covered her shoulders. Her hair had been plaited into three braids, a style favored by some of the women. Her head had not been flattened.

The old man talked eagerly to one bystander after another. None had any time for him, and he seemed to be making a pest of himself. David pointed to him and asked Luke what the old boy was up to.

"Puyallup," Luke said. "Wants to bet *mistshimus*,

girl slave. Three hundred blankets. Too much.''

"The girl with him is his slave?''

"Sure. Rich man. Many canoes. Five-six slaves.''

"He wants to bet her against three hundred blankets?''

"Sure.'' Luke gave David a sharp, curious look. "Too skinny,'' he muttered.

Aware that they were looking at him, the old man stared back at them, hesitated, and then came toward them.

"Ask him about the girl,'' David said to Luke. "Where did he get her?''

Luke asked the question and the old man began to jabber. Puyallups spoke a Nisqually dialect, but the old man was toothless, and Luke had difficulty understanding him; so it took a while to get a translation.

It turned out that he had bought the girl from some Bella Bella traders when she was a child. They had raided some of their northern neighbors and he had brought their captives south to Puget Sound to sell. The old man's wives had raised the girl like a daughter; she was prodigiously accomplished in cooking, sewing, basket-making, and the like. Wouldn't the young *t' kope tyee* like to wager three hundred blankets against her?

"*Hyas hyiu,*'' Luke said. "Too damn much.''

The old man slapped the girl on the stomach, spun her around, slapped her on the behind. She was very strong and worked hard, he said.

The girl was plainly used to being treated as merchandise, and she bore the inspection with a sort of patient amusement. David found himself avoiding her eyes; yet he was amused by the old man's efforts to

55

bargain and reluctant to put an end to them. Just to egg the old fraud on, he touched the girl's hair and asked if she had *inapoos*, lice. The old man swore that every member of his household bathed every day, washed their blankets regularly in urine, and that there wasn't an *inapoo* in his house.

"How old is she?" David asked.

"*Tenas*," the old man said. "Young."

"How many winters?"

The old man produced a shrug that indicated his lack of concern with such details. He patiently counted on his fingers and said he had bought her eight winters ago. Maybe ten winters ago. She was about waist high then, maybe six winters old. Maybe seven. The girl frowned and looked off into the distance as if trying to remember who she was and where she came from.

"Ask him if she's a virgin," David said to Luke. He hoped it was a routine question.

The old man considered a moment and then replied that the girl always returned from berry-picking with her basket full to the brim. David didn't see the relevance until Luke explained that there was a sort of joke about this. A girl who returned with her basket only partly filled was apt to be accused of spending part of her time in the bushes with a boy.

Then a strange thing happened. The girl pushed in front of the old man and, eyes fastened on David, spoke for the first time. The words came slowly and precisely, English words.

"I—am—seven—years—old."

The old man, who had no idea of what language she had spoken, was annoyed by her behavior. He shoved her aside and took up his jabbering sales talk. David put

56

his back to him and drew the girl aside.

"You speak English?" he asked her.

Painfully, she repeated the words. "Speak—English."

"Do you understand what I'm saying?"

"I—am—seven—years—old."

"Where did you learn to say that?"

She didn't understand. She smiled. Her eyes were frightened, confused.

"Where do you come from?" She didn't understand that at first, either, and he repeated it.

She pointed to the north. *"Siah,"* she said.

Faraway. Somewhere faraway to the north, sometime long ago, someone had taught her to say in English that she was seven years old. Surely, she must have learned more than that. But the Bella Bella had captured her and sold her as a slave. What did that do to a seven-year-old mind? From what smothering earthslide of despair did it have to rise and remake itself?

"What is your name?" he said.

She scowled into the darkness and understood. Her lips groped silently with words before she spoke them.

"My—name. My name—Tsil-tsil."

"Tsil-tsil," he said. He smiled at her. It was the name the Puyallups had given her and Luke translated, pointing at the sky. It meant *star*, he said.

The Puyallup team won a point and chanted their lucky song into the wind. The old man became impatient, demanding.

"I don't have three hundred blankets," David said. "I don't have any blankets at all."

The old man stabbed him in the stomach with a

finger and pointed out that there were many thousands of blankets at Fort Nisqually, great bales of blankets. Surely the *t' kope tyee* could make marks on a paper that would get him as many as he wanted.

"Suppose I buy her," David said. "Buy, not gamble." He wondered if there was a possibility of his talking Will Triplet into giving him enough credit for three hundred blankets.

The old man said he would sell the girl outright for four hundred blankets. Luke pointed out that the old man intended to bet on the Puyallups, who were ahead. So it was reasonable that the amount needed to cover the bet be less than full value. But both prices were foolish. The girl was worth a hundred blankets at most. The old man was a thief at heart and maybe a little bit crazy.

Tsil-tsil suddenly thrust her hands in front of David, holding them side by side. The left hand was stunted, half the size of the other. It was a shocking thing, but there was no malformation, no ugliness. Some early accident or disease had simply arrested growth and left her with the hand of a small child.

Luke fairly crowed at the disclosure. The old man was furious with the girl and raised a fist over her head and struck at her. She was ready for that and easily avoided the blow. He began jabbering again and made her flex the fingers of the dwarf hand to show that it was perfectly serviceable. Then he had her grip one of David's fingers. David looked into the dark young face, and it was a moment of union. Then he was quickly frightened by what he might be getting himself in for.

She's a trap, he thought. All women are traps, and

ten thousand years of civilization don't mean a thing.

"Two hundred blankets," the old man said.

"Fifty," Luke said.

David withdrew his finger from Tsil-tsil's grip. "I have no blankets. No one at Fort Nisqually would honor my paper."

He turned, avoiding the girl, and made his way through the crowd. A light in Dorothy's window dimmed and disappeared as he walked toward the house. She had left a low-burning lamp for him in the parlor, and he used it to light his way to bed.

For a time he lay sleepless, tormented by the wild song of the gamblers as it rose and fell with the wind.

Chapter 5

Dorothy came to breakfast in a riding dress, saying she meant to visit the sick baby again. She was in a hurried mood. David was sleepy and sullen. They agreed that no one should feel he had to be chatty at breakfast.

"Alex is sometimes very expansive in the mornings," she said. "Sometimes it's more than I can bear."

She usually found a way to mention Alex, he thought, and to belittle him.

"At other times he's very glum. He snaps at me if I *breathe*."

He sipped his coffee and added more of the rich cream. "He never does anything right, does he?"

She fastened a look on him and stared until he met it. She smiled impishly. "I deserved that."

"He gets himself mixed up with God," David said.

"Exactly. That's what I—" She gestured and didn't finish.

"That's what Will Triplet says."

"Perhaps he does. Why do you always mention Will?"

"We're getting awfully chatty," he said.

"Yes. Shall we just sit and grunt for a while?"

"Ugh," he said.

He watched from the door as she rode off into a bright morning. After a while he went to the barn and found Luke cleaning out the stalls. David asked about the *slahal* game. Had the old Puyallup put up Tsil-tsil? Luke shood his head and said the old man was a *la-ah*, a cheat. When the Puyallups were three sticks away from winning the game, he had come down to fifty blankets. In view of his original price, he hoped this would seem a good bet. The truth was that fifty blankets was close to the girl's full value. But the people around here were onto him, Luke said. No one had taken the bait.

David lazed around the rest of the day, spending a good deal of the time browsing in Alex's library. Dorothy didn't return until twilight, and she had Will Triplet with her. They dined on Hudson's Bay ham that Neena had baked to tender perfection. Will did most of the talking, holding forth on women's rights, the Free Soil Party, and a proposal made by some settlers down around Astoria that the northern part of Oregon break off and become a new territory.

David found himself wondering if Dorothy had spent the whole day with Will. There was something between the two. Not necessarily a sexual affair, but something, some sort of private understanding. It showed in darting glances and unfinished smiles. It showed especially in Dorothy's small frowns when Will was becoming unbearably dogmatic—and in his quickness to catch the cue and soften voice and opinion.

They went into the parlor, and Will lighted his clay pipe. David excused himself, saying he wanted some air. He strolled aimlessly over the grounds and found himself in front of the church. Following an impulse, he went inside, groped his way through darkness to the nearest bench, and sat down.

He breathed the musty silence and asked himself what he was doing here in a lonely mission in a remote territory among people who irritated him fully as much as the people back home. Adventure. That was the easy, stupid answer. A young man of good family, uncertain and unsettled, went to remote places in search of adventure. He was supposed to come home in a year or two with the restlessness worn out of him. Of course, he might get lucky and come home rich. Or he might not come home at all.

With his eyes adjusting to the darkness, he could make out the interior of the church in a dim and shadowy way. High, narrow, paneless windows let in shafts of starlight that laid frail patterns across the benches. Between and beyond were pools of darkness. He could not make out the pulpit.

I've come to God's house to find composure, he thought. Father would be pleased. He would nod smugly and turn it into a personal victory.

A sound jolted him, a sigh, a rustling. A seep of wind through faulty chinking. A bird roosting on a ledge. A mouse. He peered closely, knowing it was none of these. Something was there in the blackness near the pulpit, someone.

He got up and moved down the aisle, scraping his feet. Even before the huddled figure on the front bench looked up at him, he knew who it was. He took her hands and raised her to her feet. Her left hand was tiny in his palm.

She was frightened, trembling. There was the awful gulf of language, the difficulty of explanations in over-simple Chinook. She had run away from the old man. She had been hiding in the church all day. She had been talking with God.

He led her out of the church and through the night to the house. He took her into the parlor and introduced her, being rather formal about it.

"Mrs. Cargo, Mr. Triplet, this is Tsil-tsil. She's a slave. She's run away. My guess is she's had nothing to eat all day."

Will grunted curtly. Dorothy got to her feet. She looked startled but quickly recovered.

"Well, goodness. We'll get her something to eat. Neena!"

Neena appeared, wiping her hands on her apron. She regarded Tsil-tsil sullenly.

"Take her to the kitchen," Dorothy said. "Feed her. *Mamook muchamuck yahka.*"

Neena muttered in Nisqually and turned toward the kitchen. Tsil-tsil followed her. Dorothy stopped David with a hand on his arm.

"David, this is serious business."

"I suppose it is."

"Her owner will be around to get her. He'll be furious. We'll give him a present, a considerable present, and ask him not to beat her. Runaways are sometimes killed, you know."

"She's not going back," David said. "I'm going to buy her."

"That's preposterous."

He turned to Will. "I want three hundred dollars' credit at Fort Nisqually. Will you arrange it?"

Will laughed and shook his head. "You're barking up the wrong tree, lad. I can do nothing for you."

"You won't do it?"

"Of course not." He laughed again. "Alex would

have apoplexy. His hot-blooded young protégé buying himself a squaw!''

''You're wrong,'' David said. ''Alex would approve.''

''Nonsense.''

''I want three hundred dollars' credit at Fort Nisqually tomorrow morning, Will. I insist on it.''

''Insist all you like. You'll not have it.''

David turned and strode into the kitchen. The Hudson's Bay ham was still on its platter and less than half gone, but Neena had given Tsil-tsil only scraps. She sat at the table and ate these with her fingers. David carved a thick slice and put it on her plate. He got her a knife and fork and showed her how to use them, both of them laughing at her awkwardness. He added beans to her plate from a pan on the hearth, got bread and butter for her, and asked Neena to bring her coffee and cream and sugar.

Neena made no secret of her feeling about waiting on so inferior a person. She slopped coffee as she set a cup at the girl's elbow. *''Mistshimus!''* she hissed.

David poured himself a cup of coffee and sat down. Will and Dorothy came into the room. Dorothy stared at Tsil-tsil's efforts with knife and fork. Then she turned to David.

''You said Alex would approve. What gave you that idea?''

''The way I'll put it to him, he'll approve.''

''David, what are you going to do with her?''

''You don't really have to ask that, do you?'' Will said.

''I'm going to set her free,'' David said. ''I'll make it clear to her that she can go north to her people if she wants, whoever they are. Or she can stay here. She learned a little English somewhere when she was a child. I have an idea she could pick it up quite easily. If she stays, I'm going to teach her."

"What for?" Will demanded. "Will speaking English solve her problems for her? You're a romantic idealist with a considerable capacity for self-deception. You'll make a preacher yet."

"All I want to do is free a slave."

"With a *sitkum siwash* in her belly, like as not."

"Will!" There was more amusement than reprimand in Dorothy's tone. "David—let's see, how do I put it delicately? Do you have a *romantic* reason behind your philanthropy?"

"The hell with delicacy," David said. "If I put a *sitkum siwash* in her belly, I'll accept responsibility for it. I won't abandon her."

"Lord help us!" Will said. "Lord preserve us from the schemes and pledges of a hot-blooded young man!"

"It's nice to hear you calling on the Lord," Dorothy said.

"Pure blasphemy."

"Well, we'll take care of the girl for tonight," Dorothy said. "Neena will look after her."

"I want her to stay in the house," David said.

"David—"

"If there are any lice, I'll clean up. I'll wash the bedding and do whatever else is necessary."

Dorothy sighed noisily. "All right. Neena and I will give her a bath, clean clothes—"

"She doesn't need a bath. I don't want her humiliated."

"Lord help us," Will said again.

"David, you've got to be reasonable," Dorothy said. "The Indians have a class structure, you know: chiefs, the rich upper class, commoners, and slaves. Tsil-tsil is a slave. She's used to humiliation. She expects it. We'll have plenty of time to think about restoring her pride. Tonight she gets a bath."

David remembered how he had shamelessly treated the girl as a piece of property the night before, just because the situation amused him. Dorothy was right. Tsil-tsil thought of herself as property. Humiliation was her way of life. Still, she ran away....

Neena was sent for a washtub, which she set down with an unnecessary clatter. Tsil-tsil gave David a questioning look and a small smile.

"I believe she thinks you're going to bathe her," Will said.

"We'll leave her with the ladies. Come on. I want to talk to you."

"Not much," Will said. "If I can't watch 'em bathe her, I'm on my way home. And I'm lending you no money. That's final."

Dorothy gave David a wink. "We'll see. Now you two clear out."

Will left by the back door. David went into the parlor. He began to be plagued by second thoughts. In freeing the girl, mightn't he raise hopes in her that would turn to disappointments? And Will was right, of course. What did a man do with a pretty slave girl besides teach her English? There was no fooling himself about the answer to that one.

She came in wearing a calico dress that hung to her ankles. Her hair hung down her back. Dorothy came behind her.

"Nary an *inapoo*," Dorothy reported. She motioned Tsil-tsil to a chair near the fire where she could dry her hair. "I'm going to put her in the bedroom next to yours. Dare I? David, I think you may be right. I think she's an unusual girl."

"I didn't say that."

"My, you're grumpy. *Yahka chako solleks*—right, Tsil-tsil?"

Tsil-tsil smiled and said nothing. Dorothy said she would be right back and went upstairs. Tsil-tsil turned sideways to the fire, throwing her hair forward over her face. He watched her, aware of her slender body under the loose dress.

Dorothy returned, hands clenched in front of her. She opened them to reveal three paper-wrapped cylinders that she placed in David's lap.

"Three hundred dollars in gold," she said.

Chapter 6

The next morning David sent Luke off toward Chebaulip, the principal Puyallup village, to find the old gambler. He was back in an hour, having met the old man and several of his male relatives on the trail. They were armed with sticks they had cut along the way in anticipation of giving the runaway the beating she deserved. David saw them coming, Luke in the lead. He told Tsil-tsil to stay out of sight and met them in the yard.

With Luke's help, he got the price down to two hundred and fifty blankets. They all traipsed over to Fort Nisqually, where he bought the blankets, leaving the old man and his entourage with the problem of transporting them.

Back at the mission, he gathered them all in the parlor—Dorothy, Luke, Neena and her husband, and Tsil-tsil. He announced to Tsil-tsil that he was setting her free.

"Do you understand?" he said in Chinook. "You are no longer a slave. You can do as you like. You can go north to your people if you wish. Do you understand?"

The scene fell flat. There were no tears of joy, no vows of eternal gratitude, not even a smile. She nodded that she understood, but she looked disappointed.

"Or you can stay here," David said. "We—I'll see

that you're taken care of."

"*Nesika*," Dorothy said. "We."

"I don't think she catches on," David said.

"She slave," Luke said. "Don't know how to own herself."

Tsil-tsil spoke then, slowly and matter-of-factly in Nisqually, pausing now and then for Luke to translate.

God had spoken to her. Not from the sky but from here—she touched a finger to her breast. He had told her to run away and hide in His house. It had been quiet there and He had told her to listen and wait. After a long time she had heard David come into the church. Had God also spoken to him?

"Maybe," David said. "*Klonas*."

God had never spoken to her before, she said. She had dreamed dreams in which the star spirits had spoken to her. And once a dog fish spirit had got into her and she was sick until a medicine man scared it off with a rattle. But this business of hearing God speak was new and alarming. He had meant her to become the slave of the *t' kope tyee*. She understood that clearly. To find herself set free was puzzling.

The best reply David could think of was that under the white man's law in this part of the country, he could not own a slave. That amazed her, and he had to do a lot of explaining. Finally, she seemed satisfied—or at least resigned to her new, free status. But she had no wish to go north to her people, whoever they were. God had said nothing at all about that.

That seemed to settle it. David was disappointed by the lack of an emotional climax. Dorothy came to the rescue, saying that they would all celebrate by having lunch together.

They ate in the dining room, with Neena's husband assigned to Alex's chair at the head of the table and Neena at the foot. Dorothy did as much of the serving as Neena. She was doing her best, David realized, to erase caste lines.

It was an impromptu party with warmed-up ham and beans. Effortlessly, Dorothy kept a conversation going in Chinook. There were jokes, teasing, much laughter. With its many onomatopeic words and childish combinations, the jargon itself was often comic. This was at least as true for Indians (who had invented it) as for whites.

That afternoon David began to teach Tsil-tsil English. The weather was pleasant and they walked around the mission grounds pointing at things and saying the words for them. From time to time as the lesson continued, more words and phrases from long ago were stirred out of her memory. "Tell—us—a—story," "Here—I—come," "Good morning, Mrs. Wing." They popped up suddenly and startled her as much as they did him.

It was Mrs. Wing who taught her, she thought. She also remembered a girl her own age, Louise, who might have been Mrs. Wing's daughter. They were white, she thought. She wasn't sure.

Then she smiled and came up with the most startling words yet. "C-a-t—spells—cat," she said.

He picked up a stick and scratched the letters on the ground. She copied them, naming each letter.

He took her into the house and printed the alphabet on a sheet of paper.

"A-b-c's," she said.

She was able to name only a half dozen letters at first,

but in two hours' time she knew them all by sight and could print most of them.

Dorothy dug up a map with the names of many of the coast tribes on it. She read off those north of Vancouver Island in hope that Tsil-tsil would recognize one as that of her own people. It was a small chance, of course. Often as not, the white name for a tribe was not what its people called themselves.

Tsil-tsil's only reaction was to the name "Haida," which brought fear into her eyes. This meant nothing, Dorothy pointed out; it merely reflected the fear of the Puyallups for the mysterious raiders from the north.

Haltingly, Tsil-tsil recalled a number of log buildings surrounded by a palisade. She could remember no name for it. She could think of nothing except Fort Nisqually, which had taken its place in her mind. They went over the map names again. She didn't think she was Bella Coola or Kwakiutl or Takulli. Cowichan? Tsimshian? Salish? She had no idea.

"Nusskay," she said suddenly. She thought it was the name her people called themselves.

He took her to the fort the next day, walking along the bluffs above the creek. They found the factor, a friendly Scot, overseeing the counting of about fifty Chilkat blankets that had arrived on the Hudson's Bay paddlewheeler *Beaver*. They were to be held here until they could be put on a ship for England. He was much pleased with them and spread one to show its colors and intricate, angular design. Foot-long fringe hung from its edges, and he explained that it was designed to be worn, not slept under. He draped it over his shoulders to demonstrate.

There were many blankets like this in the country of

her birth, Tsil-tsil said.

David asked the factor if he had heard of a tribe called Nusskay, but he had not. It was not the name of a major tribe; he was sure of that. Probably the name of a village, he said. Maybe a chief or a clan. He asked her the words for blanket, canoe, and water in her native tongue. This was difficult for her; at first she could think only of the Puyallup words. When she finally came up with others, they were strange to him. His guess was that she came from far to the north. He called in a clerk and an educated Delaware who had spent some time with interior Canadian tribes, but neither could be of help.

David took her back to the mission, and they spent the rest of the day indoors, continuing with her lessons. The next day, the third of her freedom, followed much the same pattern. On the fourth day, he loved her.

It began with a walk to the fort with the sun glistening on the creek and fragrant lilies in bloom on the prairie. He bought her presents from among the trade goods: a looking glass, a hairbrush, a comb. And, after a bit of haggling, one of the Chilkat blankets.

The *Beaver* was still anchored here, and they walked to the shore and looked down on her, a strange little snub-bowed, square-sterned craft with twin sidewheels. She was loading from a raft, hauling aboard barrels of flour to be distributed to other Hudson's Bay posts.

"She sails north from here," David said. "She stops at Hudson's Bay posts all the way up the coast. If you want to seek your people, you can go with her."

"Do you want me to go?" She had lost much of her shyness, and there was a teasing note in her voice.

73

He replied with great seriousness. "You must do what you truly believe is best. The ship will leave as soon as it is loaded."

"I will do what you say."

"I say nothing at all." He struggled with the inadequacies of Chinook. "You must decide. Think carefully and decide."

"What good am I to you?" she said. "You seldom touch me."

"Are you going?" he demanded. "Decide."

She shook her head, tipping her chin in challenge. He took her hands, raised the stunted one to his lips, and kissed the tiny fingers. She was in his arms then, warm and eager, and he led her into the woods that grew along the bluff.

He led her to a tiny clearing, a sun-speckled place of grass and moss, and he spread the Chilkat blanket. There was a time of soft laughter and of silliness as he taught her how to kiss. There was the time of tender seeking and then of surrender and of taking. When he had loved her, they slept and woke and he loved her again.

It was dusk when they got back to the mission and walked hand in hand into the parlor. And Alex was there.

He was pale and bone-thin and moved stiffly, but he was on his feet. He had just completed an inspection of the entire mission and was pacing the room and barking criticisms to Dorothy and Luke.

"...needs a mopping out. It had better be done tonight. I had expected the small pasture fence to be repaired by this time and the roan mare turned in there. She is going to foal any minute. I want lye put down the privies behind the church. . . . Hello, David. This is your slave, I take it."

"Her name is Tsil-tsil and she's free now. This is Dr. Cargo, Tsil-tsil."

Alex beamed at her. "Tsil-tsil. Star. She's a pretty thing. I can't approve, you know. This is a mission. I can't approve of your keeping a slut here."

Bitter words rose in David's throat and he put them down. He wanted to stay now. He wanted the job at the mill. Damn it, he *had* to stay; he had lost the advantage of not caring. He had a feeling that Alex wouldn't be fooled by a bluff, but he made it anyway. He took Tsil-tsil by the arm and turned back toward the door.

"Where are you going?"

"Out from under this immaculate roof. I'll try to get quarters at the fort."

"You're offended," Alex said, looking pleased. "That suggests you've got yourself into a situation you don't know how to deal with."

"You don't have to use words like 'slut.' "

"David, the girl is behaving in a perfectly acceptable way for a Puyallup Indian. She is a moral person. You are not. What do you think it's going to do to her when she realizes—fully realizes—that by white standards she is a slut?"

"My God, Alex, this is the frontier. Your eastern prudery doesn't apply."

"A very temporary condition. The tide of settlement will be here before you know it. We'll get families— wives and daughters and what you call eastern prudery by the wagonload. But the awful thing, David—the *awful* thing is that you're going to teach this girl white ways, aren't you? You're going to make her completely

75

vulnerable.''

"I'll take care of her. I'll not desert her."

"Yes," Alex said thoughtfully. "You've got it bad, haven't you?"

"Maybe I have."

"Yes. When the machinery gets here, we'll move Will to the new claim. You and the girl can move to his cabin....I keep thinking of your father. He'd be shocked, shocked."

Chapter 7

It was a good spring. In March and April there were long spells of bright dry weather, with the fort thermometer climbing to the high sixties in the afternoons. As soon as his shoulder was well enough, Alex took to tramping the prairie and shooting grouse. Luke put in a three-acre vegetable garden. Tsil-tsil and David made love and studied English.

Dorothy spent much time on horseback, visiting villages on the rivers or along the shore. She did this routinely, almost dully, and yet persistently. David wondered about her. It seemed to him that she was deliberately driving herself, tiring herself. Sometimes it seemed that she was close to the breaking point and trying to get there in a hurry.

As the weeks wore on, Alex became impatient for the arrival of the new mill machinery and increasingly critical of everyone. He insisted that David put in at least four hours a day at the mill. David grudgingly obliged him. After all, he was going to take over the operation when Will moved to the new site, and there was a lot to learn. He disliked the work, though, and especially resented Will's habit of leaving him in charge and going down to the shore to work on a small sloop that was in the final stages of construction. The boat would serve him well when he moved to the new site. Will said. He wouldn't have to rely on Indian canoes for transportation.

Once Alex saw the speed with which Tsil-tsil was learning English, he began to make plans to use her as a teacher. They had tried to get a school started but had failed, he said. It had been attended by both children and adults, but after a few weeks everyone had lost interest. He was certain, however, that an Indian teacher could make a success of the project.

David usually read to Tsil-tsil in the evenings, going slowly at first, pausing to explain unfamiliar words. He read a good deal from the Bible, which she liked, and then tried some other books from Alex's shelf. With patience, he got her interested in *Oliver Twist*. By the time they were halfway through, she was completely caught up in Oliver's adventures and fascinated by the strange life of a great white city. Lamb's *Tales from Shakespeare* was also a success.

The last days of May and first days of June were gloomy, with the sky almost constantly overcast. Then summer came in on a north wind. Days were long and warm and died slowly with magenta sunsets. Nights were cool. Sometimes there was fog in the mornings. Indian families from the back country trailed past the mission afoot and on horseback to spend the good weather on the beach. Some would stay with relatives; most carried a supply of reed mats that they would lay over a pole framework for shelter. Then, on the last day of June, the trek was reversed by a rumor that sent the people into the back country again.

David was at the mill when the frightening word reached Nisqually. He was directing the combination of manpower and oxpower that dragged the carriage through the saw. Tsil-tsil was there, too, having arrived on Dorothy's mare. She was in the mill office now, working on a lesson David had prepared for her. He put his back to the screeching saw for a moment and stepped to the door to ask, shouting through the noise, how she was coming. He got his smile and his answer and turned back just as the saw came to a stop. The crew clustered around a boy who had brought the news; then they surged down the trail. One thought to turn and fling a one-word explanation to the boss.

"Haida!"

Tsil-tsil heard and was at his side. He thought at first that raiders must be on the beach below, and he led her through the trees to a place where they could look down on it.

Indians were tearing down mat shelters and packing possessions into baskets, but there was no sign of war canoes. Will Triplet's little sloop, which he had been taking out daily, was gliding toward its anchorage, and that was all.

A few minutes later Will came up the trail, puffing on his pipe. He had talked to some of the people on the shore and took a scoffing attitude toward the alarm.

"The story is that Haidas burned a village. I can't make out where. Some think it's Chebaulip, but that's nonsense. Haidas would pick a small, isolated place. If the raid occurred at all, it was most likely away up north. This happens every summer. Nothing for you to do but shut down for a while."

David took note of the "you." Apparently Will had already consigned responsibility for this operation to him. Will thought of himself, David supposed, as superintendent of the new mill even though the machinery still hadn't arrived.

Will gave a little wave of his hand and trudged off toward his cabin. David scouted up saws and axes left by the cutters, turned oxen into pasture, greased the big saw, and he and Tsil-tsil rode back to the mission.

Tsil-tsil's long-conditioned fear of the Haida was evident in the tense way she sat her saddle and in her eagerness to canter. The Indian families congregating around the fort and those moving eastward across the prairie seemed to add to her nervousness. When they reached the mission, she went directly to the church. Indians were gathering there, too. Some were preparing to camp under the long shelter behind the building.

As Tsil-tsil went in, Dorothy came out. She called to David, who waited and walked to the house with her.

Neena was waiting at the kitchen door, full of frightened questions. Dorothy assured her that they were perfectly safe, that the Haidas were probably far to the north. Even if they were close, she added, they raided only beach villages and never came inland. Neena began counting on her fingers, tolling off friends who lived on the beach. Her hands were trembling.

"I give up," Dorothy said. "Go ahead and panic. Enjoy yourself."

The girl followed them into the parlor as if afraid to be alone. After a moment she retreated to the kitchen.

"Where's Alex?" David asked.

"In the church. He's telling the people there that God will protect them if they'll mend their ways. If the Haidas raid them, it will be because of gambling and polygamy and not coming to church. Sit down, David. I haven't seen much of you lately."

"No." He sat down.

"I thought at first we were going to be close

80

friends—intimate talks and all that. My confessions to you were really a ruse, you know. What I really wanted was for you to tell some of your dark male secrets to me. But Tsil-tsil came along and spoiled it all, didn't she?"

"She's kept me pretty busy." Dorothy laughed and he joined her. "That didn't sound the way I meant it."

"It was Alex who was really thwarted, I guess. One reason he was so eager for you to stay with us was to keep me amused. I realize that now."

"Amused?"

"I hope *that* sounds the way *I* meant it," she said. "You're a nice young man from back home. Alex thought that would be pleasant for me. He thought that having you around would make up for some of the loneliness and hardship. He can be very astute and very foolish at the same time."

"He has his faults. You magnify them."

"Are you going to defend him again?" She sighed noisily. "It's no good, David."

"You remind me of my mother," he said. "Sometimes I think you're much alike. Maybe you just have the same problems."

"She must have solved them."

"I'm not sure. She never quit trying, though."

"I'm not like that, I'm afraid. For me, there comes a time to give up or go mad."

"Do you know what my mother told my sister when she got married? She said, 'Don't make the mistake of seeking out your husband's weaknesses so you can overlook them.' "

Dorothy smiled without enthusiasm and got to her feet. "I'll have to think about that one. Excuse me.

Neena is going to stand around and tremble and not do a thing about supper unless I prod."

She went into the kitchen. It was the last time he had a chance to talk to her. The next day she rode off and didn't come back.

She left in midmorning on horseback, as she had left so many mornings before. It was not until suppertime that it occurred to anyone that something might be wrong.

They delayed the meal an hour and then ate without her. Alex questioned Neena, who remembered that Dorothy had taken two carpetbags with her. This wasn't unusual; she often carried food and presents to families she visited. Later he questioned Luke, who said she had ridden off toward the fort.

"She's probably run into someone who's sick," David said. "Or she's helping deliver a baby."

"Probably," Alex murmured. His manner had become strained, restless. He asked Luke to saddle a horse for him. David said to make it two, that he would go along.

They rode to the fort in the long summer twilight, finding it hazed by smoke from the Indian campfires around it. They discovered no one who had seen Dorothy that day.

They rode on to the mill and found Will's cabin deserted. Dorothy's horse was in the barn. Will's sloop was gone.

David sensed the truth then and he supposed Alex did, too. He tried to be reassuring. "There's very little breeze tonight, Alex, although there was a brisk one earlier. They may have gone for a boat ride and are having trouble getting back."

Alex seemed not to hear him. He mounted and led the way back to the mission at a dead gallop. They found Luke, Neena, and her husband seated around the kitchen table and eager for news. David followed Alex through the house and up the stairs to the large bedroom that he and Dorothy shared.

The room was paneled horizontally with foot-wide spruce. Alex lighted a lamp and took it to a corner near the head of the bed. Here he knelt and pressed against a bottom board that pivoted upward to reveal a hiding place in the wall. He reached into it and lifted out two small, bulging canvas bags. He ran his hand the length of the opening as if he expected to find more. When he did not, he let out a roar and got to his feet.

"She took half! There were two more bags—over six thousand in gold! Only she and I knew about this hiding place. She took half. *They* took half! She and Triplet."

Tsil-tsil had come into the doorway and stopped there. Alex looked pleadingly from David to her and back again. He dropped the bags on the bed.

"I brought it on myself," he moaned. "I trusted a godless scoffer and I'm getting what I deserve. But Dorothy—I trusted her, too."

David gestured helplessly. "Easy," he muttered. "Easy, Alex."

"He talked her into it. I know that."

Jerking open a drawer, Alex swung out the gunbelt with the two parrot-bill pistols holstered on it and buckled it around his waist. He untied the string around the neck of one of the bags and took out a paper-wrapped roll of coins that he dropped into his coat pocket. He shoved the bags back into their hiding place and pushed the panel into place.

Tsil-tsil slid out of his path as he strode through the doorway. David followed, pausing to kiss her.

"Go to bed," David said. "I have to look after him."

They rode to the fort again, running their horses recklessly in the darkness. They reined up at the Indian camp, with Alex bellowing in Nisqually at the top of his voice. He quickly had a crowd around him, a staring, frightened crowd. David stayed a short distance away. He strained to understand the Nisqually words and gathered that Alex was shouting for a canoe and crew to take him to Port Townsend.

Will and Dorothy had chosen their moment carefully. Pursuit, it seemed to David, was going to be well-nigh impossible. Surely no Nisqually would be willing to risk a trip the length of the Sound as long as there was talk of Haidas on it.

As it turned out, he was wrong. As Alex upped the price he would pay, a few young men grew interested. Finally, half a dozen of them agreed to take him, provided he arm them with rifles that they could keep as payment in addition to three blankets apiece. In spite of his entreaties, they refused to leave at once, however. They would meet him on the beach at dawn, they said.

He made arrangements at the fort for the rifles and reluctantly agreed to go back to the mission to try to get some rest. By the time they reached the house, a change in his mood was taking place. He was calmer and wanted to talk. With the Indians sent to bed, he and David sat at the kitchen table and sipped coffee.

"I've got to go after them," Alex said. "It's the only thing to do, isn't it? I'll follow them to hell if I must, but

I've got to bring her back."

"What will happen when you face Will?"

Alex thought about that for a moment, staring at the table and pursing his lips. "I'll let him keep part of the money. Yes, that will disillusion Dorothy. Yes, that will do it. I know him. I know them both."

"Alex, leave those pistols behind."

"You're afraid I'll kill him?"

"I'm afraid you'll try."

"No. No, I shan't do that. There'll be no need for it. You see, Dorothy is—well, an utterly cold woman. I'm speaking of the connubial relationship, you understand. By the time I catch up to them, he'll have found that out."

"That's too bad," David said uncomfortably. A man had no right to say that about his wife except perhaps to a doctor, he thought. He added almost hostilely, "I'd have guessed she was rather passionate."

Alex gave him a sharp look. "Yes, I suppose you would think that. She's a bit of a flirt, of course."

"And a warm person."

"A warm person and a cold woman. Ever since our child died. Will will have no patience with her. He's a lecherous man—you must know that. He's been sleeping with half a dozen different squaws. Uses my trade goods to pay them off, as a matter of fact."

"Leave the pistols behind," David said.

"Yes.... I'll wear them on the trip, of course. I'll take them off when I face Will. I'll make Port Townsend tomorrow night if it costs me fifty blankets. They'll still be there, surely. It would be a miracle if they caught a ship at once."

"Alex, if it doesn't go exactly as you anticipate, you'll lose your temper and start shooting."

"Good heavens, is that what you think of me?"

"I think anyone in your situation might act emotionally."

"Yes. I dare say I haven't been making a great deal of sense. David, should I do nothing? Should I let them go?"

"I think you should think about it."

"Do *nothing?* No, I'd never forgive myself. I'll bring her back. For her sake. Do you realize what she's doing to herself?"

"I'll go with you," David said.

"I need you here. You'll have to conduct services Sunday. I know you don't want to. You said you wouldn't do it again. But this is dire emergency. I implore—"

"All right, Alex, I'll do the best I can." David sighed. "On one condition. You leave those damn pistols with me."

Alex nodded slowly. Then he sprang to his feet and doffed the pistol belt, dropping it on the table with a clatter. David gathered it up and felt a little easier.

"I'm going up to bed," Alex said. "I won't sleep, of course. I need to be alone, though, don't I? I need to pray."

David went to his own room and found a low-burning lamp there and Tsil-tsil asleep in the bed. He touched her cheek and woke her.

"We're going to get married," he said.

The words surprised him almost as much as they did her. This was a time when he should have been distrustful of marriage. But he was thankful he had said the words, whether they were sensible or not.

"We'll have Alex do it before he leaves in the morning," he said.

She sat up and he held her. "I not leave you," she said.

They were married in the church before dawn. Luke and Neena were witnesses. Alex was at first full of petulant objections, but he beamed on them in appropriate fashion during the brief ceremony. No one had a ring that would do for the tiny third finger of Tsil-tsil's dwarf hand. She improvised one by sewing together the ends of a little strip of buckskin, and they used that.

After the ceremony, she and David rode to the shore to see Alex off. The crew was waiting on the beach, six silent, shadowy figures beside a canoe in the thinning darkness. A shifting fog lay over the bay. A Hudson's Bay halfbreed was waiting with the rifles and a supply of powder and lead. He would let no one touch the guns until Alex had signed a receipt for them. Alex issued them then and oversaw the loading of each. As the canoe shoved off, he waved his own weapon in the air in a warlike farewell.

"Feed my sheep," he called to David.

"My God," David said under his breath.

"What does he mean?" Tsil-tsil said.

The canoe disappeared into the rolling fog. They could still hear the chant of the paddlers, and it gave David an eerie feeling.

"He means to look after his congregation."

"Congreg—?"

"His people. He is a strange man."

"Close to God," she said.

"That would please him. That is what he would like

you to think.''

"You think not?''

"No closer than anyone else.''

She frowned, staring into the fog.

No doubt, many Nisquallies and Puyallups came to church that Sunday in hope of supernatural protection against the Haidas. Others probably came because they were afraid to go fishing or clam-digging and had nothing else to do. In any case, the gathering was the largest David had seen.

With the help of Luke and Tsil-tsil, he did his best to put on an adequate show and was mildly satisfied when the day was over. In the evening he strolled out to watch the gambling, although he found that he was of two minds about it now. He enjoyed the excitement of it. At the same time, he was annoyed that the Indians considered it a suitable climax to a day of worship. Most of all, he guessed, he was annoyed with himself for being annoyed.

The next day the Indians organized a watch from a bluff north of Nisqually Landing that provided a long view downsound. If Haida canoes were sighted, the watchers would touch off a smoke signal. Thus encouraged, men ventured to go fishing again, although most families still spent nights away from shore. It seemed to David that he might get the mill operating again. He visited it one morning in hope that some of the crew would hear he was there and return.

He took Tsil-tsil with him. They inspected the cabin that had been Will Triplet's and might now be theirs. Some of the trees behind it had been cleared away to provide a view of the bay from the rear window. This was paneless, closed by an inside shutter that he swung back to let in light and air. His exclamation brought Tsil-tsil to his side. They watched a bark round a point and creep into the bay.

"She'll want logs. I'll have to scare up a loading crew."

Two Nisqually canoes escorted her. A tall figure stood at the ship's stern rail, shouting at the canoes, waving his arms. Tsil-tsil recognized him first. She pointed excitedly.

"Look! It is Alex."

Chapter 8

They met him on the beach as he stepped out of one of the canoes. He was alone. He shook hands with David and gave Tsil-tsil a smile and a touch of his hat.

"How did services go?"

"Well enough, I guess."

Alex waved his hand toward the bark. "The mill machinery arrived. It was there aboard the *Cecropia* when I got to Port Townsend. We unloaded it at the new site. Now the captain wants all the logs and squared timbers we can give him."

"We'll need a loading crew," David said.

"The Indians on the island were as terrified as our people. They were all gathered at one big camp in the interior. We finally got some of 'em to build a raft and float the machinery ashore."

"Fine." David asked the burning question. "Alex, what about Dorothy?"

"Gone," Alex said very quietly. He turned away, apparently interested in the beaching of the second canoe. He sighed and went on. "They caught a ship that sailed a few hours after they got there. Will must have known about that ship, though I don't see how. She's bound for the Sandwich Islands and Shanghai. They'll leave her at Honolulu, I suppose, and catch another back to California. There was no use in following, David; it might be months before I caught up to 'em. And here was the *Cecropia* just arrived with my equipment. It was a sign, a reminder that I have work to do here....Look here, I believe we have the start of a loading crew right here."

The Indians from the two canoes gathered round. Alex hired them all with a minimum of barter and began explaining the work to them. Logs would be floated out to the ship and hauled aboard with her crane. Squared timbers would be carried down from the mill by hand and rafted out.

That night at supper Alex was full of talk about the new mill. He had left word with Murchison at Port Townsend to keep his eye out for an experienced sawyer who understood steam milling. In the meantime he and David would go to the new site, build a cabin, and perhaps set up some of the machinery.

"I'm making you a full partner in *both* mills now," he said. "Call it a wedding present."

"You're very generous," David said.

"You're going to make us both rich. We'll get the new man to take out a claim and give us an option on it. We're going to get control of all the timberland we can. Most of my share of the profits will go into the mission. My personal needs are few now. In fact, I shall live quite austerely. Yes, austerity has its rewards. But you—by the time your child is knee-high, you'll be a rich timber baron."

"My child?" David glanced at Tsil-tsil, who smiled shyly and shrugged.

"When do you expect it?"

"Alex, we're not expecting a child."

"Oh? I assumed— Well."

"You assumed that's why we got married."

"I jumped to conclusions. Yes. Well, my apologies."

The two men took their coffee into the parlor while Tsil-tsil and Neena were clearing the table. They sat in front of the fireplace as they had done so often with Dorothy. A fire was laid but not lighted.

"I suppose there'll be children sooner or later," David said.

"Does that scare you?"

"My commitment is made, Alex."

"She's a fine girl. She'll make a good teacher. It will be difficult for her at first. She's an ex-slave, and there's a stigma attached to that. But she'll win the people over. I'm sure of that." Alex rose, stretched, yawned. "I'm suddenly very tired. David, I had to let them go, didn't I?"

"Yes," David said.

"I keep thinking of Dorothy. I must be the blindest man God ever made."

"We're all blind."

"Yes. Yes, we are.... I wish it hadn't been Triplet, though. Blast it, he isn't what she wants. He offered her a way out of here, that's all. A way to get away from me—"

The *Cecropia*, hold and deck loaded, sailed on Saturday morning. On Sunday there were new Haida rumors and another big congregation. In spite of the uneasiness, Alex used the time between services to hire a canoe and crew to take him and David to the new mill site. It was again an expensive bit of negotiation that required him to furnish every man with a rifle.

Monday morning they shoved off, packed to the

gunwales with tools, food, lanterns, camping gear. David would have liked to take Tsil-tsil with them, but Alex pointed out that they needed every inch of space for baggage. They would be gone only for the rest of the week, he said, and would be back at the mission for Sunday services. He hoped in that time to clear a site for the mill and to get started on the construction of a cabin. They would continue to commute weekly until the machinery was assembled and the mill operating. By that time he hoped Murchison would send him a qualified sawyer who would take over day-to-day operation of the project.

There were six young men in the canoe crew. Because of the heavy load, they were reluctant to raise the mat sail and they paddled the whole distance. They worked steadily, their chant subdued and spiritless. They made no effort to hide their nervous eagerness to get to the island as quickly as possible. They reached it well before noon, keeping the canoe close to its shore until they came to the little bay David had last seen on the trip to Port Townsend.

They beached. The man in the bow leaped out to pull the canoe more solidly ashore. Instead of doing so, however, he froze, pointing to their rear. He barked a short and fearful word.

"Haida!"

Five hundred yards behind them, in open water just outside the bay, a great canoe glided past. It was broadside to them, red and black in the sunlight, fast-moving, high-prowed, and packed with men. A standing figure in the bow sighted them and swung an arm in their direction. The canoe immediately curled into the bay.

"Get ashore!" Alex yelled. "Take your guns!"

The crew was on its way over the sides in a panic. They remembered to snatch up their rifles but nothing else. David and Alex gathered up powder flasks and bullet bags out of the tangle of cargo, personal gear, and dripping paddles. The crew headed across the beach toward the low bluff above it. Alex began shouting orders in a mixture of languages.

"Get back here! Here! Form a line. We'll stand them off, blast it. The best way to invite an attack is to run. David, you take charge of those three. Line them up. We'll fire in volleys. I'll take these three."

The Indians hesitated, torn between their urge to flee and a need for leadership. Alex gestured, smiled, spoke more quietly and reassuringly. David asserted a tenuous authority over three of the men, pushing them into a line on the beach.

The war canoe sliced toward them at a slight angle, moving fast. David tried to count the paddles on the near side. At least ten. There were men between the rows of paddlers, some waving spears. There were more than thirty men in that canoe.

It took some frantic explaining to get the idea of firing in volleys across to the crew; but they saw that it made sense and steadied down.

"Spread 'em out a little," Alex ordered. "We'll fire first. We won't try to hit them at first. I doubt if these lads can come within twenty yards at this range, anyway."

The canoe was a shade over three hundred yards away, David guessed. Alex and his men raised their guns. Ridiculously, Alex gave the command to shoot in Chinook.

"Poo!"

The four guns flashed and thundered raggedly. The canoe slowed, turned a little. Then it corrected its course and came on faster than ever.

David counted ten and raised his rifle. His three men followed his lead. Alex's men were frantically reloading.

"Aim to draw blood!" Alex yelled. "Teach 'em a lesson."

David fixed his sights on the man in the bow. "Fire!" he called and pulled the trigger. The figure in the bow flounced but kept his feet. There was motion among the Haidas, confusion. Paddling stopped. Alex finished reloading and yelled at his men to hurry. They were not adept with guns and fumbled in their haste. They were fishermen, not hunters. It was possible that none among them had fired a gun a dozen times in his life.

The paddles of the war canoe were flashing again. It turned sharply and pointed out of the bay. Alex and his men raised their guns too late for a broadside shot at it. They fired with no noticeable effect.

"By heaven, we drove 'em off," Alex said. He shook David's hand and then the hand of each of his men. There was a moment of laughter and mutual congratulations among the Nisquallies, brief and uneasy. They had driven off the terrible Haida, a thing they would tell about all their lives, but right now they had difficulty believing it.

"I think I winged one of them," David said.

"Good. They've no right in these waters. It's time they learned that."

"Will they be back?"

"Not that bunch. They'll want nothing to do with us."

The crew, obviously, was not so sure. They kept staring uneasily toward the point around which the canoe had disappeared.

"It seems to me they might land up the shore a way and come at us on foot," David said.

"Most unlikely. They'll ask themselves how many more well-armed people might be back in the woods."

They carried their gear up the bluff to a creek bank where the new mill would be built. The equipment was here, crated and covered with tarpaulins. Alex, like a child with a new toy, had to uncover it and show it off—a donkey engine, an assortment of wheelwork, belts, chains, and pulleys. There were crated tools, too—two-man saws, bucksaws, peavies, shining new axes.

They lunched on sandwiches, the Indians keeping a nervous watch on the bay. Then Alex set off for the camp where the local Indians were gathered. As soon as he was gone, David posted a lookout. The other Nisquallies lost their edginess and settled down to work, cutting post-thick trees and trimming the trunks for a small shelter.

Alex was back in an hour with half a dozen Indians from the interior. Their arrival destroyed everyone's inclination to work. They wanted to hear about the encounter with the Haidas, and the Nisquallies wanted to tell about it—over and over again.

They talked and puttered till sunset; then both groups started off to the interior to spend the night. They urged Alex and David to join them, but Alex refused.

"We gave those Haidas a lesson and they won't be

back," he said to David. "Let's show these people we're sure of that. We've got to encourage 'em to move back to the shore."

David felt the uneasiness of the Indians. Putting that aside, however, it seemed to him that the sensible thing would be to spend the night in the Indian camp, if only to make friends with more of the people here. If it hadn't been for the brush with the Haidas, he thought, that is what Alex would have done. But now he was bent on establishing their victory as an important one by proving the shore was safe.

Alone, they built a fire, made coffee, cooked bacon and flapjacks. A breeze sifted in off the water, languid but cool to bodies still damp with the day's sweat. The Indians had got corner posts into the ground for the small cabin; now the two men stretched a tarpaulin over these, laid fir and cedar branches under it, and rolled up in their blankets.

They lay snug with the faint sound of the tide-washed beach reaching them and the smells of sea and forest in their nostrils. They talked of the Haida canoe, of plans for the mill, the mission. Then Alex brought up more personal things.

"She left me," he said. "I'm alone. I'm just beginning to grasp that."

"I suppose it is hard to realize," David muttered.

"Loneliness will be good for me. I shall be celibate now, in thought as well as in deed. I see the Way now, the true Way. Our appetites dominate us, David. We are their slaves. We must subdue the beast within us in order to be more than beasts. That is man's purpose on earth, isn't it? To become more than a beast. To realize his godly potential—"

"Mortification of the flesh?"

"Yes. Are you laughing at me? You're a young man, newly married. You're content to be a prisoner of your senses a while longer. Perhaps that's as it should be . You married Tsil-tsil, and that was a good thing, a commitment to the child she will bear."

"You keep talking as if she were pregnant."

"She is. I'm quite sure of it."

"Alex, she would have told me. I know she would."

"Quite possibly she doesn't know it herself. Or isn't sure yet."

"But you are."

"There are signs an observant person learns," Alex said. "They are much easier to spot in a young woman than in an older one. A certain texture of the skin about the eyes. A slight fullness of the tissues, especially in the face. A radiance—"

Restlessness stirred in David. He wanted to get back to the mission and ask Tsil-tsil point blank. "You have the damnedest way of trying to establish truth by declaration," he said.

There was a brief silence, with only the sounds of their breathing and of the steady whisper of the waves in the distance. Then Alex said, "Explain that, please."

"The Haidas are driven off forever because you have declared it so. You are no longer a prisoner of your appetites because you have declared it so. And now you have declared Tsil-tsil pregnant."

"I see. Yes. Pride—a great weakness. My dominating demon. It's what drove Dorothy away, I suppose."

They talked no more. Sinking into sleep, David came alert with a start. Some small foreign sound had

99

touched an alarm in some deep part of his being.

He tried to identify the sound, to relate it to the sting of fear it brought. It had been sharp, harsh, brief. The grinding of a canoe nose on the beach? The thought brought a new stab of fear that he rejected. He had dreamed the sound. Yet he could not be sure. He listened for a long time, hearing only Alex's heavy breathing and the distant lapping of the tide. He dozed and came solidly awake again, unable to smother a residue of fear. Damn it, if he wanted a decent night's rest, he had better calm himself with a look at the beach. He quietly unwrapped himself from his blankets and got to his feet.

They had left their rifles against a post a yard from where Alex slept. He took one of them and stepped out of the shelter. He wound among the trees until he could look down on the concave reach of shore in frail moonlight.

The tide was nearing flood. Shining black mass of water nibbled with silver lips at narrow rind of beach. Dull mass of forest laced unevenly into night sky. He scanned the beach and found a shadow that seemed strange to him, a long dark mass indistinct against the rise of shore. He studied it a long time before he was sure it was a canoe.

He raced back through the trees, stumbling in the soft duff. He reached the shelter, bent over Alex, shook him.

"There's a canoe on the beach, a big one. We're getting out of here. Don't argue. Just move quietly."

Alex staggered to his feet. David turned to the post to snatch up the other rifle. It wasn't there.

"Alex—"

He saw the shadows pressing in on them then, tall, vague forms at first and then grotesque creatures in helmet-masks that added as much as three feet to their height. They came from all sides of the shelter in a circle, converging slowly, spears and axes in their hands. They halted at the edge of the shelter. David dropped his rifle, sensing that one small threatening move with it would bring him a spear in the back. Alex drew himself up, hands on hips, and demanded in Chinook to know what was going on.

No one paid the slightest attention to him. Four men advanced on them, prodding them out of the shelter with spears. Others swarmed over them, throwing them to the ground, tearing off their clothing. Alex struggled for a moment, flailing wildly with his arms, but he was quickly knocked limp by a blow from a war club. With a spearhead at his belly, David offered no resistance except to try to cling to some of his clothing.

Naked, they were pulled to their feet and prodded toward the shore. Alex was dazed and could move only at a slow, staggering pace. When they reached the beach, two of the weird masked figures seized him by the arms to support him. They all jogged along the beach then. No one spoke. The only sounds were those of feet on gravel and an occasional clatter of wooden armor.

They reached the great canoe and David and Alex were forced aboard. The Haidas shed their armor and their elaborate helmet-masks and were suddenly human—tall, broad-faced and broad-shouldered men with hair bobbed to shoulder length, arms and legs covered with tattooing. They took their places in the sixty-foot craft with practiced efficiency and shoved off. They had hardly spoken during the entire raid. Now, afloat, they began to laugh and talk. As soon as they were out of the bay they burst into a triumphant chant to the rhythm of their paddles.

Chapter 9

There were three dozen men in the canoe. Ten manned paddles on each side. Others sat between them on the thwarts or on carved black boxes that filled much of the craft. A lookout stood in the bow behind the elaborately carved-and-painted bowsprit. From time to time he extended an arm in signal to the helmsman, who steered with a seven-foot paddle.

David and Alex sat in the bottom of the canoe, shivering in nakedness and washed by bilge water. David had been cut in several places by spear points. The wounds were shallow, the result of prodding; but a small blood vessel at the back of his thigh had been cut, and his leg was drenched with blood. He clamped a hand against it, and after a while the bleeding stopped. Alex sat with knees drawn up and head thrown back, a stunned emptiness in his hawklike face.

"You were wrong," David said. "My God, how you were wrong!"

Alex looked at him as if surprised to find him there. He said nothing and returned his gaze to the night sky.

"You're always wrong. I should have learned that by this time."

Alex seemed not to hear.

"What do we do?" David demanded. "Try to buy our way out of this? Offer them blankets? Where do we get blankets? How do we arrange for payment?"

"Immortality," Alex said, "is merely perception of ourselves by a timeless consciousness."

David studied the upturned face, not quite believing his ears. He raised a hand to Alex's bony shoulder and clasped it gently. "Alex, snap out of it. Do you know where we are?"

Alex smiled sadly at the stars. "The black night of the soul."

"Alex, we're prisoners."

"Yes. We must escape."

"The first chance we get, we've got to make a run for the woods. I have a feeling they won't follow far into the woods."

"We are prisoners of ourselves," Alex said. "We are estranged and gone backward."

"Alex, for God's sake, snap out of it. We're prisoners of the Haidas. Don't you understand that?"

"Ye see indeed, but perceive not."

It was useless. Alex was out of his head. It's up to me, David thought. I've got to try to treat with them. If that doesn't work, I've got to make a break for it.

They traveled for about an hour, swiftly angling across the channel east of the island, bearing northward until the red eye of a campfire came into sight on the mainland shore. Using this as a beacon, they put in on a narrow rim of beach in front of a low, grassy area. Four Haida youths waited here, boys in their early teens, tending the fire and guarding three Indian prisoners. These were two women and a man. They lay in the knee-high grass, the man naked and bound hand and foot, the women with blankets over them. All had ropes tied around their necks, free ends held by a guard who sat with a war club in his lap.

David and Alex were led to this group and motioned to sit down. Alex obeyed docilely. David put his hands on his hips and turned to the Haida nearest him.

"Who is chief here?" he inquired in Chinook. "I ask to speak to him."

The man made a threatening gesture with his war club. Two others seized David and threw him to the ground.

"I wish to speak of payment. Many blankets."

No one paid the slightest attention to him. They bent his arms behind his back until each palm touched the opposite elbow; then they bound them tightly. His ankles were tied with a short length of rope left between them so he could take very small steps. Then a rope was knotted around his throat and the end tossed to the guard. Alex was tied in the same mannner.

David lay on his stomach next to one of the women prisoners. In an effort to ease the pain in his arms, he rolled slowly and sat up. The woman also sat up, keeping her blanket over her. She was not tied except for the rope around her neck. She spoke to David in Chinook.

"Talking to them is no good. They do not hear."

"Don't they speak Chinook?"

"When they wish. But they don't like to speak it. They consider it degrading."

She was young, under twenty. She wore her hair in one long thick braid that emphasized the strange shape of her skull, severely elongated in infancy.

"What tribe are you?" he asked.

"Snohomish. The Haidas came in the night and burned our village. Everyone got away except us three. This is my sister beside me. The man is her husband."

"Your hands and feet are not tied," David said.

"My sister and I have been friendly to the young men and they no longer tie us."

"Why don't you untie the rope from your neck and run away?"

"I'm afraid," she said. "And where would I go? I cannot go back to my people. I am degraded."

"How long have you been a prisoner?"

After a moment, she said, "This will be the fourth night. It is greatly degrading."

"Who is chief here?"

"There are two families," she said.

"And two chiefs?"

"One is very tall, the tallest man here. He is called Kat. The other is called Skow. He was wounded in the arm by a bullet today. Were you among those who fired on us?"

"Yes."

"You must understand that the names I have given are short names used by their relatives. They have other names—chief's names."

"I mustn't use the short names?"

"They would consider it degrading."

The Chinook word for degrading or degraded was *keekwulee*. The girl was clearly trying to adjust to the realization that she herself was suddenly and hopelessly *keekwulee*. She was greatly occupied with the word.

"There are many things that they consider degrading," she said. "When we had to run away from your bullets we came here and made camp and everyone was degraded. Kat and Skow promised they would make slaves of you."

Slaves. He had thought of himself as a prisoner, that

was all. But now he faced it. He was a slave. Someone owned him.

"They will take us to their land far to the north," the girl said. "I have heard it's a shadow land where the sun never shines. I don't know if that is true."

The Queen Charlotte Islands. How far had Alex said they were from Puget Sound? Seven hundred miles?

"I hope it's not true," she said. "I hope the sun shines sometimes."

David lay down on his side, facing her. He found it impossible to relieve the ache in his tightly bound arms. And the night was cold. Both he and Alex were shivering violently.

"Your hands are free," he said to the girl. "Pull some of this grass and throw it over us."

With a glance at the guard, she tore up some of the tall, coarse grass and laid it tentatively on David's thighs. When there was no objection from the guard, she gathered more, crawling naked out of her blanket. The woman on the other side of her joined her and they collected armfuls of grass and piled them over David, Alex, and the Snohomish man.

The grass was slightly moist with dew, but it trapped body heat and provided a degree of warmth. David and Alex lay back to back. David maneuvered until his right fingers touched Alex's trussed arms. The cord was slick and soft, the knots wire-tight. Working one-handed with numb fingers, David found the task of untying the knots monumental.

The Haidas bedded down in rows, all sleeping with their heads pointed northward. Only the guard remained awake. He sat with his knees drawn up, clutching the ends of the neck ropes. Sometimes he chanted a gruff, rhythmic song, perhaps to keep himself from falling asleep.

At last a knot slipped in David's fingers, and in a little while, another. There was slack in the cord then and Alex was able to slowly work himself free. Keeping as much of the long grass over them as he could, he rolled over and began to untie David. When the job was finished, David cautiously drew up his knees and undid the cord that hobbled him.

"There's brush off to the left," he whispered. "Beyond that there's rising ground and what looks like timber. If we can get into it, we ought to be all right."

It seemed to him that darkness was already beginning to fade. There wasn't much time left. He whispered to Alex to remove the rope from his neck. He left his own as it was.

"I'm going to try to get close to the guard. As soon as I hit him, you beeline for that slope. Alex, do you understand?"

"Yes, of course. But I say—"

"Don't argue. Just do it."

"Yes, of course.

There was a vagueness in his voice David didn't like; he could only ignore it and hope for the best. With arms behind him as if he were still tied, he got to his feet.

The guard was instantly alert. David said in Chinook that he wanted to make water. The guard, on his feet now, pointed to a spot a few feet to his right. David minced through the grass as if his ankles were still tied. He stopped half the length of the tether rope from the guard. He dared not turn his back for fear of exposing his free hands. The guard held the tether ropes in his left hand, war club ready in his right. He was alert, tense.

David struggled with a leaden uncertainty.

Then Alex sat up, shedding grass, yawning noisily. David leaped at the instant of diversion. He seized the war club with his left hand and swung hard at the guard's jaw with his right. The blow landed solidly. The man went down, dropping the ropes, but not before he had called out a warning monosyllable.

Whirling, David lost his grip on the war club and didn't try to pick it up. He ran toward the slope, stumbling in the tall grass and cursing the stiff reluctance of his legs. There were sharp voices behind him and he glanced back at a confusion of shadows, none of them very close. Alex had not followed. David glimpsed his tall naked figure, arms extended, moving slowly toward the beach, commanding the attention of the roused sleepers and drawing some of them toward him.

David had a fair start on the others. He reached scattered brush at the foot of the slope and could see now that there was indeed heavy forest not far ahead. Hope flared and was smothered as figures rose in the brush about him. He veered right. His feet tangled in something that felt like a blanket and he careened into a crouching man. They both fell. David flailed wildly at the man and rolled to his feet. He was wrenched flat by a jerk on the rope that still circled his neck.

Men swarmed down on him, falling on top of him. With a sense of utter distaste, he understood that not all the Haidas had slept in the vicinity of the fire. Some had spread blankets here on the slope, perhaps with the idea of cutting off the most feasible course of escape. He tried to fight back as men seized his arms and others kicked and beat him unmercifully. He lay helpless in a

109

world of jolting pain and blinding light that at last faded into nothingness.

He floated back slowly and for a time was not himself but the things he sensed: sloshing bilge water, the smells of sweat and sea, the rhythm of a chanted song. He was warmth of sun on skin, mother comfort of silken flesh, the adze-marked inside of a canoe hull painted red. Slowly, existence expanded. Chinook words brought him fully to comprehension.

"You are alive," the Snohomish girl said cheerfully.

He stirred and groaned and sat up, pierced by stifling pain. Nearly naked men sat on thwarts above him. The girl was beside him; he had been lying in a twisted position with his head on her thighs. He closed his eyes against stinging sunlight.

"Where's Alex?" he said.

She didn't understand. He raised himself, gasping with pain, and looked up and down the rows of men. He glimpsed a white body a few feet behind them and saw that Alex was manning a paddle. He was glistening with sweat but appeared to be in good spirits. His lips moved as he tried to catch the words of the Haidas and join in their chant.

"We have been traveling north all day," the girl said.

David looked over the gunwales. They were several miles offshore and moving swiftly. He looked down at his naked body and saw great bruises on his arms, trunk, thighs. No bones were broken in his arms or legs, he decided; the sharp pain was somewhere in the middle of him. Ribs, probably. There was a ringing in his ears and a terrible dryness in his throat. His voice was that of a stranger.

"Is there water?"

The girl shook her large, strangely shaped head. She smiled at him with her eyes and pulled him toward her. He leaned against her and closed his eyes.

They traveled until dusk, when they landed on a wooded island. Cramped and pain-torn, he had difficulty getting out of the canoe and then in walking. The girl steadied him across the beach to a campsite on grass-speckled sand.

The prisoners were herded to one side and made to sit down. They were guarded by three young men, one of whom was the guard David had slugged the night before. David was gasping for breath. Alex reached out and laid a hand on his forehead.

"You took a brutal beating, but I guess you were lucky. They were angry enough to kill you."

"I think I have some broken ribs," David groaned. "I don't think it's anything worse than that." With the sun gone, he was beginning to feel cold.

Alex was himself again, David thought. At least he was rational and knew where he was. Yet there was something different about him, something odd about his voice and manner.

"Alex, we've got to make another try," David said. "If somehow we could steal the canoe—"

"That's impossible. It's always guarded. It's too big for two men to launch, anyway. No. I want you to promise me you'll make no further try until I say so. Give me your word."

"Alex—"

"Your word. At least for tonight."

"All right. I guess I'm not up to it tonight, anyway."

Haida camp-making was an exercise in quiet efficiency. Each man had his task and did it without delay. Food and gear, stored in boxes, were unloaded from the canoe. Wood was scouted, stones ringed into fireplaces. Water was boiled in cooking boxes by adding hot stones. Roots and cakes of inner spruce bark were stirred in along with seaweed gathered fresh. The result was a lumpy soup that was served in wooden bowls.

The prisoners were served after the others had eaten. The broth had a strong musty taste but David found he was suddenly ravenously hungry and drank his portion quickly. The food warmed him for a few minutes, but as darkness thickened he began to shiver.

The women prisoners were taken away, led off down the beach by a group of young men. David, Alex, and the Snohomish man huddled together for warmth. After a time, a man brought ropes to the guards, who approached the prisoners to tie them. Raising his eyes to the man who had brought the ropes, Alex spoke slowly and calmly in Chinook.

"There will be no attempt to run away tonight. We will promise."

The man threw back his head and looked down his nose haughtily. He had the broad-shouldered, broad-hipped, thin-legged build of the other Haidas, but he was unusually tall. He must be the chief called Kat, David realized.

"We're on a small island," Alex said. "How can we run away?"

Kat took back several of the ropes from the guards, leaving just the neck ropes. These were secured, but hands and feet were left free. Alex spoke his thanks, promising that he would begin at once to learn the Haida language so he could address a chief properly. He pointed to David and made another request.

"This man needs a blanket. He is sick and must be kept warm."

Kat regarded David with haughty lack of concern. He spoke to one of the guards, who translated the words into Chinook.

"He is a fool. Let him be sick. Let him die."

"Alex," David said. "This man is a chief. Try to buy our freedom from him. My God, offer him a thousand blankets."

Kat had already turned away and was on his way back to the fires.

"I tried that this morning," Alex said. "They're almost impossible to negotiate with because they're very proud and they have an aversion to Chinook. And they are plainly taken with the idea of bringing home white slaves."

Two of the guards followed Kat. The other sat down with the neck ropes in his hand.

"We could jump him," David said. "He has a knife at his belt. We could get it before the others could get here. We could hold it at his throat and keep them off. We could get to the canoe."

"No. We gave our word."

"Alex, that blow on the head did something to you. We're slaves. They're taking us to the Queen Charlottes."

"That chief would like us to try something. I could see it in his eyes. I guarantee you he'll be ready for us. Accept, David, accept. Consider this an adventure." He laughed happily. "Think of it! We're with the mysterious Haida!''

''My God,'' David muttered.

They stretched out close together. David lay between Alex and the Snohomish man. They were both concerned for him and felt it was important to keep him as warm as possible. Grateful, he drifted into strange and fitful dreams. He was wakened when the women were brought back.

They both had blankets. The Snohomish man moved away and lay down with his wife. The other girl took his place, spreading her blanket over David, Alex, and herself.

Chapter 10

There was little activity in the camp until after sunup, and it turned out that the day was to be spent leisurely. Everyone, including the prisoners, began the morning with a plunge in the icy water of the Sound. Breakfast was the same musty porridge as the last meal. Afterward, some of the Indians took the canoe a little way offshore to fish for cod. Then everyone just lazed around and talked, smoked, dozed. They passed around bricks of a coarse greenish tobacco that they called *gwul*. Two or three stuffed it into carved black pipes and smoked it. The others chewed it.

David was steadier, but the pain in his ribs was crippling until the Snohomish girl improvised a corset for him. She begged a piece of ragged and dirty buckskin, washed it in seawater, and scoured it with sand. When it had partially dried in the sun, she bound it around David's middle. Shrinking a bit as it dried, it gave support to his ribs and greatly eased his breathing.

The girl's Snohomish name was a yard-long combination of sibilants and gutturals. A short form of it sounded something like "Tsooktsee," which was close enough to "Susie" so that he called her that. The Haidas addressed all prisoners as "*huldinga*." It meant "slave," Susie said.

From time to time she and her sister were taken off down the beach, a demand that they accepted matter-of-factly. Susie, in fact, sometimes seemed to encourage it with flirtatious glances.

She had a way of picking up information during these sessions. She learned, for instance, that the party was waiting here for another canoe to join them for the long voyage north to their village. She also reported that there had been an argument between the two chiefs, Kat and Skow, about the white prisoners. Kat wanted to kill them and take their heads home on poles. Skow insisted that they be kept alive.

In the afternoon some of the Haidas began to gamble, playing a two-handed game called *sin*. Short marked sticks were juggled under a mat by one player and the other tried to guess their position. David sat down near one of the games to watch. An Indian approached and halted squarely between him and the players, throwing back his head and looking down haughtily.

"*Huldinga*," he sneered.

He was about David's age, well built, heavily tattooed, naked except for a loincloth. His upper left arm was bandaged with coarse cloth. He stood with arms akimbo, dipped a foot into the loose, dry sand, and kicked some into David's face.

David rolled away. Wiping his eyes, spitting, he got to his feet. The man laughed, spoke in Haida, and pointed to the ground. David realized from the bandaged arm that this must be the chief called Skow, the man his bullet had grazed. Alex called softly from a few yards away.

"He wants you to sit down."

"Why doesn't he say so in a language I can understand?"

"*Mitlite!*" Alex said, enunciating the Chinook

116

word. "You understand and now he knows it. Do it, David."

David obeyed. Skow promptly dipped his toe into the sand and kicked more of it on him. This time David was ready and raised his hands to protect himself.

"*Huldinga!*"

"How many blankets for our freedom?" David asked.

Skow beckoned to the young guard David had knocked down two nights before. He spoke crisply. The boy translated into Chinook.

"Your hair will grow long. It will turn gray. You will be a slave as long as you live."

"You would be wise to ask my people for blankets. If you do not, they will come for us in ships with many guns."

"Stop it," Alex said. "You're inviting him to kill us."

Skow spoke again, a look of amusement on his face. Again the boy translated. "If iron people come after you, we will make slaves of them all."

"You don't understand their numbers or the numbers of their guns," David said.

"For God's sake, stop it!" Alex hissed.

Skow now motioned for David to get to his feet. He did so, thinking that perhaps Alex was right, perhaps he was to be killed. He looked Skow in the eye, smiling to hide his fear and then realizing that the smile might be taken for insolence.

Skow and the guard held a brief conversation. Then the guard said, "You caused me dishonor by striking me with your fist. Skow Hungay has spoken with your owner. They agree you should be punished."

"Who is my owner?"

"Haidamasa Kat, who is also a chief."

Kat, the tall one. The one who wanted to kill the white prisoners and be done with it. Men seized David's arms from behind, bringing racking pain to his chest.

"Easy," Alex called. "Show respect. That's what they want."

Skow raised a fist above his head and struck an awkward, hammerlike blow at David's face. David rolled away as best he could, but the fist caught him solidly in front of the ear. His knees buckled, and he collapsed on the sand.

He got slowly to his hands and knees, shaking his head, pretending to be hurt worse than he was. He was pulled to his feet and his arms pinned again. The young guard stepped forward; now it was his turn to strike, it seemed. He looked almost apologetic as he raised a fist. He swung more from the side than Skow had done, striking with the inside of his fist. It was a painful blow, but not so hard as the one Skow had struck. David could have kept his feet but made no effort to. He lay still for a moment, then began to get up slowly. Skow and the guard had turned their backs and were walking away. David sat on the sand, touching his numb face with his fingertips. He was not badly hurt. He understood vaguely that the pride of these people made it necessary for him to be struck in the manner in which he had struck. They seemed to have forgotten that he had taken a murderous beating at the time.

In a few minutes Skow came back. He did not stand over David now but quietly sat down near him. Even more surprising, he spoke in Chinook.

"You come from the east," he said. His tone was almost friendly. "All iron people come from the east. Is that true?"

"True," David said.

"They are of many nations?

"Yes."

"You are a *Boston?*"

"Yes." *Boston* was the Chinook word for a citizen of the United States.

"In the north we see very few Bostons and then only on ships. At Fort Simpson there are King George men. Would they pay blankets for a Boston?"

"Yes. Then my people would pay them for the blankets."

Skow considered this, nodding thoughtfully. His manner had changed completely. Having demonstrated his authority, he could now sit down and talk in a friendly fashion.

"Why did you come from the east?" he asked.

Groping for an answer that would make sense, David smiled and said, "I wish to become rich cutting trees and selling them to ships."

Skow returned the smile. "To become rich. And now you are a slave."

David laughed uneasily. He puzzled about this proud young chief and about the world that had shaped him. He considered the tattoos that covered Skow's arms, thighs, and chest. There was a large eye high on his chest, balanced on the hilt of a knife. Below that was a monster with a wolf's head, split in two and done in back-to-back profiles. The rest of him was covered with animals, fish, birds. All were neat and symmetrical and conventionalized. Here were the things Skow valued. Here were charms against the things he feared. Here were his legends, his experience, his good name. And high on his left arm was the bandage. The wound under it must be slight: it didn't interfere with the use of his arm. But what part of the man's being had been torn by that bullet? What proud crest mutilated? What careful magic flawed?

"Cutting trees will make you rich?" Skow shook his head as if this were beyond comprehension. He touched the tattooed eye on his chest. "I am rich. All the chiefs of my people are rich. My family owns many thousands of blankets, many slaves, many canoes. We own four copper shields that have been brought down from the north. Each is worth ten thousand blankets. No, you will not be set free for a few blankets. There will be no more talk of buying freedom."

"You said that you're not my owner. Perhaps he'll see the wisdom of selling me back to my people."

"Haidamasa Kat is also rich, almost as rich as I. There are many rich men in our village. You will see for yourself."

"I've heard much of your people," David said. "They are great warriors."

"We go where we wish. We take what we like. Do the iron people think they will not be taken for slaves when they come within our reach?"

You damn fool, David thought. In another generation the iron people will have your islands and your goods and your souls.

Skow got to his feet. He reached down and touched David's shoulder with his fingertips. It was a pat such as a man might give a horse or a dog, David thought.

Late in the afternoon, the second canoe arrived. It

was a few feet shorter than the other but had about the same beam of seven or eight feet and carried almost as many men. It was in command of a relative of Skow, a middle-aged man with a drooping mustache. He had seven prisoners: four women, an old man, and two small boys. They were Nootkas, taken in a raid on a Vancouver Island village. Two of the Haidas were wounded, and it was clear the Nootkas had put up a considerable fight.

There was a medicine man with the new party, a spindly old codger who wore a polished bone through the septum of his nose, a necklace of shark's teeth, an apron of puffin bills, and did his hair up in a tight knot on top of his head. He was much concerned with the wounded men. One had a spear wound in the stomach. The other was unconscious from a blow on the head. The old shaman got them stretched out on the sand and chanted and shook his necklace at them while others cleaned the blood off them and covered them with blankets. Suddenly he noticed the white prisoners and hurried over for a closer look.

Taking off the necklace and holding it in front of him, he circled them warily, muttering to himself. Glaring, he moved closer, shaking the necklace. He made a careful inspection of David first, looking into his eyes, shaking the necklace at him, making him open his mouth and peering into it. He did the same with Alex and then turned to Kat and Skow, who had come up to watch. He held a terse, tense conference with them, never taking his eyes off the prisoners. With a last shake of the necklace in their direction, he went back to his patients.

He then embarked on a series of incantations that

kept him the center of attention for the rest of the day. He danced, chanted, and circled the camp, chasing away spirits with a stick. Next he came up with a bag of dried herbs that he sprinkled in a circle around the two patients and then in a larger circle around the entire camp. As an afterthought he trotted over to David and Alex and sprinkled a pinch on each of them. After that he shook an elaborately carved rattle over the patients and then went into some mumbo-jumbo with a hollow tube with stoppers at both ends—a spirit-catching tube, Alex said.

Finally, he ordered a sweat hut erected on the beach, a temporary affair swiftly built of poles and mats. Stones were heated and placed in a trench inside. Water was poured over them to produce great clouds of steam. The warrior who was in a coma was then placed inside and the medicine man went into a rattle-shaking dance around the hut. Within minutes the patient stirred, groaned, turned over. The medicine man spoke to him. The man crawled out of the hut, looking shaky and confused. Men helped him across the beach and into the icy water. He came out sputtering and was dismissed as cured.

The other wounded man was now semiconscious but still moaning constantly. The medicine man changed the poultice that had been put on the ugly stomach wound. He danced and rattled and sang. Twilight came. A meal was cooked and eaten. The man grew worse. The medicine man ordered the stones in the sweat hut heated up again. When the steam was ready, he ordered the patient put inside.

"No!" Alex strode forward, raising his arms in protest, barking Chinook words. "You don't sweat a man with a stomach wound!''

All activity stopped. The shaman gave a reflexive little shake of his rattle in Alex's direction.

"The man is cut up inside and must be kept quiet. He should be given no food for several days. That is the only chance he has."

The old man began a new dance, sidestepping around Alex, pointing a finger at him, shaking the rattle. David sensed disaster. Remarkably restrained until now, Alex had picked the worst possible moment to assert himself. He was putting himself in competition with this old humbug.

"You are surely a great man of magic," Alex said. "I have no magic. I know a little bit about healing, that is all. There is no evil spirit in the warrior to be sweated out. He is cut up and must be left to heal. He should not be moved."

The old man continued his slow, weird dance. The men who had come to lift the patient hesitated. There was low-voiced talk among the others.

"You are warriors," Alex said, rolling his preacher's voice out over the camp. "You have seen many men wounded. Have you ever seen a man with a hole in his belly helped by sweating?"

Skow came forward, calling out sharply to the medicine man. The two held a short discussion. They were joined by the mustached chief and then by Kat. Skow was calm and businesslike, asking brief questions and listening thoughtfully to the medicine man's answers. The mustached chief occasionally put in a word or two. Kat said nothing. He stood with his hand on a knife he wore at his side. He kept throwing ugly glances at Alex.

In the end, the medicine man got his way. The wounded man was carried to the sweat hut and put inside. He had begun a weak, intermittent moaning, interrupted by coughing and a struggle for breath. For a while he could be heard inside the hut. Then he was silent. They lifted him out and he was dead.

His body was laid out on a blanket. The company gathered in a circle around it and took up a plaintive chant. The medicine man danced, moving arms and body more than feet. Then he began a harangue, pointing accusingly at Alex. Alex was brought to the center of the circle. David watched helplessly.

The medicine man seemed to be expounding some occult logic that made Alex responsible for the warrior's death. The mustached chief interrupted with a brief comment. Some of the other Indians put in a few words. They seemed not to agree with the medicine man and to be presenting their arguments in a polite and low-key way.

David was startled to find Skow standing over him. The chief had circled the camp and quietly come up behind him. He sat down beside David.

"Your friend put the death spirit into the wounded warrior," he said, speaking slowly in Chinook. "That is what Kwawlang says."

"Kwawlang is the name of the medicine chief?"

Skow nodded. "He is of my household. He is more than a hundred years old. He has died three times. Each time his spirit has gone into a living man who has taken his name."

"Perhaps it is true," David said. "Who can be sure?"

"It is true. He has told me of things he remembers

from a hundred years ago. He's a good man, a good friend, although we don't always agree." Skow was silent for a moment, then he said, "Your friend is my property. I don't want him killed. Is it true that he has power over the death spirit?"

"No, it's foolishness."

Skow nodded thoughtfully. David stared through the darkness to where Alex stood in the firelight, surrounded by seated figures, a shadow among shadows. None of it was real. This puzzling young chief beside him was not real. The right words spoken convincingly and privately might save Alex. But how did you speak meaningfully to a proud young Haida about spirits?

"Kwawlang says he did it to show his power over the death spirit," Skow said.

"Then why would he tell you he has no magic? You heard him say it."

Skow nodded again. He wanted to be convinced. David fumbled for the Chinook words to express a complicated idea.

"I, too, have no knowledge of magic. But it seems to me that the death spirit was in the first warrior, the one who was unconscious. It came out of him in the sweat hut and he didn't die. The spirit remained in the hut when he came out. When the second man was put in there, it went into him and he died."

It was a desperate attempt, but it worked.

"*Anguh!*" Skow said. "Kwawlang did not drive it away! Hah! I will tell them that."

"He shouldn't have put the man into the sweat hut. Alex tried to tell him that."

"*Anguh!*" Skow got to his feet. He touched David on the shoulder as he had done earlier. This time, in the

125

darkness, the gesture seemed more friendly than patronizing.

Skow did not go directly into the circle. He walked around it, speaking to certain men and gathering a little group around him. Then they all moved in together.

Skow spoke rapidly and calmly. He pointed to Alex, to the medicine man, to the body of the dead man, to the sweat hut. The medicine man seemed to be caught off guard. When he tried to speak, Skow's group pressed in on him and overwhelmed him with their arguments. Skow laughed and clapped the old man on the back. Alex suddenly raised his arms and called for attention. He praised the medicine man for bringing the first wounded man back to consciousness. He called this a great feat of magic. For once, he spoke the right words at the right time. The shaman's pride was saved. He stalked off to scatter another circle of crumbled herbs around the camp.

Chapter 11

They broke camp at dawn. It was a day of swift dark clouds and whitecaps, not a good day for travel. They took the big canoes northward in the lee of the island; then a strong wind from the west hit them and David judged that they were at the head of the Strait of Juan de Fuca. A good part of the day was spent angling into the wind, fighting it with all the force human arms could get into paddle strokes.

Alex and the Snohomish man had been given paddles and put to work. Because of his sore ribs, David was not pressed into service. This was hardly the result of kindness but simply because he would slow them down.

By midafternoon they were in the Strait of Georgia and among the San Juan Islands. Now there were rain squalls. The tide changed and was against them and they camped early. They made a meal of soup, slept in shelters of mats and boughs. The next morning was dark and gusty, but in the afternoon clouds turned white and lazy and a summer sun came out.

In the long monotonous days that followed they had generally fair weather, though the nights were damp and chilly. David developed a stabbing cough that kept alive the soreness in his ribs. Discomfort nagged the hopelessness within him until at times it was almost unbearable. There was no telling when the Nisquallies they had left at the mill site would get up the courage to make the trip back home. What story they would tell and whom they would tell it to were beyond speculation. Eventually the news would reach Fort Nisqually. Eventually it would be reported to the territorial authorities at Oregon City. By that time it would be regarded as rankest rumor. Alex seemed to be in good physical health; yet the mental change that had come over him persisted. He seemed almost content. He had picked up the words to many of the crew's chants and he joined in, not lustily as David would have expected, but softly and unobtrusively. In camp, he spent a good deal of his time just sitting and staring at the sea or at the sky. Sometimes he wrote Haida words in the sand with a stick, spelling them phonetically and pronouncing them aloud.

He had a way of making abrupt, abstract observations. These bursts usually came after a long contemplative silence. They might have been the result of careful composition; yet he himself seemed surprised at them, as if they had come from nowhere.

"Man is the only creature whose nature is divided against itself," he said suddenly one night when they were camped near the mouth of a creek. He and David had been given the task of washing the wooden bowls from which the company had eaten. Each bowl was intricately carved. He had been studying the carving on one closely. Now he laid it aside, patently pleased with his own words.

"So?" David said.

Alex repeated the words. He translated them into Chinook and tried them out on their guard, who stood a few feet away. In response he got a blank stare.

"He thinks you're crazy as I do," David said.

"I dare say," Alex said.

When they had wiped the bowls out with grass, they carried them to the center of camp and laid them on a mat to be claimed by their owners. Alex spotted Kwawlang, the medicine man, and went over to speak to him. David considered the man a vain and dangerous old fraud. He had been humiliated and was probably nourishing a grudge. But Alex had a strong curiosity about him and a strange respect for him. Kwawlang, who responded with insults at first, now tolerated his company.

Tonight they held a long conversation. Alex then accompanied Kwawlang on his herb-scattering trip around the camp. When he rejoined the other prisoners, he had two extra blankets.

"I begin to see method in your madness," David said. "Did you convince him the spirits want us to have these?"

Alex, not amused, spoke distantly. "His world of spirits is at least as real as our world."

David stretched out and yawned comfortably. He was getting used to going around naked, he supposed, building up a resistance to cold. To have a blanket all to himself seemed a great luxury.

"Ah, yes," he said flippantly. "We are all toys of the spirits."

"'Spirit' is a word," Alex said. "'Time' and 'space' are also words. They have no actual existence. They are not aspects of the universe but aspects of the mind of man."

David closed his eyes to ponder the man beside him. Rejection by Dorothy, the blow on the head, the shock

129

of sudden slavery—one or all had torn Alex to pieces, and he had come together not quite the same. His strangeness had seemed a temporary thing, the result of shock or concussion or bewilderment. But now there was no doubt. The change had to be accepted as deep, maybe permanent.

There had been change in himself, too, David realized. It was surely nowhere nearly so severe as that in Alex, but it was there and it was confusing. There were the desperate times when he felt that any effort at escape was worth the risk. But after the first days of the long voyage north, these moments were infrequent and he was able to console himself with the thought that in time there must come an opportunity when he would have a chance of making it. The important thing was to stay alive until the chance came. In the meantime he found himself resigned to his place as an inferior member of this company. Sometimes he existed almost in mindless contentment. He would come out of the mood with a start, reminding himself that the arrogant, half-naked, tattooed people around him were not a meaningless fantasy that would go away. They were real. They owned him. They were his future.

The feeling of fantasy was intensified by the stupendous beauty of the Canadian coast. Here a great range of mountains met the sea in a chain of inlets, fiords, island-dotted channels. Mile-high cliffs towered above their shimmering reflections. Sea-sculptured rock formations, sometimes tufted with scrub trees, jutted out of naked beaches. Barren buttes rose out of richly timbered hills. Snow-capped peaks glistened in the sun like massive jewels. Glaciers reached down to emerald bays. Mile after mile, vast ungraspable splendor overwhelmed the mind.

They passed a few villages at the mouths of rivers but did not stop. Usually there was a large group of armed men waiting on the shore. It was clear that the people of this country knew in advance that the war canoes were coming and were ready for them. Moreover, the Haidas had no interest in making raids now. Their expedition was over; they thought only of getting home.

For several days they were in the Strait of Georgia, which narrowed into a maze of narrow passages and finally broadened out again. Then they were past the great long island of Vancouver and in turbulent water. They hugged the coast closely. One night they put in at a Kwakiutl village. The chief was a friend of Skow, it turned out, but there was much making of the peace sign and calling back and forth to shore before they landed. Amid palpable tension, there was a feast of baked halibut and then a bit of trading. The Snohomish man and the Nootka children were sold here. The price was four large boxes of dentalia, which, like slaves and blankets, were universal currency. The only source of these tubular shells was off the tip of Vancouver Island and a monopoly of the rich Kwakiutls.

The villagers were amazed to see white slaves in the group. David spoke to several of them, asking them to notify the British of what they had seen. He promised rewards, but no one gave him any reply at all.

The Haidas made camp half a mile down the shore from the village. They posted extra guards, and David had no doubt that the village was well guarded, too, tonight. If there was old friendship here, there were also old grudges and distrust.

Susie and her sister were in anguish at being separated from the latter's husband, as were the Nootka women by the sale of the children. After initial shrieking and wailing, they settled down to keening, as if the man and children were dead. No one paid much attention to them, even though their mourning went on most of the night.

The next days were long ones, with the canoes shoving off at first light and landings not made until dusk. They passed Bella Coola country. Sometimes they saw fishermen in small canoes; these invariably headed for shore when they saw the Haidas. On the third night they camped on a lonely cape, and Alex learned that they were in the country of the northern branch of the Kwakiutls. That meant the Queen Charlottes were to the west of them across sixty miles or more of open sea. They lay over here for a day, not liking the look of the weather. On the next morning, well before dawn, they began the crossing of tempestuous Hecate Strait.

The wind was hard against them. Waves were high and ragged. The canoe took them gracefully, seldom shipping water, but everyone was drenched with spray. Susie, huddled in the bilge beside David, was terrified and spoke of the danger of the canoe splitting. She claimed it was not a rare thing for a large canoe to split down the middle in very rough water. *Tamanohuses* were mixed up in it, of course, the way she explained it, and she sang a soft song to keep the evil ones away. The Haidas seemed to have some similar belief. Kwawlang stood in the bow of the lead canoe and shook his rattle at waves he didn't like the look of.

They spent most of the day out of sight of land. Then they watched a shrouded sunset behind distant black mountains that rose out of the sea. David knew nothing about the Queen Charlottes, and Alex knew little more. He did recall looking at a map of them and remembered they were a long, tight, triangular archipelago of two very large islands and countless small ones.

As they approached the shore it was clear that the party had hit the islands exactly where it planned. David had come to realize that this precison was true of the whole voyage. Every campsite had been selected in advance. This was uncanny when he considered that it was done without compass or maps; those who had made the trip before simply had the country in their heads.

The canoes swept past two small islands and around a tentacle of land into the calm waters of a bay. They camped on the beach, eating a skimpy meal and going to bed early. The great reach of violent water they had crossed gave a new dimension to David's loneliness, and he lay awake for a long time staring at the night sky. Desolate, moonless, its few stars dimmed by fast-moving clouds, it seemed empty of meaning and a reflection of his soul.

In the morning they pointed the canoes northward. The day was overcast, Stygian, the water choppy. They followed the bold coast of a large timbered island. They passed a small bay and for miles were off a windswept spit, desolate except for a speckling of brush and scrub trees. They maneuvered around its point, crossing a series of bars raked by breakers. Then they were in a big triangular bay that funneled down to a wide, ragged inlet. They paddled up this, hugging the north shore, racing the canoes, singing wildly.

The surroundings here had an etched quality that

reminded David of illustrations in some old volume of Milton or Dante. There was a soft haziness to the whole, yet details were crisp. The shore was forested. A mist-crowned mountain rose above the green-black sea of trees to the north. The inlet was spotted with miniature islands, perfectly round, banded at their steep bases with accumulations of yellow kelp.

The canoes skirted a brushy point and suddenly a line of brilliant color was staring out of the forest. It was half a mile long, half a mile of tree-high totem poles gaudily painted in red, white, green-blue, yellow, black. Each towered above a single-gable house front decorated with a huge symmetrical image of some bright monster.

Terrifyingly beautiful, the Haida village was like nothing David had ever imagined.

Chapter 12

The canoes curled in toward shore. Men, women, and children streamed out of the bright houses and down a bank to the beach. Dogs barked. Large black birds circled the beach, screaming raucously. The villagers began a chant, a welcoming song. The men in the canoes joined in. A small group on shore wailed a discordant song, a death song. They were relatives of the warrior who had been killed. They knew of his death before the canoes reached shore because his paddle had been lashed upright beside the thwart he had occupied.

Each man had his own place in the canoe and his assigned turn to board and disembark. These were determined by his rank, and they were strictly observed. It would not have been surprising if now, as canoes nosed onto the beach and relatives of the warriors pressed in on them, the disembarking order had been disregarded. But it was not.

In general, the welcoming was restrained, ceremonial. There were a few quick embraces, a few shouts of greeting. But everyone fell silent as a gray-haired man in a Chilkat blanket and a tall wooden headdress came down the bank. He was old and unsteady and was supported by two young men. Kat, Skow, and the chief with the drooping mustache walked forward to meet him. He touched each on the shoulder, spoke a few

135

words, and began a chant in which everyone joined.

The loot that the raiders had brought home was laid out on the beach: baskets, blankets, shell money, copper ornaments, Alex's watch, skins, bits of clothing, the rifles taken from David and Alex. It was distributed to the families of the raiders without quibbling; the division had been determined by the chiefs beforehand.

The prisoners were paraded onto the beach and separated into three groups. David and Susie belonged to Kat, her sister and Alex to Skow, the Nootkas to the third chief. The white men were the objects of silent staring at first and then of whispered comments and snickering.

Naked except for the binding he wore around his ribs, David tried to meet the eyes of the people who came close to look him over. It was not easy for him; he was tempted to bow his head and stare at the ground. There was no reason to be embarrassed, he assured himself. Many of the village men were as naked as he was. Women wore nothing but short hide aprons. But it was not really his nakedness that shamed him, he realized. It was being on display, being studied and appraised as an animal, a piece of chattel. That and his whiteness. These people had not known much contact with white men. Still, like all Indians, they must see whites as rich, domineering people who considered themselves superior to red men. And now they had white slaves among them and could stare and prod and smirk and reverse the myth of superiority.

He stared back at them, smiling as if he could be amused at his predicament. They were a strange-looking lot. They were taller than Puget Sound Indians and maybe a bit lighter skinned. Their heads had not been flattened. Women wore their hair long, letting it hang down their backs. Men wore theirs short, varying in length from shoulder-length bobs to trims as short as his own. A few of the older men had mandarin mustaches and skimpy chin whiskers.

Both men and women were heavily tattooed. Both sexes wore colorful ornaments: shell earrings, bracelets and anklets of animal teeth, neck pieces of polished copper. Some of the men had abalone shell pendants dangling from their noses. Medicine men could be distinguished by polished bones in pierced septums. But the most curious personal decorations were the lip plugs worn by the women. The flesh of their chins had been pierced an inch below the mouth and a plug inserted. In teen-agers this was a small polished bone pin. It increased in size in older women. Some of the mature ones wore shell-inlaid oval plugs two inches wide. In very old women the weight of the labrets caused their lower lips to hang down so that their teeth were exposed.

Three medicine men came up to peer at him. He met their eyes, hardly seeing them, staring through them. He thought of them as *skaggies* now—the Haida word was *skahgilda*, but in informal speech it was often shortened to *skaggy*. Two of them took a brief look at him, shook their rattles, and went away. The third remained, and David saw suddenly what should have been apparent from the first. Naked from the waist up, this *skaggy* was surprisingly but undeniably female.

She wore her hair in a topknot as the others did and she had the same sort of carved bone through her nose. She carried a circle of puffin beaks, which she carefully kept between him and herself. She was unabashedly

137

curious, moving around him and looking him over from head to toe. When he and Susie were led up the bank, she and some other women accompanied them.

He walked on stiff legs along the broad path in front of the houses. There was a stiffness in his mind, too, he thought, a reluctance to accept what his senses recorded. The village was a spectral place in both meanings of the word. It blazed with colors of painted totem poles and house fronts. At the same time, on the edge of a forest on this remote island, this avenue of grotesque art seemed an illusion, a mirage.

The group stopped in front of a large house and began to enter one at a time. This was his owner's house, he supposed—Kat's house. Like the others, it had a towering pole at the center of its gabled front. The bottom figure of the pole was a wolflike creature. An oval hole in its stomach was the entrance to the house. Obeying the gestures of one of the women, David got down and crawled through.

The interior was one large, dim, smoky, smelly chamber. The floor had been excavated to three levels to form a tiered pit—an inverse pyramid. At the center of the lowest level there was a square of stones with a fire glowing in it. The framework of the house was rectangular, which left extra space at the far end at the top level. Part of this was screened off by stacked boxes with Chilkat blankets draped over them.

Susie was taken aside and David was surrounded by jabbering women. They poked him, touched his beard, made him open his mouth. Some of them scowled at him, others giggled.

"All right, girls, I'm a naked white man. Have a good look."

The strange words brought a startled silence. The *skaggy* shoved others aside and confronted him, her expression grim. She was a little afraid of him, he realized. They all were.

"I have no magic." He spoke in Chinook now, smiling. "If I had, I wouldn't be here."

There were whispered questions among the women as if they didn't understand. Someone gave the *skaggy* a knife, a short iron blade set in a carved bone handle. She quickly cut the laces on the deerskin around his ribs and removed it. There was a gasp from the onlookers. Most of his body was well tanned, but it was dead white where the binding had been. The *skaggy* threw the deerskin aside and shook her circle of puffin beaks at it.

"No magic," he repeated. "Speak to Kwawlang."

Reaching through the circle of beaks, she touched the pale flesh over his ribs. It was as if she thought there might be some magic in keeping part of himself so white. She placed the knife between her teeth and touched him with both hands. She then stepped back and stared at his privates. She raised a hand and made a grabbing motion in the air. She took the knife from her mouth with her other hand and made a cutting motion. The pantomime was clear enough. Behind her an old crone cackled.

Panic touched him. He tried to hide it, to face the woman stolidly. He knew nothing of these people or their ways. It was possible that they did this to slaves, that the *skaggy* was supposed to do it to him now. If she tries, I'll fight, he promised himself. I'll get that knife from her and kill her and anyone else who touches me. I'll fight until somebody smashes my skull or puts a spear through me.

139

"Who in hell do you think you are?" he said.

The *skaggy* turned and motioned to a girl in the crowd. The girl moved up beside her. She was about fifteen, slender, full-breasted, pretty. She wore a small polished plug beneath her lips. She looked David straight in the eye, raised a fist, and struck him hard on the side of the head. She stepped back. The *skaggy* made the grabbing and cutting gesture again. The girl stepped up and lit into him with both hands. He raised his hands to protect himself and was hard put to do it without grabbing her arms or in some way giving the appearance of fighting back. This, he sensed, he dare not do.

It was over then. He was taken to a place on the top tier that, after considerable gesturing on the part of the women, he understood was to be his sleeping place. He sat down. He was left alone except for Susie, who was sitting a few feet away.

He didn't entirely understand the significance of what had happened but he got the gist of it. He had been put in his place. If he forgot it, punishment would be swift and horrible.

Susie was sitting with her knees drawn up, staring at the mat floor. He spoke her name and smiled at her. She gave him a look of agony in return.

"The sun is not shining," she said.

For a time David sat quietly and let his eyes rove over the details of the house. It was built on a framework of giant crossbeams and supporting posts. There was little furniture except for scores of carved storage boxes. Some were in neat rows along the walls; others were scattered around and used for stools. There were larger chests, too, and one thronelike settee with storage space beneath the seat. Everything was carved with conventionalized figures in low relief.

It was not clear to him how much freedom of movement he was permitted, and he decided to find out. He stood up, stretching and yawning to attract attention; he didn't want to appear to sneak away. He walked to the small oval doorway and dropped to his hands and knees. No one tried to stop him, and he crawled through.

There was spotty afternoon activity around the village—children playing, women cleaning fish on the beach, two men skinning a seal. At the near end of the line of houses, men were putting wall boards on a new house. Four men with blankets over their shoulders watched. The tall Kat was easiest to identify. The others were Skow, Kwawlang—and Alex. David sauntered over to join them.

Alex pointed to him and said, "David." He pronounced the name slowly and then repeated it. Kwawlang and Skow both said it after him. It was the first time he had been called anything by Haidas except "*huldinga*."

Alex was in the midst of a conversation with Kwawlang—a mixture of Chinook and Haida that was difficult to follow. Skow was interested and sometimes put in a word or two. Kat remained aloof.

Where there was a pause, David touched the trade blanket that Alex wore over his shoulders. On the trip, the blankets they had used at night had always been taken away in the daytime.

"How'd you get it?" David said.

"Asked for it. Tomorrow I shall try for a loincloth."

Alex turned to Kat and with word and gesture indicated that David needed a blanket, too. Kat replied haughtily and at some length. Kwawlang took it upon himself to interpret. David missed the fine points, and Alex explained.

"You can have the use of a blanket, but you must understand that a slave can own nothing. If you pick a berry or dig a clam, it is his. You breathe only by his permission."

David nodded at Kat and said he understood.

"I think I'm a bit luckier in my owner," Alex said. "The tall one appears to hate us both."

Kat pointed to the men at work on the house.

"He wants you to join them," Alex said. "It's his house."

David went over and joined the workmen. All but one wore their hair long, the mark of a slave. He saw no way to be useful, and he stood waiting to be told what to do.

The siding was put on vertically. The edges of each board were smoothed with a crude drawknife until they fitted against the adjacent board. There was no great precision about this; cracks between boards provided ventilation. Holes were drilled near the tops of the soft cedar boards with a bone drill skillfully operated between the palms. Pegs fastened top ends to a crossbeam. Bottoms were embedded in the ground.

Feeling a little silly, David picked up a knife and a sharpening stone and began to dress the edge. After a while, the man with the short hair motioned to him to go with three of the others and get more boards. They went to a place behind the village where a man was splitting boards off a log with wooden wedges. Two others were smoothing them with adzes. David and the men with him picked up the boards that were ready and went back to the house. The man with the short hair had them pile the boards inside the house. It seemed that work was over for the day.

That night there was a celebration at the house David and Susie had been taken to. There were speeches by Kat and some of his relatives. David and Susie were displayed, along with the rest of Kat's loot from the trip south. There was group singing, then pantomimes by dancers in huge wooden masks. Course after course of food was served on beautifully carved wooden dishes. Slaves were allowed to help themselves after each dish had made the rounds of the family and guests.

Some of the food was readily identifiable, some not. There was roast salmon, boiled cod, fresh salal berries and blueberries, assortments of roots, herbs, seaweed. The seaweed was mixed with salmon roe. The other vegetables were served in a fish-oil sauce.

As near as he could make out, there were six other slaves attached to the household besides himself and Susie. Four were men and easy to pick out because of their long, shaggy hair. All were expected to stay at the top of the tiered floor when they were not busy. The next lower shelf was used as sleeping space by the less important members of the family. Chiefs slept in the center, close to the fire. Kat, however, had a private space behind the screen of boxes and blankets at the back of the house.

There were at least a dozen members of the household besides slaves. These were Kat and his two wives, his mother, his younger brother and wife, an aunt, a married nephew and his family, and two teen-age nephews, who had been on the raid. Kat had two sons, but according to custom they were being raised in the house of a maternal uncle.

This information was given to David by one of the slaves who had been working on the new house. The family had grown too big for this house, he explained. Some of it would move with Kat to the new house; some would stay here with Kat's brother.

The slave was a middle-aged man called Necoon. He had been born in bondage in another village on the islands. He had been traded around quite a bit and had belonged to a Tsimshian chief on the mainland for a while. He had picked up Chinook there and even a word or two of English from the Hudson's Bay people at Fort Simpson. He spoke to one of Kat's wives and got David the blanket he had been promised.

There was great uneasiness among Kat's slaves, Necoon said, because of the new house. In a day or so the carved totem at the entrance of the house would be erected. He had seen the pole, and at the bottom of it there was a figure of a man upside down. That meant that a slave would be killed and thrown into the hole in which the pole was to be set. This was an old custom often observed by rich chiefs and was supposed to bring good luck to the house.

Of course, Necoon said, the slave wasn't always actually killed. Sometimes he was taken away and sold and everybody pretended he was dead and buried under the pole. But Kat was very rich and very proud. It was feared that he would be strict about the tradition. None of his slaves felt safe.

When David changed the subject to the possibility of escape, Necoon seemed stunned. Apparently, he had never considered the idea for the simple reason that he had no place to escape to. Anyway, there was no way it could be accomplished, he said.

David didn't see why a slave couldn't slip out at night, steal a small canoe, and be on his way. Necoon pointed out that the village was guarded at night. The man in charge was a slave. It would be impossible to bribe him and very difficult to slip past him. He would be rewarded if he caught a slave trying to run away; he would be severely punished if he did not catch him. And even if a person made it out of the inlet into open water, he would never get across the strait to the mainland. If the weather was good, fast canoes would pursue and quickly overhaul him. If it was bad, a small canoe couldn't survive. There were other objections: the hazard of being captured by mainland tribes, the dreadful prospect of being traded to the Tlingits of the northern wasteland if caught by the Tsimshians, the certainty of cruel punishment if overtaken by Kat.

In the morning the village stirred with daylight and became a beehive of activity. Everyone began the day with a plunge into the numbing water of the inlet. Then, for three or four hours, everyone was busy. Men pushed off in canoes to go fishing or seal-hunting. Others worked with adzes on cedar logs they were shaping into canoes. Women wove baskets, washed blankets, gathered seaweed. Behind the village, the woodworkers were busy splitting boards, carving totems, building watertight boxes.

David went to work with Necoon and the others on the new house again. By noon they finished putting on the siding and quit for the day. Most of the other activity ceased, too, at least as far as the male sex was concerned. They sat around the rest of the day and dozed or talked or played *sin*.

The sun broke through about noon and the afternoon was warm and pleasant. The inlet was calm, glasslike. The round little islets rose from it with picture-book neatness. David was pleased to see Susie working in the sun. She and another woman were washing and stripping spruce roots that were to be split and used for weaving. He thought the sunshine would have put her in good spirits, but it had not. The new house pole would be put up the day after tomorrow, she said, and she was terrified.

Chapter 13

The next day David helped dig the hole in which the great pole would be set. The hole was a little more than a yard wide and about seven feet deep. It was deeper than usual, Necoon said—confirmation that a slave would be buried here.

The soil was moist and sandy with many rocks in it. Digging was done with wooden shovels. The slaves spelled one another in the hole. As the hole got deeper, the work became cramped and skittish, and David found himself dreading his turn. It was necessary to loosen dirt with a shovel, hunker down, fill a basket with his hands, and pass it up to those on the surface. Soil kept trickling down on him, and it seemed as if the sides might collapse and bury him. There was also the panicky thought that one of the other slaves might drop a rock on his head. That would provide a corpse and settle once and for all whose grave this was to be.

The work was finished by the middle of the morning. The slaves and their short-haired boss traipsed over to the place behind the village where the totem pole lay. It was not quite ready. A craftsman was putting the last touch of paint on the carved figures, already bright with a variety of colors. He used a brush with flat bristles cut at a slant. Off to one side, a slave ground clam shells with a stone pestle. These had been baked, Necoon explained, and were pulverized to make white paint.

Black was made from soot, red from a special clay, and yellow from a residue scraped from boxes in which urine had been stored.

The pole would rise five fathoms above the roof of Kat's new house, stabbing the sky with figures that symbolized his family lore. The figure of a raven with spread wings was at the top. Its breast feathers formed the headdress of a human figure below it. Next was Wasco, a sea beast with the head of a wolf and body of a whale. Then came the figure of a frog, mother of the world. Below that was Beaver, another myth hero who played a part in family tradition. At the bottom was a very tall figure with a masklike face. This was Kat himself. He was clutching a replica of a copper shield to indicate his great wealth. Beside one foot was a tiny human figure upside down, a representation of the slave who was to be buried under the pole.

One of the craftsmen gave Necoon a bit of news that took away his apprehension about who was to be killed. Kat had bought the old Nootka man taken on the raid. The man was too senile to be of much use, and Kat had got him cheap. It seemed pretty clear that he was to be the victim. The change in Necoon's attitude was abrupt. Smiling his relief, he began to talk as if he looked forward to the event and to speculate as to who would do the killing. It was quite possible that he himself would be asked to do it, he said. He sounded as if he hoped he would.

They went back to the new house and found Alex, Kat, Skow, Kwawlang, and some others standing outside. Alex was wearing a belt with sealskin aprons fastened to it, front and rear. The female *skaggy* was inside the house, going over the place to scour out any evil spirits that might have taken refuge there.

Two women stood close to the entrance to the house. One was old and wore a blanket over her shoulders. She had no lip plug, so David supposed she was a slave. The other, naked from the waist up, was the girl who had struck him when he first arrived. She turned and met his look, steadily, languidly. He had not brought his blanket to work with him and was suddenly very conscious of his nakedness. Alex touched his arm to draw his attention away from the girl.

"No," Alex said. "Of all the taboos in this village, she is the biggest. She is taboo for everybody."

"What do you mean?"

"That's the daughter of Kaigyet, the lady *skaggy*. The girl is a virgin. That's a thing the Haidas don't ordinarily put a great deal of emphasis on, I gather, but in this case Kaigyet is making much out of it. She claims the girl's purity gives her special powers over certain spirits."

Kwawlang grumbled at Alex to stop speaking in English. Alex clapped him on the shoulder and apologized in Haida. Kwawlang nodded and mumbled something. Skow moved closer, looking amused. There seemed to be an understanding among the three of them. Alex was treated almost as a friend.

"How do you do it?" David said. "How come they haven't put you to work?"

"They'd rather listen to me talk. We'll discuss it later. Meanwhile, speak Chinook. Throw in as many Haida words as you can."

Alex turned to the others and explained what he had just said. Skow and Kwawlang both nodded, looking at David as if he were backward. Kat ignored them all.

Kaigyet shuffled out of the doorway, carrying her *clechadarran*, her circle of puffin beaks. She began to go around the house in a sort of dance, backing off and then going close to peer under the overhang of the roof as if she saw something suspicious. The others followed her at a little distance. David and Alex lagged behind.

"Damn it, Alex, you're enjoying yourself."

"Well, yes. In a way, I am."

David scanned the village and the beach below it. For many, the working day was over. Several *sin* games had begun around the houses and on the beach.

"You ever counted the houses here?" David asked. "There are more than forty. And in front of every house there are two or three canoes. All we've got to do is steal one."

"Well, not quite all," Alex said. "We've got to have a good start and we've got to know exactly where we're headed. Meanwhile, I urge you to enjoy yourself, too—if only to put them off guard a bit. Look around you. It's like a look at ourselves ten thousand years ago. Well, something like that. Mankind took a wrong turn somewhere, David. Perhaps if we look closely, we can see where."

"Sure. We'll discover the answers to all the ills of civilization."

Alex encompassed the village with a sweep of his arm. "Look at those magnificent totems! The art and literature of a people. It's the beginning of a system of picture writing."

"A beginning that will come to nothing."

"Yes," Alex admitted with a sigh. "But it has a meaning. It's a look into the dark past we

150

carry inside ourselves.''

Kaigyet had reached the back of the house. She took a small box from a bag that hung at her waist, unfastened the lid, and set the box on the ground. She pointed at a place under the eaves and began an elaborate pantomime in an effort to catch the spirit she claimed was there. She stole up close to it, shook her *clechadarran* at it, and motioned to her daughter to get on the other side of it. The girl extended her arms and jumped this way and that, taking cues from her mother. The spectators stared in fascination. The two women, arms outstretched, worked closer and closer to the box. When the *skaggy* was satisfied that the spirit had gone into it, she slapped on the lid and inserted pegs to hold it tight. She then casually dropped the box back into her bag of paraphernalia.

''No doubt she'll keep it for a pet,'' David said.

''Don't scoff, David. There is a spirit in that box.''

''You don't sound much like a Christian minister.''

''Jesus drove out demons. Something has happened to me, David. I'm seeing—''

''I think you're still suffering from that wallop on the head.''

''I'm seeing with a new clarity. Spirits exist in the mind. These people draw no line between the inner and the outer—it's all the same world. Who is to say that way of seeing is inferior to yours?''

''You should have been born an Indian,'' David said. ''You'd be the greatest *skaggy* of them all.''

''Perhaps I would,'' Alex said, completely serious. ''I have a religious nature.''

''Plus a bit of humbug.''

Alex pressed his lips into his polite, dutiful, pastor's

151

smile. "Here again there is another way of looking at it. Kwawlang, for instance, is rather good at sleight-of-hand tricks. Deception? Certainly. But a trick is an art form, a form of communication. There is a special kind of truth to it."

"It will be interesting to see how you'll rationalize the killing of that slave tomorrow," David said. "Is that an art form, too?"

"What are you taling about?"

Alex had heard nothing about the custom of burying a slave under a totem pole. Apparently no one in Skow's household had thought it worth mentioning. He became greatly upset as David told him about it. Then, as Kaigyet and the others completed their circle of the house, he approached Kwawlang and questioned him.

The old *skaggy* replied with a shrug and a few mumbled words. Alex then approached Kat, who gave him a scornful look and turned away. Alex pursued him, touching his arm. Kat whirled and struck him backhanded in the face, almost dropping him.

Skow strode forward, shouting angry words at Kat. The white slave was Skow's property, and it seemed that Skow didn't want Kat hitting him. Kat pointed to David, who had once (with Kat's permission) been struck by Skow. Apparently Kat claimed he had a right to a blow at Alex in return. Skow seemed to accept the logic of this. He examined Alex to see if he was damaged, decided that he wasn't, and the incident was over.

David had thought that work was finished for the day, but it wasn't. The men who were in charge of raising the totem pole showed up. They wanted a trench sloping up from the bottom of the hole, and Kat's slaves were put to work digging it. The idea was that the pole would be much easier to raise if it was laid in the trench with its base in the hole.

As they worked, Necoon explained that there was a lifelong rivalry between Skow and Kat. They were cousins but members of different clans, Kat being a Raven and Skow an Eagle. All members of upperclass Haida society belonged to one group or the other, and Necoon tried to explain the intricate matrilineal system that dominated Haida life. A man inherited property and clan status from his mother's side of the family. Since he could never marry within his own clan, his children always belonged to the other clan. Sons usually were raised by their maternal uncle. There were subclans within the larger groups and also a system of secret societies.

It was all much too complicated for David to understand in detail, but he gathered that the village chief was the great-uncle of both Skow and Kat. Both were in line to succeed him. According to Necoon, Kat was the favorite. He was ten winters older than Skow. Moreover, the Raven clan was a shade more powerful than the Eagle.

Skow was a great warrior and very rich, Necoon admitted. Still, he must be uneasy about the potlatch Kat would give tomorrow at the dedication of the new house. Kat would give away great wealth—most of it to Skow and his family. This was the way chiefs ''made war,'' the hard-bitten old slave explained. They and their families spent years accumulating wealth so they could bestow it on their rivals. This brought great honor to the giver and an embarrassing obligation to the receiver. The latter was expected to give an even bigger

153

potlatch. He was expected to give more than he received and thus shift the obligation back to his rival. The ''war'' went on until one or the other failed to outdo his rival and was thus disgraced.

Tomorrow's potlatch would not be held in the big potlatch house behind the village but in front of Kat's new house. Stores of goods had to be carried to the site—stacks of trade blankets, oolaken oil, boxes of dentalia, baskets of ornaments and charms. Much of it was stored inside the house for the night. Some was left outside and covered with mats.

In the morning David was sent to help carry the totem to the house. It took about twenty men to transport the pole, lifting it by ropes that had been tied around it. They removed the short ropes when they reached the house and used longer ones to lower the pole into the trench. The whole village gathered quickly. Everyone was invited to the outdoor part of the affair.

Two young men beat drums and sang Kat's family songs. Masked dancers appeared and acted out some of the legends that the young men chanted. David stood beside the trench with the rest of Kat's slaves. The old Nootka man was among them now, staring dimly at the dancers in a way that made David wonder if the old boy even suspected why he was here. Kat and the feeble old village chief sat in front of the dancers. Other chiefs formed a half circle around them, sitting on mats and blankets. The rest of the villagers stood in a tight crowd that reached up the avenue in front of the houses and overflowed onto the beach.

Kat got to his feet, a towering figure in a long sea-otter robe and a tall wooden hat carved with the face

154

of Raven and decorated with plumes of white fur. His brother and his nephews, wearing Chilkat blankets and many ornaments, rose and joined him. They called out names and presented gifts of trade blankets, harpoons, fishing gear, paddles. These were unimportant presentations, Necoon explained, made to the unimportant people of the village. There was no obligation to repay at a later date. The goods were sort of a bribe, David gathered, payment for attending the ceremony and bearing witness to the honors that Kat claimed for himself.

Practically every adult male in the village (excepting slaves and the chiefs who were to receive large amounts of goods later) was given some sort of gift. When this was done, Kat made a brief speech, pointing to the house and the pole. He was followed by a professional speechmaker, a man Necoon said was well paid to extol the wealth and power of Kat and his family. After that the drummers chanted a new song of praise composed especially for the occasion.

Kat rose again and gave an order to Necoon, who took the old Nootka man by the arm and led him to the edge of the hole in which the totem was to be set. The crowd was silent, motionless. Another of Kat's slaves stepped up and handed Necoon a foot-long stone club. The old man, puzzled at first, suddenly caught on to what was to happen to him. He began to tremble pathetically. He seemed to want to speak but to be unable to.

There was a shout from deep in the crowd. Alex pressed forward, waving his hands over his head. He stopped directly in front of Kat and turned to face the crowd.

"I have a message for the Haida people, a great truth

that my people have discovered. No man is greater than another. He may be richer or braver or wiser, but that does not make him greater. The words are strange to you, but think! All men are born the same. You know in your hearts this is true. And a slave is a man like any other. That, too, you know in your hearts. In the eyes of Nekilstlass, the God of everyone, who takes the form of Raven, a slave has the right to live. The same right—''

Kat strode forward and struck him with his fist, a great arcing blow that caught him on the ear. Alex lost his balance and fell to one knee but quickly rose and tried to go on.

''There is a world beyond this world where men go when they die,'' he shouted. ''There it shall be done to you as you have done to others.''

He dodged another blow from Kat and whirled away from Kat's brother, who came forward to seize him. He leaped in front of the old Nootka man and again faced the crowd.

''Kill *me*. I offer myself in his place.''

Kat's brother and some others pressed in on him. Trapped between them and the house, he jumped down into the hole. David joined the group that ringed its edge.

''Alex, come out of there. You're acting like a madman.''

Alex looked up, turning in place, making a complete circle. Then he sat down at the bottom of the hole.

''Tell them to raise the pole,'' he said.

Kat pushed through the crowd around the hole, muttering petulantly. He picked up a handful of gravel and flung it into the hole. Alex sat with knees drawn up and head bowed and didn't even flinch. There was discussion between Kat and his brother. Then the chief made a chopping gesture.

"*Tiuh la-ah!*" he said. "Kill him. I will buy him from Skow."

Skow came forward, looking into the hole and shaking his head. Kat repeated his offer to buy Alex. Skow named a price. It was too much. They haggled briefly and came to an agreement.

"Give him his way," Kat said, pointing to Alex. "Raise the pole."

Alex got to his feet and extended a hand to David, who helped him out of the hole. Alex faced Kat, throwing his arms wide and then pressing his hands against his chest. He spoke in a voice that all could hear.

"I must have time to purify myself. Man is part good, part evil. If I do not purify myself, Kat will forever have evil spirits at the door of his house."

The logic of this was overwhelming. There was not a Haida present who would deny that Alex was possessed by spirits. There was a silence. Kat looked at his brother and spread his hands in a gesture of indecision.

"I will need a day—two days—to purify myself," Alex asserted.

Kaigyet, the female *skaggy*, had joined the group. Unobtrusively, she took the stone club from Necoon's hand. Approaching the old Nootka man from behind, she raised the club and smashed it down mightily. He grunted once and collapsed, the shape of the club pressed into his skull. Kaigyet motioned to Necoon to help her, and they dumped the body into the hole.

It all happened so quickly that no one could grasp it at once. Alex stared into the hole open-mouthed, his

157

hands still pressed against his chest. Skow shook his head and turned away. Kat made a little gesture of resignation and then a large one that was a command to raise the pole. Eyes on the ground, Alex stalked through the crowd.

The top of the pole was pried out of the shallow end of the trench. A small log was slid under it and across the trench. David and some others lifted the top of the pole higher. Its butt slid into the hole, crushing the body of the dead slave. Using long, stout poles, they raised the big column to an angle of about fifty degrees, bracing it with the log. A long rope that had been fastened to the top was now seized by a score of volunteers, and the pole was pulled upright. Dirt was tamped into the hole around the edges, and the job was done.

The hired speechmaker made another speech. The singers chanted another song. Then the important gift-giving began.

Some of the goods to be distributed to the chiefs were stored away and would be delivered later; so a good part of the ceremony consisted of Kat's merely naming the recipients and announcing what they would be given. He did this in a boastful way, taking the attitude that parting with rich gifts meant nothing to him.

A chief received ten boxes of oolaken oil and some dentalium ornaments. Another was given a hundred blankets and a canoe. A third chose to be offended by his present of two hundred blankets. He and his family were richer than Kat believed, he said. He would soon give a potlatch in honor of a dead relative and would return this insulting gift ten times over. Kat immediately doubled the gift and the chief seemed satisfied.

Three men sat off to one side and kept tally. Two did it by cutting notches in small sticks, one stick for each recipient. The third, a slave, relied entirely on his memory. He could tell you, Necoon insisted, exactly what had been given away at every potlatch he had ever attended. The three could be called the tribe's public accountants, David supposed.

Kat's first gift to Skow was a huge war canoe. Skow sat facing his rival across a small fire. He accepted the canoe with a toss of his head and a snort. Kat then pointed at the canoe, which some of his relatives were paddling in toward the beach. It rode low in the water and was loaded to the thwarts with carved and painted boxes. When it had landed and had been drawn up on the beach, one of the crewmen opened a box and dipped his hand into it to show that it was filled with oil.

The crowd gasped, impressed by the extravagance of the gift. Skow snorted again. He got to his feet and said drily that he had expected his first gift to be blankets. Kat already owed him five hundred blankets, he said— the price agreed upon for the white slave called Alex. This brought another gasp from the onlookers—it was an enormous price for a slave. It was clear, Skow chided, that Kat had run out of blankets and was not so rich as he would have the people think.

The remark was the first of many insults that the two chiefs exchanged. Under different circumstances they could join their families into a raiding party and share a canoe. But now that it was time for them to bring their rivalry into the open, it was thoroughly bitter. David understood why Necoon had said there was "war" between them.

The more Skow received, the more he would have to

repay at exorbitant interest. So Kat was trying to embarrass him by giving as much as possible, parading his own wealth and ''generosity'' as he did it. He promptly met Skow's challenge by presenting him with a thousand trade blankets. Then there were gifts of a large carved chest filled with more valuable Chilkat blankets, an even larger chest of furs, a number of boxes of dentalium shells, a female slave....

When the last presentation had been made, Skow pretended to be surprised that this part of the ceremony was finished so soon. He turned to look at the new totem pole and gave a little shake of his head. It was too bad that a family as given to boasting as Kat's had so little to boast about, he said. He himself had more oil and blankets than he knew what to do with. He would soon return many times over the things Kat had given him, and he would have handsome gifts for everyone else as well. In the meantime he would demonstrate how little today's gifts meant to him.

He pointed to the oil-laden canoe on the beach and ordered it unloaded and turned over. Dry wood was piled against it. Some of the oil was poured over it. The rest, still in its boxes, was stacked around it. Then Skow seized a firebrand and walked down and touched off the whole pile. The crowd cheered. Flames were quickly reaching fifty feet into the air. Everyone had to retreat, murmuring in awe, cheering when a new box of oil caught and flared.

Necoon shook his head sadly. Skow was getting the best of it. He was trying to goad Kat into breaking a copper, the slave explained. These were rare, shield-shaped plaques that had been brought from the north. Their value varied according to their individual histories, but even the least was worth thousands of blankets. If a copper was broken, however, it became next to worthless. If Kat broke one now, Skow could meet the challenge only by breaking a copper of his own. But Kat would lose a copper-breaking contest, Necoon said. His family owned only two coppers. Skow's family owned four.

It didn't happen—not that day. Kat made a little speech in which he sneered at Skow's arrogance. He said he looked forward to the time that Skow gave a potlatch. He hinted that he might break a copper then. The people seemed disappointed.

The chiefs and their families went inside the new house now, and there began a session of feasting and boasting that lasted far into the night. David selected a place for himself on the top tier where he could watch unobtrusively. In a few minutes a tall figure moved through the semidarkness and sat down next to him. It was Alex. He sat with knees drawn up, head on arms. After a time he produced a soft sound that might have been a sob.

"I wish I had never climbed out of that hole, David. I wish my body had been crushed by that pole and that old man were alive."

"I doubt it," David said. "I think that's what you wish you wish."

"I meant to die. I truly did. Then it came to me that nobody had to die, that I could talk the people out of a useless waste of life. I could have, too, if I'd had a minute or two longer. They were listening, David. I was making sense to them. If that confounded female hadn't smashed the old man's head just when she did, I'd have pulled it off."

161

"I doubt it."

"I was meant to be crushed into the earth by that pole, David. I failed."

"Damn it, Alex, I wish you'd stop treating this whole miserable ordeal as if it were a mystic journey for the benefit of your personal salvation."

There was a silence during which David was aware that Alex was breathing heavily and fast. Then Alex said, "There were barriers I didn't know how to overcome. Dorothy. The mill. The chance to be rich. Then they were all swept away. I was stripped of every material tie—"

"So was I."

"The world is nothing, David. Try to see that."

"Right now it's worse than nothing—it's hell. But it's all I'm truly sure of."

"God give us eyes," Alex said. "We are prisoners of ourselves."

"And of these damned Indians."

"We can be free if only we *will*. Free of ourselves. We can rise above the beast and be free. The beast, the idiot brother, must die. There can be no compromise. Blast, it, David, I compromised."

"The old man never knew what hit him," David muttered. "There's that consolation."

"Next time I won't. I swear it."

"Make a martyr of yourself if you want to, Alex. Just be sure you really want to. And be jolly well sure you leave me out of it."

"God give you eyes," Alex said. He sighed and fell silent. David stretched out and went to sleep.

Chapter 14

There was a new prominence for Alex now. A good many of the villagers were afraid of him—or of the evil spirit with which he had threatened to haunt Kat's doorway. Others were shyly attracted to him, as if he might have knowledge worth listening to. Most, though, seemed to admire him just because he had put on a good show. He had offered his life and had angered Kat into buying him—at an unheard-of price—in order to kill him. Yet he had survived. That made him sort of a hero.

Kaigyet, an important member of Kat's family group, now arranged for Alex to be put in her charge. She lived in the new house, but she also had a sanctum of her own, an unpretentious slab building where she kept her herbs and paraphernalia. She spent much time there. So, now, did Alex.

He admitted he was afraid of her. "Kwawlang is a reasonably honest man," he said one night. His and David's sleeping places were a few feet apart in Kat's new house now. "He was furious when I tried to stop him from putting that wounded man into that sweat house, but he got over that. We've become something like friends. But this female treats me like a beast to be probed and experimented with and kept under her control."

"What do you do at her hut all day?"

"Some of it is very humiliating."

He would give no details. When David pressed him, he shook his head and said nothing.

"Maybe you'll agree now that we've got to get away from here in a hurry," David said. "Summer is going to end early up here. There's sure to be weather that will make that strait impossible to cross. We've got to move quickly."

Alex made no comment. David reached out and shook him.

"A canoe," David said. "A sail, some fresh water, a good start. That's all we need. Of course, there are some other things that will help if we can get them. These people have a few firearms. If we could steal a couple of rifles, some powder and ball—"

"Dorothy doesn't approve of firearms," Alex said.

David was jolted by the irrelevance of the words. Something was wrong with the man, something more than moodiness. It was as if a switch snapped within him and he was somewhere else, in some strange realm of his own.

"Go to sleep," David muttered.

David was put to work for a craftsman, a relative of Kat who made watertight boxes. David, Necoon, and other slaves did the preliminary work, splitting boards off logs, adzing them, polishing them to a satin finish with sharkskin. The craftsman then steamed them, molded them into the four sides of boxes, and sewed the joint together with spruce withes. He fitted and sewed the sides into grooved bottom boards. He covered the boxes with carved figures. Finally he painted them black, sometimes with touches of other colors.

While they worked, David pumped Necoon for information and learned a good deal. There were at least twenty villages scattered around the maze of islands, some no larger than two or three houses. The closest was a little way up the inlet. Another was less than half a day away on the east coast of this big island. There was still another, a large one, on the north coast. It was a day and a half away by canoe. Necoon supposed it could be reached overland, but no one ever went that way. The Haida were a seafaring people. They knew nothing of the mountainous, forested interior of their island. There was no reason why they should. There was little game except bears, and these came down to the river mouths during salmon runs and were hunted there. So nobody ever went into the forest farther than necessary to gather herbs or find a cedar suitable for a totem pole or canoe.

The only Hudson's Bay post the Haida visited was Fort Simpson. It was on the mainland a bit north of these islands in the country of the Tsimshian. It was two or three days away, more if the weather was bad. People from this village visited the Tsimshian country in the spring when the oolaken were running, Necoon explained. They fished at the mouths of mainland rivers and rendered their catch into oil on the spot. They also did a little trading at the fort then.

One midnight when the household was asleep, David rose and slipped outside to appraise the chances of stealing a canoe. He crept down to the beach and walked along it, examining canoes along the way. A small dark motion on the bank above him told him he was being watched. He'd expected this; part of the purpose of this night stroll was to learn who the watchman was and where he would be. But another shadow moved on the beach a little way ahead of him, sliding into the deep darkness of the bank.

He hadn't expected there would be more than one. He walked to the edge of the water and stood looking absently acrosss the inlet as if on a casual stroll. He tossed a rock into the water. He moved on leisurely and heard a faint crunch of gravel somewhere behind him. He stooped for more rocks, using the opportunity to look back, and saw a dark figure sink down behind a canoe. There were at least three of them and they were all around him.

He went back the way he had come. He climbed the bank and found a man standing near the doorway of Kat's house. He was a big, long-haired man, a slave, and he carried a war club. He smiled toothlessly and stepped aside. He spoke with a show of good humor.

"I thought you might be the *gow geek,* the monster who comes at night to steal children."

"I couldn't sleep."

"You could be mistaken for the *gow geek* and be killed. Midnight is a bad time to die."

David went into the house and sank down on his blanket, the Haida words ringing in his head. He rolled to his stomach and buried his face on his arms, engulfed in hopelessness.

Something touched him and he found Susie beside him, laying her blanket over him as she had done in the cold nights when they were traveling. She took him into her arms, pulling his head against her breasts. How did she know? he wondered. How did she know he needed her until she was beside him? She was a thick-built little Snohomish girl with a pointed head, a slave used by a dozen of her captors, but she sensed the call of his despair and obeyed it. Later, half waking, he thought he was beside Tsil-tsil and loneliness had been a foolish dream.

In the morning Kat came to the woodworker's place behind the village, carrying an inch-thick alder stick. David was seated on his blanket in the sun, smoothing a board with an adze. Without a word, Kat began to beat him with the stick.

David sprang to his feet, adze and board in his hands. For a moment they were face to face, man to man, motionless, glaring.

"Hit me again and I'll kill you," David said.

He spoke in English, and even as he said the words he knew he couldn't mean them. Sometime, some way, there would be a chance to get off this island, and he wanted to live to do it. In the meantime the work was not hard, there was plenty to eat, and the humiliation and pain of an occasional beating were bearable. They had to be bearable. He had to stay alive.

He tossed the adze to the ground. The tall chief raised the stick and struck again. David was still holding the board and he blocked the blow with it. Then Necoon seized him from behind and threw him, holding his legs while Kat struck half a dozen sharp and painful blows.

"You are not to walk about the village at night," Kat said, speaking as if to a child. He snatched up David's blanket and walked away.

Being deprived of the blanket was the worst part of the punishment. It seemed a petty thing at first, but by sundown he knew it was a great loss. It was warmth, dignity, modesty. Without it, he was a shivering animal.

Susie doctored his bruised back and shared her blanket with him at night. Alex moved ten feet away from them and slept near the door. An effort to remove himself from carnal distractions? There was no telling. In a few days Susie wangled another blanket and gave it to David. No one made any objection.

He took no more night walks. He did spend some of his free time exploring the environs of the village by daylight—the sweat huts and smoke ovens up the beach, the scattered shacks and storage houses that reached a little way into the woods, the sizable cemetery that was studded with carved posts as elaborate as those in front of the houses. One or another of Kat's male slaves was always near at hand. Usually it was Necoon, who seemed to have been given special responsibility for David's custody.

Sometimes he talked to the big slave about freedom, questioning one man's right to own another. Necoon invariably scowled and seemed offended. Loyalty to a master was his supreme ethic. To challenge it was to challenge the whole of his being. David had little hope of arousing a spark of rebellion, but it amused him to disturb the man. Yet there was more to it than that; there was the matter of his own morale.

Something was happening to him. He thought perhaps it was something of the same sort that had happened to Alex—or the first nebulous beginning of it. He was here. He was not free, but then he had never been free. He had not been free in New York or at college or aboard the *Maria Kane*. At the mission there had been glimpses of freedom—his buying Tsil-tsil, his marrying her. Perhaps even the glimpses had been illusions. Perhaps by taking on a wife and a sawmill he

168

was committing himself to a lifetime of slavery. But at least he had made the choice.

That's all the freedom there is, he thought—a choice of masters. Often a man chooses even when he does not realize he has chosen. Often he has not chosen when he claims to have chosen. Necoon at least knew clearly who his master was; in a way, he was to be envied. Kat was the meaning and purpose of his being, and Necoon put no other gods before him.

Chapter 15

Fall was a time of food-gathering, of feasting, and of preparation for the long dark winter that quickly followed. Several kinds of berries were picked and dried. Crabapples, found in the swamps, were boiled and stored away. Salmon were caught in nets and weirs and smoked in great numbers. Bears came to the river mouths to feed on the salmon and were caught in scissorlike log traps that broke their necks. Their meat was roasted, their skins cured for winter clothing. Geese and ducks were hunted with bows and arrows and with bolas. They were roasted whole without being drawn or plucked. When they were cooked, skin and feathers were peeled off and entrails removed.

Haidas paid little attention to bad weather except to put on more clothes. The poor wore skirts and capes of cedar bark—the inner bark shredded and woven into fabrics. Upper-class people wore fur or garments made of elkskin obtained in trade with the Tsimshians. Everyone had a conical rainhat of tightly woven spruce root. Everyone went barefoot. Moccasins would only have been a bother in the constant wet weather.

Susie wove David a cedar-bark skirt and cape that were better protection against the rain than his trade blanket. To the amusement of everyone, Alex made his own clothes. He picked up the rudiments of weaving, but he was awkward at it and lacking in patience. He produced stiff, shapeless garments that he seemed in danger of walking out of. His conical hat was lopsided, and he had trouble keeping it on. He disliked going barefoot, and he talked Skow into returning the boots that had been taken from him when he was captured. They flopped against his naked shins and, along with the ill-fitting clothing, caused much laughter.

Sometimes the rain was studded with sleet. Sometimes it turned to snow. The temperature now often dropped below freezing, but it didn't stay there for long periods. Snow seldom stayed long on the ground.

In the first weeks of captivity, David had lost all track of time. Alex still had no interest in it. David began to mark off days by notching a stick, but he could only guess that they were in December or perhaps getting into January.

Day itself was only a dreary five or six hours of lesser night; it was often almost unnoticeable in the dark weather. The people of the village slept when they were tired, ate when they were hungry, worked when they felt like it. No longer determined by the sun, the pattern of life was set by the elaborate ceremonies with which the Haidas passed the winter.

There were feasts, dances, dramatic presentations. Much of it had to do with the initiation of young men into secret societies, fraternal organizations that brought together men who were under the influence of the same spirits. There was the Seal society, the Salmon society, the Bear people, and so on. The most active and influential group called itself the Cannibals.

Some of the people claimed that the eating of human flesh was not longer practiced. Others hinted that, on secret occasions, it was. In the public part of the initia-

172

tion, members of the sect ate raw flesh that they said was human. According to Necoon, this was a pretense; it was actually dog meat. During the ceremonies, the Cannibals also pretended to be obsessed with a craving for flesh and ran around biting onlookers. Such antics were accepted in a spirit of play. Everyone had a good time at the initiations.

Potlatches were frequent. The family of each initiate was expected to give one in his honor. They were given, too, on the occasion of a death, a birth, the taking of a new name. Enormous though the wealth of the village was, it became clear to David that some of the same goods were given away again and again. Families borrowed blankets, oil, dentalia, even slaves and canoes, in order to give them away at a potlatch. . When it came his turn to give a potlatch, the creditor called in the debt, with interest, and often borrowed more besides. And the potlatch itself, of course, was a kind of borrowing in reverse. Every recipient of a large gift was expected to pay it back eventually in greater amount. It seemed as if the system must break down sometimes, and David gathered that once in a while it did.

Sometimes, as was now the case with Skow and Kat, rival chiefs attacked each other with potlatches. If one could thoroughly outdo the other, if he could overwhelm him with obligations, he could disgrace him and reduce him to impotence. According to Necoon, an outpotlatched chief sometimes felt that the only recourse left to him was to murder his adversary. It rarely happened, Necoon said, but it was not unheard of.

By the time Skow gave his potlatch, days were getting noticeably longer and there was the feeling that winter might be nearing its end. The village gathered in front of Skow's house. Kat, in typically haughty fashion, didn't appear until the preliminary gift-giving was over. Then he pushed through the crowd and sat down in the front row of chiefs, a smile frozen on his face.

Skow stood erect and elegant in a white fur cape. It was fitting that Kat was so happy, he said. He was about to receive great wealth. He would receive more than he could match in ten years.

The first gift was two thousand blankets. Kat scoffed. Skow raised it to four thousand. He gave two slaves, two war canoes, a dozen chests of Chilkat blankets. Then he pointed to two canoes that were paddling in toward shore. Both were loaded with boxes of oil, a twofold return of Kat's gift.

The villagers were tense, silent. The canoes nosed onto the beach and the crews climbed out. Would Kat match Skow's disdain for wealth by burning the gift? It seemed as if he must.

He rose, forgetting to smile and then quickly remembering. He said that he had been expecting more because of the way Skow had been bragging. This would do, he supposed. It would make a handsome fire. But some families in the village were running low on oil. Two moons would pass before the oolaken schooled and the people made their annual trip to the mainland to replenish their supply. So he would not burn the oil. The heads of families could go to the canoes and help themselves.

There was silence, then a small murmur of approval among some of the people. Men and women rose and began to take the oil. But these were just ordinary people of the village, poor people who did not give potlatches or sit on the village council.

A slave brought forward a flat box. Skow lifted the lid and lifted out a copper shield, the first David had ever seen. It was simply a sheet of hammered copper about a foot and a half long, wider at the top than at the bottom. The lower third was divided by a T-shaped ridge.

The villagers purred their excitement. Skow spoke the name of this particular copper, an impossibly long word that named some of the chiefs who had owned it. This one had a long history, he said, and was the most valuable copper in the village. Surely it was worth both that Kat was known to own. He paused to let that sink in. Then, with great effort, he bent the copper in his hands and broke it along the ridge. He broke it again and again, so that he held four pieces.

"You see how little I care for wealth," he said. "I burn canoes loaded with oil. I give away thousands of blankets. And now I destroy this priceless copper."

One by one, he dropped the pieces into the fire. Facing Kat, he said, "Can you match that? You do not own so valuable a copper. Still, I challenge you to match me."

Kat had already sent for a copper. Necoon brought it forward now, carrying it in his two hands. Kat took it, held it in the fire for a moment, and then bent it, putting it under his foot and working it back and forth until it broke. When he had four pieces, he sailed them over the heads of the crowd into the sea.

There were no cheers, just hushed words of awe. Within a matter of minutes, the people had seen two ancient coppers reduced to trash. Such destruction was a frightening testimonial to the power of the destroyers.

The story would be told all over the island. It would spread to the mainland, to the Kaigani Haida to the north, to the Tsimshian. This was a historic battle between the two chiefs, and it would make them famous.

But the contest was not over. Skow rose again and took another copper from the flat box. Evening darkness was creeping in, bringing a storm with it. A drop of rain splashed the polished surface of the plaque. Skow wiped it tenderly away. He named the copper, bent it in his powerful hands, and broke it. He did this directly in front of the village chief, who reclined on a pile of bearskins in the place of honor. During the earlier part of the ceremony, the old man dozed. Now he was restless, nervous. He muttered to himself as Skow broke the copper again and tossed the pieces at Kat's feet.

Necoon appeared with another copper. Everyone knew it was the last that Kat owned. Kat looked ill, his face a haggard mask. But he took the copper with a contemptuous toss of his head. He lacked Skow's strength. He had to heat the bright shield several times before he could bend and break it.

Triumph was at hand for Skow. He had only to break another copper and Kat would be unable to respond to the challenge.

He was brought another box, containing his two remaining plaques. He held them up for display, praised them, told a little of their history. Gradually it became apparent that he was not going to press his advantage. He was not going to break another. Not today.

Vaguely, David understood the young chief's strategy. Neither had won this contest, but Kat had no more coppers. Skow could challenge him and defeat him disgracefully any time he wanted. Everyone knew it. There was no need for him to demonstrate. He was the favorite now, the probable new chief.

Still, Kat brazened it out. When Skow had returned the coppers to their box, he faced the crowd and announced that he would give a potlatch before the days grew short again. He would show the village what a great giving of gifts was like. He would drown Skow in a sea of gifts. There was an icy determination about him that was impressive.

The storm held off and there was an outdoor feast of roast halibut, steamed clams, oysters baked in their shells, abalone simmered in oolaken oil. The old chief ate nothing and was escorted to his house. Kat, too, left quickly.

David stuffed himself, wondering where Alex was. When wind and rain finally struck, he scooped a dozen baked oysters onto a mat and took them to his sleeping place. He found Alex there, sitting cross-legged and staring at nothing.

"Kat got his sails trimmed."

"Yes," Alex said. "Kwawlang said it would happen."

David never knew when he would find Alex in a responsive mood, and he was pleased. He gave him a handful of oysters. "Will Skow be the next chief? The old man can't last much longer."

"I should think so," Alex said.

"It might be important to us. Skow's far more friendly."

"Yes." Alex slurped down an oyster. "I get the

177

feeling life's a game to him, including potlatching. He has to win, of course.''

"So does Kat. They're both hungry for power. Alex, they say these things sometimes end in murder.''

"Yes, I can understand that. Either of them might be capable of it if he should be thoroughly frustrated.''

"When there's a big affair like this, the whole village centers its attention on one spot. It seems to me we could have stolen a canoe and got a fair start before we were missed.''

"I don't know,'' Alex said. ''Anyway, the weather turned bad. Be patient, David. The time will come.''

"You sound as if it isn't especially important.''

"It's important. The world is important. It matters. It's our way of seeing it that doesn't matter. It doesn't matter at all.''

David groaned inwardly. He's off again, he thought. David snuggled into his blanket and closed his eyes. He could hear Alex breaking open oysters and sloughing them down.

Much later, Susie came in. She spread her blanket close and he woke, groaning to let her know it. Necoon had come in and was snoring a few feet the other side of her.

She had been with a man, David supposed. He rolled away from her and heard soft panting sounds from Alex's direction. He raised himself and gaped at vague, shapeless undulations in the darkness. He turned to Susie and touched her.

Someone is in bed with Alex," he whispered. She said nothing. He poked her gently. "You passed them. Who is it?"

"I saw nothing. It's too dark."

He didn't believe her. She was a curious girl; she would know. "Shall I crawl over and look for myself?"

She was frightened, trembling. "It's Skyil."

"Skyil? The daughter of Kaigyet?"

"Shh! You'll wake Necoon."

"Surely you're mistaken. It can't be Skyil."

"I am not mistaken. It's Skyil, the famous virgin. I saw her with him once before. They will get caught."

David turned away from her, appalled by the risk Alex was taking. At the same time he wanted to laugh.

After a time a dark figure rose from Alex's blanket. Swift and lithe, scarcely perceptible, it stole in perfect silence along the wall and dissolved in the thousand shadows of the house.

Chapter 16

Spring in the Charlottes was a mere hint, a feeble promise. It came undramatically with more daylight, slightly milder temperatures, a few buds, a subtle brightening of grass. Violent storms were frequent. Overcast was almost as constant as ever. The rare clear days were usually also cold, and there was ice on the puddles in the morning.

Halibut fishing went on all year round, but it was especially good now in certain places off the east coast of the archipelago. Equipped with wooden hooks and baskets of cuttlefish for bait, many families made trips to the fishing ground. They returned with canoes loaded to the gunwales with the large flat fish.

Alex now worked with David and Necoon at the place behind the village where boxes were made. The work was tedious but it seldom lasted more than half a day. Sometimes when it was finished they were given special tasks. Quite often they went into the forest with other slaves and women in search of the first pale sprouts of salmonberry, fireweed, miner's lettuce, and other edible shoots. Sometimes they stripped bark from spruce and hemlock, separating the tender inner bark, which was eaten fresh and also dried and pressed into cakes. These excursions seldom took them as much as a mile from the village.

One morning they were hurried into a canoe and

taken up the inlet by Kat's brother and several male members of the family. Necoon and another slave, called Kwung, went along. After they'd paddled for about an hour, they passed a place where the inlet narrowed down to about fifty yards. David thought at first that they must be nearing the head of it; but it broadened out again and he realized it was really not an inlet at all but a strait between the two largest islands of the archipelago.

Half an hour later they reached a small village of four houses. They were taken into one of these, a meal was served, and then all members of the party except David, Alex, Necoon, and Kwung headed back down the inlet.

They remained here three days and nights, Alex and David closely guarded by Necoon and Kwung. David could get no explanation until the canoe returned to take them back to the big village. Then he learned that a big ship had been sighted tacking into the inlet, a ship of the iron people, coming to trade. Kat had ordered the white prisoners removed until it left.

When they go back, David found Susie sitting above the beach, twisting fiber into line that would be used in fish nets. The sun was peeking through the clouds and she had found a place where it shone on her. She was excited about the ship.

It had anchored off the village, and those with furs to trade had paddled out to it. One night a party of whites had come ashore and feasted with the chiefs. They were *Dutchmen*, she said. In Chinook that was an unspecific term meaning any white who was not British or American. Likely as not, the ship was Russian, David decided.

"Did you speak to anyone from the ship?" he asked her.

"One of the chiefs made love to me. He paid Kat for this."

"Did he speak Chinook?"

"Only a little."

"Did you tell him about Alex and me?"

She shook her head, looking frightened. "We were told not to speak of you. Kat warned me especially about this. He said he would have me killed if I spoke of white slaves."

By David's estimate it was late March or early April when villagers began preparations for the annual trip to the mainland. The largest canoes were taken out of winter storage places and tested for seaworthiness. Cracks were caulked with pitch, hulls smoothed with sharkskin and repainted. There was fasting and dancing to assure a bountiful run of oolaken.

Early one bright morning they left, three quarters of the village in a great procession of seagoing canoes. Many slaves went along, but Necoon and Kwung were left behind, charged with guarding David and Alex. This was a disappointment to Necoon. Somewhat bitterly, he told David what the trip would be like.

Given good weather, the passage across the strait would take a day. The next day they would paddle north to the mouth of the Nass, where the oolaken schooled. The small fish came in massive schools, he said, and were trailed by seals, sea lions, and killer whales. The fishing grounds were the property of a rich Tsimshian chief. The Haida chiefs would have to buy fishing rights from him. The fish were taken in nets and rendered into oil at once. This was done by boiling them in water and skimming the oil off the top. There were certain rituals that must be observed during this process. Otherwise the oolaken spirit would be offended and the oil would spoil quickly. Normally, it would not go rancid for two years or longer.

When the run was over, there would be feasting and celebrating with the Tsimshians. Sometimes white traders visited the fishing grounds, bringing whisky. Necoon had got drunk at one of these gatherings once, he said. The next morning he remembered nothing. He was told he had killed a Tsimshian slave. He laughed now and pointed out how lucky he was that the victim was only a slave. Kat paid the dead man's owner a few blankets, gave Necoon a beating, and that had been the end of the matter.

Most of the villagers would come home when the fishing was over, their canoes loaded with boxes of oil. A few would form parties and go north or south along the mainland, raiding for slaves and loot. Skow would surely do this. But this year Necoon didn't think he would share a canoe with Kat. Their jealousy had grown too much for that.

The boxmaker went on the trip, so there was no regular work for David and Alex to do. They did a little clam-digging, a little root-gathering. Most of the time they just lazed around, always under the watchful eyes of Necoon or Kwung.

Alex's usual mood now was one of scowls, mumbled criticism, sometimes sarcasm. Skyil had gone with her mother on the expedition, and David guessed that he missed her. He was on the verge of bringing up the subject several times but didn't know how to do it without sounding like a busybody. He kept hoping that Alex would bring it up. At last he did.

They had taken their morning plunge and had found a sunny place on the bank to dry off. Necoon and others were still in the water, splashing and romping like children. Alex jogged in place and stripped water from his body with his hands.

"I have put us in a somewhat hazardous position," he announced. "Perhaps you know."

David squeezed water out of his hair, shoulder-length now. He dabbed at his body with a rotting fragment of old trade blanket, a makeshift towel that was a treasured possession.

"The girl," he said.

"Ah, you know. I thought you knew. Call me a fool, David. Get it said."

"Pure fool and a yard wide."

"I find I haven't progressed beyond the desires of the flesh. That is a terrible thing for me, David."

"I'm glad you've come down from that pose as some kind of ascetic headed for Salvation with a capital S," David said. "But why in thunderation did you have to choose Skyil?"

"Ah, David. I prefer to believe she was chosen for me. She is my future. Together we shall minister to the Indians. With my timber claims to support us, we shall teach them the true meaning of Jesus, not the usual codified mishmash. We shall stand with them against the white encroachment. This is my destiny. I see it clearly—my worldly destiny."

"Seems to me your worldly destiny might be to get your head knocked in for seducing a sacred virgin."

"A sacred virgin. A charming way to think of her.

But seduction? There was none on my part, David. That's the truth. She came to my bed. I didn't invite her. I had scarcely spoken two words to her previously.''

David laughed, shaking his head. "You're hopeless." He tossed the piece of blanket to Alex, who began to rub himself with it.

"If there is blame in this, it falls on Kaigyet," Alex said. "A fiend, a harpy. Sometimes she tied me hand and foot and tortured me. She cut me, burned me, whipped me, stuck thorns in my flesh. It was all done in an experimental way, as if I were a strange new specimen to be studied.

"I know what you think of me, David. I'm a windy visionary, a pretentious hypocrite. But at that time I truly hated my body. I swear it. I welcomed the torture. It was God-sent. Truly, David. I would lie there and deny the pain and try to separate my true being from the physical. At times I was quite successful. Not for long, but there were moments when I was truly detached from the pain. Kaigyet seemed to know, and it made her furious. She stopped the torture and began to do other things to me, sexual things. I refused to respond. She's an ugly old hell-cat—that helped. Then she brought in Skyil. The girl never touched me. She was just there, watching, looking into my eyes. After a while I was unable to deny my body any longer. Kaigyet knew. She understood. She delighted in my humiliation.

"Eventually, she lost interest in this sort of thing and it stopped. Then she lost interest in me entirely. Then one night there was Skyil, crawling into my bed.''

"Is there a chance Kaigyet put her up to it for some

reason?'' David said. ''She's a tricky one.''

''Never. That girl's purity is an obsession with her. Kwawlang tells me there's some kind of minor tradition behind it. A virgin is believed to have power over certain spirits. The Haidas don't ordinarily pay much attention to that sort of magic, but Kaigyet has built this thing up. She protects her daughter from so much as a touch by a man. The old woman who guards the girl has no other duties. She's with her every moment that Kaigyet isn't. But she's pretty old. When Skyil sees that she has an active day with no chance to cat-nap, she sleeps like the dead at night. The girl has no trouble slipping away.''

Alex tossed the towel to David, who spread it on the ground in the sun. ''Susie and I have already got onto you. Others will, too, sooner or later. Word will get to Kaigyet. Alex, you've got to put a stop to it.''

''Yes. Well, I'm working on a plan for our escape. I'm giving all my thought to it.''

''I've thought of very little else.''

''It's a bit complicated,'' Alex said. ''There are a few details I haven't worked out yet. But by the time Skyil returns, I'll have it. She's part of it, David. We're taking her with us.''

David stared, scowled, laughed. ''God Almighty damn, Alex! No. I'll have no part of it.''

''Ah, David. You haven't even heard it.''

Necoon came up the bank, puffing from his swim and pausing to shake himself like an animal. He seemed to be able to loosen his skin and vibrate his body inside it. He sat down with his back to the sun. Kwung came up the bank and sat beside him. Kwung was a silent, solemn man who had been captured from some northern tribe when he was a child.

"How do we get away from these watchdogs?" David said.

"We'll see. We might be able to slip away at night. The beach is closely watched as you know. The back of the village less so. As for these two, perhaps we'll have to overpower 'em."

"Brilliant. You can have Necoon."

Necoon, hearing his name, scowled at them. David grinned and spoke in Haida. "How do you stay in that icy water so long, Necoon? I'd turn blue."

As usual, the big slave was pleased by a compliment to his physical prowess. He took himself very seriously. Sometimes, just to goad him, David still spoke to him of freedom and of the right of all men to it. Far from stirring either pride or reason, such talk seemed only to offend him.

I've become rather fond of the old gorilla, David thought. We're friends and yet we're enemies. He'd knock my brains out if Kat ordered it, and he'd enjoy doing it. On the other hand, if I had to kill him in order to escape, I guess I'd do it. But I'd remember all my life that I had killed a friend.

Kwung got to his feet. He pointed to the east, squinting, "*Kloo*," he announced. "*Stan-sung kloo*."

Four canoes. They were black splinters far down the channel, hard to make out in glistening sunlight on choppy water.

"They come home early," Necoon said. "It's been a good run."

Kwung, excited by being the first to sight the canoes, hurried down the street shouting the news. Alex was staring eagerly. Villagers on the beach climbed to the

188

bank for a better view. Others came out of houses to join them. Long before the canoes beached, Necoon identified them as belonging to two families who lived at the far end of the village. Alex looked disappointed.

The old chief came out of his house, tottering between two slaves. When the canoes reached shore, he croaked the formal words of welcome. The people sang the homecoming song. The canoes were heavily loaded with boxes of oil. David and Alex helped unload them. The boxes were dead heavy, filled almost to their brims. The oil hadn't spilled during the trip because of the carefully crafted, tight-fitting lids.

As he worked, David listened to the chatter of the travelers, picking up bits of news about various persons whose names he recognized. Kwawlang had been ill but was recovering. Skow had been lucky at gambling. He had tired of the fishing, however, and had taken a war canoe north to raid a Tlingit village. Kat had become very friendly with the great Tsimshian chief who controlled the fishing rights. . . .

Alex listened to the talk, listened carefully, and David knew he was hoping for some word of Skyil. The old fool was in love, and he was as eager and as defenseless as a teen-ager.

Chapter 17

Other villagers returned in small groups during the next several weeks. Many of them stayed only long enough to store away their oil and get a night's rest. Then they moved to the beaches on the east coast of the island or to the great sandspit that guarded the approach to the inlet. The latter was only a few miles away, but they set up mat huts and lived there for weeks, fishing, digging clams, gathering oysters and abalone.

The boxmaker returned and David, Alex, and Necoon found themselves back at work for him. Kat's brother was also among the early arrivals. Kat himself remained on the mainland with the Tsimshians. There were various rumors that rich Tsimshian chiefs would back him in his "war" with Skow. One story had it that he was negotiating for a copper. Another had him about to take a new wife. She was a widow, it was said, and her infant son was the heir of the great chief who controlled the Nass fishing grounds.

Alex reacted so eagerly to Skyil's return that it was a wonder someone didn't notice. He had been keeping a watch for her for days, and when he saw the girl and her mother in an approaching canoe he fairly raced down to the beach to meet it. When it was unloaded and the travelers had gone into Kat's house, he followed. He sat down on the upper tier, choosing a place where he could see the girl's face in the crowd that clustered around the fire in the low center of the house. David joined him.

"Alex, go over to your sleeping place. Everyone in the village will know you're gone on her."

"I must talk to her."

"Well, don't sit and stare at her like a big love-sick oaf. Come on."

"Yes. No. I didn't realize."

They moved around the perimeter of the house to their sleeping places and sat down. Skyil's back was to them now.

"You can talk to her when she crawls into bed with you," David said.

"Yes, you're right. I'll be patient."

Necoon crawled through the doorway, scowling in the dim light. He stalked over to his sleeping place and sat down.

"It will be soon now," Alex said.

"What will?"

"We'll be leaving."

"If you really have a good plan, we will."

"You and I and the girl."

"No," David said.

"It's a good plan. We'll not move until circumstances are just right. It will be foolproof."

Necoon scowled in their direction. He was always irritated when they spoke at length in English. He had learned a word or two on the mainland but not enough so he could follow a conversation.

"Alex, have you ever spoken to the girl about escape?"

"Not a word. But I can persuade her to go with us."

"I can imagine what you'll tell her. You're a great

192

chief among the iron people. You'll promise her a big house, servants, a horse and carriage. You'll tell her she'll be a princess."

"You have a way of seeing things in the worst possible light," Alex grumbled. "I have the plan pretty well worked out now."

"The foolproof plan. I'd sure like to hear it."

"It's rather simple really. We wait for a rainy night and head into the interior of the island. The rain will cover our tracks. We'll double back and work our way up the inlet to that place where it narrows down to fifty or sixty yards. It will be an easy swim. We'll hide in the woods on the island across the way. They'll never think of looking for us over there."

David had to agree that they very likely wouldn't. "So far, so good," he said.

"We'll hide till the search slows down. Then we'll swim back across. We'll go on up the inlet to the four-house village where they held us when that ship was here. There's no night watch there; we'll have no trouble stealing a canoe. We'll come down the inlet in darkness, staying close to the far shore. The canoe won't be missed till morning. Then it will take at least a couple of hours for the news to reach here. We'll have an excellent start."

"Not bad," David said.

"I've stolen a couple of blankets, some fishline and stuff. Got 'em stashed behind the box factory."

"It all sounds good, Alex, very good, except for the girl. Taking her along is utterly asinine."

"David, you must see—"

"It will turn the search into a holy crusade."

Alex sighed sharply and shook his head. "She and I

193

have a destiny together in this world.''

"Bah. This world, the other world—which one are you in?''

"Ah, David. They're one. The division is in ourselves.''

Skyil did not come to share Alex's blanket that night or the next or the next. On the fourth night David woke and heard whispering and knew that she was there. Alex was whispering eagerly and much too loudly. David turned for a look at Necoon, asleep in his usual place ten feet on the other side of him. Susie had not returned from the mainland, and there was no one between them.

It was a great relief when the whispering stopped and, a bit later, the girl rose and slipped away.

The next morning Alex was taken on a root-gathering expedition. He didn't get to the boxmaker's until work was almost finished for the day. He picked up a board and a piece of sharkskin and sat down beside David.

"She visited me last night.''

"I know,'' David said. "You were whispering loud enough to wake the dead.''

"She was excited by the prospect of going with us—quite excited.''

"You told her our plan?''

"Not in detail, not yet. But she'll go with us. She likes the idea of getting away from her mother.''

"I can't blame her for that,'' David muttered. "But Alex, it's foolish. We don't need her.''

"Oh, but we do. She can easily get hold of things we'll need—more blankets, food, knives. We'll be in the woods a while, you know. And she

194

can help us get away—"

There was no use trying to talk Alex into leaving the girl, David realized. He might as well reconcile himself to that. The rest of the plan was all right. Fleeing into the woods to the north, circling back south, crossing the inlet at the narrow place, and then hiding for several days on the island across the way was a good idea. The Haidas would make some kind of search of the forest on this island, no doubt. It might very well not occur to them to look across the inlet.

Kwawlang came toward them, hurrying as if eager to greet them. He had just now arrived from the mainland. He had been ill, he said, and had not gone with Skow on his slave raid to the north. He had hoped that Skow would be back by this time. He had news for him. Very serious news.

Kat was truly going to marry a Tsimshian princess, the sister of the incalculably wealthy chief who owned the oolaken fishing rights at the mouth of the Nass. It was not just talk, it was true. The chief, called Pahl, was the richest of all Tsimshians, gave the biggest potlatches, owned several precious coppers. Once the marriage took place, Kat would be able to draw on this family's wealth in his potlatch war against Skow.

The ceremony would be held here, Kwawlang said, not on the mainland. That in itself would be an embarrassment for Skow. The bride and her family would arrive in a great procession of canoes. There would be a celebration lasting many days. There would be exchange of lavish gifts and much display of wealth.

They left the box-making shed and walked toward the houses. Alex and Kwawlang angled off toward Skow's house. David saw Susie on the bank above the beach and hurried to meet her.

She, too, had just returned from the mainland. She was glad to be back here, she said. She spoke excitedly of the crossing from the mainland, the feasting, the oil-making, and she was full of woman talk about Kat's bride-to-be.

She was a young widow with a tiny baby who was heir to all Pahl's wealth. Her name was Kweenu. She was a very important princess, and there were already many songs and legends about her. Susie had even spoken to her. Even though she had a dozen slaves at her command, Kweenu had sent for some of Kat's slave women and had talked briefly with each. This was preparatory to choosing some of them to serve her when she came here for the wedding. Susie fervently hoped to be among them.

Kweenu had great magical power, Susie said. She had come under the influence of a friendly spirit when she was very young. When a smallpox epidemic struck her village, the spirit got inside her head and led her away and saved her. The disease killed Pahl's brothers and nephews and left him without an heir. As Kweenu grew up, the spirit stayed inside her head and looked after her. It found her a husband, who got her pregnant and then was killed in a slave raid. The spirit then led her home to her brother. When she bore a son, he was overwhelmed with gratitude. Now he had an heir. He gave a great potlatch. It was there that Kweenu met Kat.

"Stop it," David said irritably. "Why must you always dress up a story with spirits?"

Susie was hurt. "I am only telling what was told to me."

196

He laughed and patted her arm. What had Alex said? It was your way of seeing the world that mattered. And wasn't seeing the influence of spirits in everything as good a way as any? Who knew exactly what the word *spirit—nok-nok* in Haida—signified to the people who spoke it? It really wasn't an exact term at all, just a convenient approximation. Was there really much difference then in seeing events as spirit-determined from seeing them as the result of Destiny, Divine Will, Chance, or the Law of Averages? These were convenient approximations, too.

"I'm sorry," he said. "I spoke foolishly."

The other women of the village were as full of chatter about the princess as Susie was. No doubt she represented a fulfillment of their own wildest, most secret dreams. She had given Pahl the heir that saved his prestige. She would marry Kat, allying him with Pahl and giving him victory over Skow. It was a woman's story.

A few days later Skow returned. He had raided a Tlingit village and had four prisoners, along with many bundles of deer, elk, and mountain goat skins. Ordinarily, it would have been an impressive amount of loot. But now the people regarded it a bit patronizingly. In their minds, Kat would win the battle of wealth now. Skow's raid had been an exercise in futility.

He had a new wound, an ugly spear cut on his upper arm near the scar left by David's bullet the summer before. It was swollen and festering, but he pretended to ignore it and made a point of standing straight and moving briskly. When the victory ceremony was over and the loot and the prisoners were being taken to his house. he let Kwawlang look at the wound. To David's

surprise, the old *skaggy* beckoned to Alex, who also
had a look and suggested hot compresses. Kwawlang
grunted as though he disapproved. But David knew
him well enough now to suspect that, along with chanting, dancing, rattle-shaking, and sweat baths, Alex's
treatment would be followed.

That evening the story went around the village that
Skow had laughed when he was told of Kat's coming
marriage. Late the next afternoon, returning from a
sweat bath, he saw a group on the beach that included
some of Kat's relatives, and he paused to make a
scoffing speech.

"Kat is so poor that he must take a rich wife! A
Tsimshian at that! Pah! I am a warrior. There is no end
to wealth for a warrior. When my storerooms run low, I
will go on raids and fill them. If it pleases me, I will
even raid the Tsimshians. I will take the blankets and
slaves of Kat's wife!" He laughed mightily, as if this
were a great joke. "If it pleases me, I will make slaves
of her relatives. I will hold them for ransom. What will
Kat do then? Will he come against me dressed in
armor? Pah! He will pay the ransom. He is no warrior.
He is a marrier of Tsimshians!"

It was an overreaction, David thought, a bluff. The
man was deeply worried. Alex agreed, although without showing much interest.

"Boasting will only make his defeat harder to accept," he said.

"He won't accept it. He'll fight."

"I rather imagine so. It isn't our concern, David..
Not any longer. Our plan is complete."

"You've talked to the girl again?"

"She came to me very late last night. She has put

198

aside everything we'll need. Blankets, food, everything. We'll leave the first rainy night."

David turned his eyes to the sky. Directly overhead, there was only pale overcast. But to the northwest, just above the treetops, lay a mass of threatening black clouds.

Chapter 18

He went to bed early, before Alex or Necoon or Susie. They, along with other slaves and members of the family, were gathered around the fire at the low center of the house. Some of the women were singing. There was no ritual to the singing, no purpose except to entertain.

David lay in the warmth of his blanket, breathing the rich smells of the house, listening to the songs and the beat of the rain. The songs were clean and plaintive and separate from the moiling protoplasm that produced them. The hawk song was a favorite.

Birds with pretty feathers
Sing songs in the sky.
The hawk is silent.
He is a war chief.
He hunts the musicmakers
And makes silent the sky.

Skyil was in the group, sitting beside her mother. As if cued by a gust that rattled rain against the house, her clear, sweet voice led the others into the wind song.

T'Kul, the wind spirit,
Chooses the way for the wind to blow.
He calls together the winds.

They push the clouds around
And make a great storm.

By their songs ye shall know them, David thought.
And they sing with humility and wonder.

Nekilstlas made the world
By stomping down the darkness.
He stole the sun and moon from a greedy chief.
He hung them above the world
And tattooed the sky with stars.

Alex and Necoon came to bed. Susie came later. She would have crawled in with David but he turned away from her, rolling up in his blanket.

He didn't expect to sleep, only to wait; but he began to doze fitfully. Several times he woke with a start, thinking it was time to go, but it was not. He snuggled back comfortably, almost wishing the rain would stop and they wouldn't go tonight.

My body doesn't want to go, he thought. It wants to lie here and be warm and not take risks. But *I* want to go. Alex would draw a moral from that. Clearly, he would say, you are not your body. . . .

The next time he woke, Alex's hand was on his shoulder and he realized he had slept deeply.

"Now. Quickly."

They snatched up blankets and rainhats and crawled out of the house. The rain was an icy shock. It was falling steadily. The wind had gone down.

Alex had on his damned boots. Otherwise, except for loincloth, apron, and rainhat, he was naked. He loped off toward the woods, boots flopping noisily against his shins. David followed closely, seeing little in the darkness. They reached the shed where they made boxes. The posts that supported the low roof seemed starkly alive, watchful. Alex slithered into dripping brush behind the shed and came out with a blanket roll.

They ran along the edge of the forest and angled across the cemetery with its carved poles, some of them with coffins mounted at their tops. They stopped at the edge of the woods behind the cemetery.

"Skyil will meet us here," Alex said. He was panting heavily.

"She'd better be quick."

"She went to the beach to get the attention of the guards and make sure we wouldn't be seen going out the back way."

"Alex, that's stupid! She'll get them on the alert. They'll watch her."

"No, no, no. She took one of her mother's spirit tubes. She'll tell the guards there's a spirit in it that must be disposed of immediately. That's not unheard of—I gather she's done something of the sort before."

"In the middle of the night?"

"Why not? A dangerous spirit demands immediate attention, I should think. She'll tell them to take it out to deep water, tie a stone to it, and sink it. That will keep them all busy."

Skyil appeared almost at once, walking swiftly across the cemetery from the far end of the village. She was wearing a rainhat and cape and short cedar-bark skirt. She was laden with blankets, a basket of food, two sheathed knives.

"They all shoved off in a canoe to sink the spirit,"

she said, giggling. "They took the matter very seriously."

They divided up the gear and struck off into the forest. For the first mile or two, there were well-worn trails. Skyil was in a giggly mood, making jokes about the guards, the rain, the excitement that would grip the village in the morning. David tried to fall in with her high spirits. He didn't feel much like joking; but he did his best and the girl responded and for a time they were like children on a lark. Alex, ludicrous in his boots and lopsided rainhat, grimly led the way and seemed not to hear them.

In an hour of travel, they were deeper into the forest than any of them had ever been. The trail was overgrown, almost nonexistent. Skyil had grown silent and was inclined to lag. David stayed close to her, still trying to be merry.

The rain stopped, then started again. They crossed a small open space. Darkness was lifting. They had difficulty finding a trail into the forest on the other side of the clearing. For a time they moved slowly through thick brush. As they got into denser timber, the brush thinned out.

Alex called a halt. They sat down on a windfall under the shelter of some branches. They ate some smoked salmon from the basket Skyil had brought. Her feet were sore. So were David's. To be barefoot in the shore area was one thing, in the woods another.

"We have more blankets than we need," Alex said. "Cut one into strips. Bind your feet with them."

They did this, helping each other with the binding. When they had finished, part of the blanket was left.

"We'll leave it here," Alex said. "In the open,

where it will be found.''

They took time to roll the other blankets tightly and tie slings to the rolls so they could carry them on their backs. Skyil walked awkwardly in her improvised moccasins. David shouldered her blanket roll, but she still lagged.

Up to this point, they had made no effort to hide their trail. The rain would obliterate much of it; following it would be slow but not impossible. Now, Alex announced, they had come far enough to convince their pursuers that they were headed to the north end of this large island. So it was time to begin circling back to the place where they could swim the inlet and find a hiding place on the forested south shore.

They backtracked a short distance and turned westward, walking backward and sweeping out their tracks with branches. Alex went last, fussing a great deal to make sure that every trace was covered. It was reassuring to remember that Haidas were seafaring people with no great skill as trackers.

They were in low foothills surrounding a mountain, still splashed with snow at its rocky crest. This was the mountain where Thunderbird lived, Skyil assured them. She was nervous about going closer to it.

They set out on a tortuous, tiring course around the mountain and over a shoulder of it. There was much climbing and descending. They traveled mostly in tall timber. They went slowly, taking pains to erase the few tracks they left on the springy duff.

In early afternoon the rain stopped. Patches of blue sky could be glimpsed above the treetops. There were occasional bursts of sunshine that penetrated the forest in hazy shafts. They were all tired, Skyil nearly exhausted. Alex called frequent rests, but these seemed to do her more harm than good. When they started off again, she was stiffer and lamer than ever.

Once they were around the mountain, travel was easier. They were headed south now, following a brush-lined creek. When the sun came out, it hit them squarely and seemed very hot. The brush along the creek was dripping, however, and there was no chance of their drying out.

Alex climbed a steep little hill and then beckoned to them to come up. From the top they could see the green waters of the inlet. They were scarcely a mile from shore.

"We dassn't go closer in daylight," Alex said. "We'll rest, wait for dark."

They descended the hill and settled down in deep forest to wait. They sat huddled in their blankets and nibbled at the smoked salmon. All the blankets were damp, some of them wringing wet. Skyil snuggled against Alex and then suddenly became very amorous. He was embarrassed and stared straight ahead.

"Would you like me to take a walk?" David said.

"No, no, no. This is hardly the time—we must rest, save our energy."

David laughed. Skyil got to her feet and in one swift motion shed her cape and blanket. She pulled Alex's blanket open and got under it with him.

"Love her," David said. "I'm going to snatch some sleep. Ah, the sleep of the pure in heart."

Alex raised his chin and gave him a stern, humorless look. David moved a few feet away, rolling up in a blanket and pulling another over him.

He woke cold and muscle-sore. It was pitch dark. He

got up and found Alex and Skyil asleep in each other's arms. He kicked Alex in the rump. Alex scrambled to his feet, startled and confused. He was stark naked and snatched up his loincloth.

"We'd better get moving," David said.

"Yes, by all means. Good heavens, how long did we sleep?"

They reached the beach in a few minutes, crossed it at a rocky place, and walked westward in ankle-deep water so as to leave no tracks. Their estimates of distances turned out to be good. In a short time they reached the narrrow place in the channel. There was plenty of driftwood on the beach, and they quickly tied several pieces together to make a raft that would float their gear and clothing.

The tide was low, close to full ebb. The swim was short but deathly cold and left them with chattering teeth. They came ashore on a small triangle of beach with a steep bank above it. When the tide came in, the water would reach the bank and their tracks would be gone. They carried their little raft into the woods and stashed it in brush behind a big cedar log. They walked on straight into the woods, moving slowly in the trail-less darkness. They came to a small creek and moved up it, walking in the numbing water. Skyil was peevish, moaning with every step. At last Alex led them up a little hill above the creek and said they would camp. They bedded down close together in a mass of damp blankets.

David was wakened by the sun on his face, beaming into the trees from high in the sky. He turned and was grateful for the sun and quickly went to sleep again. Later he thought Susie was with him, body silken, hands caressing. He came fully awake and found it was Skyil. She smiled up at him. Alex, an arm's length away, was still asleep.

"No!" David hissed. "Get out of here."

She giggled softly.

"You're his woman," he said.

She made a face. "He's old. He could be my father."

David studied the ripe, expectant young face. With a sound that was not far from a sob, he pushed her away.

"You chose him," he said.

She lay back, uncertain, pouting.

"Skyil, you must understand. Our people are strict about these things."

"Do not come into me then. We'll lie together like children."

"That's foolishness."

He got to his feet, shedding blankets, feeling that he couldn't mean it, that he had to have her. She was immediately blazing with anger.

"Pah! You'll be caught. You'll have your head knocked in and be thrown in a hole. I will marry a rich chief!"

He prodded Alex with a foot. Alex sat up quickly, then stretched and yawned.

"It's noon or later," David said.

"Yes. Is anything wrong?"

"There's work to do. We've got to sew blankets into a sail, cut a mast."

"There's plenty of time. First we ought to dry out, build some kind of shelter."

"The weather is good," David said. "We ought to try for that canoe tonight."

"No, no. Everyone will be on the alert now, night and day. The risk will be much less after a few days. I thought you agreed."

"Alex, I am afraid of the girl. She's tired of this already. She won't last a few days."

"She'll settle down, I'm sure," Alex said. "We'll make a shelter, dig some roots. She'll be comfortable enough. Anyway, she dassn't change her mind. She's terrified of her mother."

"Alex—" David couldn't bring himself to tell him the girl was already tired of him. "She's a child. She doesn't know what she wants."

"You leave Skyil to me," Alex said.

At the sound of her name, Skyil sprang to her feet. She spat on the ground in anger. David realized with a shock that she assumed he had told Alex about her crawling in with him.

"Huldinga!" Her blazing look shot back and forth between them. "I am a person of importance! I do as I please! You will obey me! Both of you will obey me!"

"You are surely a person of importance." Alex smiled gently, the purring pastor. "But we are also persons of importance. You are to be my wife. A man of God will marry us."

"Huldinga!" She pointed a commanding finger at Alex. "When I want you to come into me, you will do it." She swung her arm toward David. "You will do it also."

"There you have it," David sighed.

Alex was shaken, hurt. He gestured helplessly. "She's angry. She doesn't really mean—"

"If you have the sense God gave geese, you'll knock

209

her on her butt, Alex. Right now. I mean it."

"Speak in Haida!" Skyil shrilled. "I command it! There will be no more strange language."

"*Anguh,*" Alex said. "We will speak in Haida."

Skyil was momentarily silent, pacified in spite of herself by this ready compliance. She tried to hold onto her anger, but her tone was no longer shrill. "You will obey me," she said.

Alex began spreading blankets on bushes to dry out. David helped him. Then they all went scouting for food, Skyil in a pout. They soon had an armful of bracken roots, tiger lily bulbs, tender salmonberry leaves. They washed them in the creek, scouring the harsh outer skin from the roots with sand. Their meal was pulpy and unsavory, but it filled their stomachs.

Feeling better, they now built a low shelter by tying poles between tree trunks and covering them with branches. The result was small and makeshift, but it would shield them from the weather and keep their blankets dry. Skyil promptly crawled into it and went to sleep.

Alex undertook to sew two blankets together into a sail. He had also brought some bone fishhooks, and David went to the creek to fish. Using caterpillars for bait, he caught half a dozen large trout. When darkness came, Alex said that they might now build a small fire. They prepared a fireplace carefully, shielding it with brush and a blanket, even though they were surely deep enough into the forest so the blaze wouldn't be seen from the inlet. David worked the firestick, using a trimmed branch and a strip of blanket for the bow. They roasted the trout and baked tiger lily bulbs and had a good supper. Afterward they huddled around the embers. David urged Skyil to sing, but she made a face and refused.

It was a clear night with only a gentle breeze and he decided to sleep in the open, leaving the shelter to Alex and the girl. He took blankets a few yards to one side and spread them. Skyil was suddenly beside him, helping. Then she straightened and faced Alex haughtily.

"Tonight I will sleep here with David."

Alex shook his head soberly. "A woman has only one husband. That is true for Haidas as well as whites."

"I have spoken."

"Alex," David said, "come over here and get her. Take her by the arm and put her where she belongs. Be decisive about it. This one is a brat. The only way you are going to make her understand anything is by doing something physical."

"Ah, David. She is free of her mother and she thinks she is therefore free of everything."

"Exactly."

"She'll get over it."

"Speak in Haida!" Skyil snapped.

"*Anguh,*" Alex said. "We forgot. David, what are you doing?"

David pulled Skyil to her feet, pointed to the hut, and gave her a little push. "That is your sleeping place."

"Pah! You will obey me."

"There are no *huldinga* here," David said. "There are two men and the woman of one of them. The woman is a person of importance but very foolish. We have had enough of her foolishness."

She glared at him. She would have sat down on his blankets again, but he caught her in midair. He dragged

211

her to the shelter and set her down hard in front of it. When she sprang to her feet, he tripped her and set her down again.

She looked up at him, and her expression was the puzzled one of a chastised child. She crawled into the shelter. When David had gone back to his blankets, she crawled out, dragging a blanket with her. She stalked off and laid it on the ground near the ashes of the fire.

"Amen," Alex said.

"Take her into the hut with you," David advised. "Or join her where she is."

"Let her sleep there if she wishes. You made your point. She understands now that you don't want her."

"I do want her and she knows damned well I want her. Alex, if she comes to me in the night—"

"You'll call me, of course."

It was useless. David rolled up in his blankets. Alex brought another blanket and spread it over Skyil. Then he went into the hut.

David slept restlessly, wondering what he would do if the girl came to him. He tried to tell himself that he didn't want her, and there was a small amount of truth in it. He was beginning to think of her as not quite bright.

When he got up in the morning, she was no longer by the fire. He assumed she was in the hut with Alex. Women always did the unpredictable, he reminded himself. Then Alex came out of the hut, asking for her.

They waited. They looked around. Finally, they had to accept the truth. She was gone.

Chapter 19

They considered the possibility that she was playing some feminine game and was hiding nearby. They wasted time looking for tracks and finally discovered that she had gone to the creek and down it. She had headed straight for the inlet.

They raced through the woods, Alex crashing ahead like a madman. The sun was more than an hour into the sky. She had probably left at first light, David thought; if so, there was no chance of catching her. Yet they had to go as far as the shore to be sure. Alex would probably want to go farther. He'd want to swim the narrow place and continue after her on the far side. We'll stop at the shore, David promised himself. I'll stop him if I have to brain him.

They kept up a leg-twisting, breath-stealing pace through the underbrush, traveling too fast to avoid brambles and nettles. At last, staggering to the crest of a small hill, they glimpsed water through the foliage ahead. They descended into a gulch where the big trees were a bit thinner and the brush thicker. The sound of something ahead sent David loping up to catch Alex by the arm.

"Wait! Listen."

"I heard," Alex gasped. They were both panting noisily. "She must be just ahead."

"Something is. If it's Skyil, she's surely heard us.

213

She may hide in the hope we'll pass her." David was stabbed by an ugly doubt. "If it's her."

"Who else would it be?"

"Go quietly," David said.

They chose a careful course, watching their footing, avoiding brush instead of crashing through it. Then she was there, Skyil, fifteen yards ahead, coming around the trunk of a large cedar. She flung out an arm and pointed at them accusingly.

"Kill them!"

Men rose from the brush, brandishing clubs, knives, paddles. David snatched his knife from his loincloth and stripped off the sheath. He pivoted and darted back the way they had come, but a man appeared a few yards ahead of him brandishing a club, moving directly into his path. David waved the knife and charged. Someone threw a paddle, hurling it like a spear. It stabbed neatly between David's legs and tripped him hard. He rolled to his knees, slashing futilely at agile brown legs. Something heavy struck him on the back, low and with crushing pain. He was flat on his belly, breathless. A bare foot came down on his head, pressing his face into decaying vegetation. There was an endless time of smothering, of blows on his back, of writhing pain. At last he was pulled to his feet, sick and dizzy.

He was taken to the beach, aware only of the prodding points of paddles and the need to make his legs work. There were more men on the beach. He was dumped into a canoe on top of Alex, who looked at him from a bloody, swollen face.

Thoughts were tumbling irrelevancies, with the past as immediate as the present. He was in his bed at home, down with a fever and longing for Mother's cool hands.

He was in a hard cot in a college dormitory. He was beside Tsil-tsil under a tree, beside Susie in coarse grass. Then he was where he was, lying twisted in a canoe. Skyil must have left very early, he thought. She must have got to that four-house village and brought the whole male population with her.

The paddlers were chanting triumphantly. He raised himself and saw that they were approaching the large village. People were gathering on the beach. Dogs were barking. The people of the small village had captured the runaways and were returning them. There would be gratitude, honor, rewards.

Alex was lifted out of the canoe and dropped in a heap on the beach. David stood beside him, hands raised against the fists and spittle of outraged women. Kaigyet came up and the other women backed off a bit. Skyil was beside her, pointing, jabbering. Kaigyet prodded Alex with a foot. Satisfied that he was alive, she spat on him and turned to David, shaking her *clechadarran*. Her eyes were murderous. Skyil was jabbering that they had carried her away, kidnapped her. David found himself denying it, his voice strange in his ears.

Ask the night guards, he said. Skyil had distracted them so he and Alex could escape. She had met them later. Had Kaigyet trapped a spirit to be buried that night? Speak to the guards.

Skyil screamed that he was a liar and threw herself at him, clawing at his face. He caught her wrists and pushed her away.

Someone had handed Kaigyet a knife. Her eyes were on David's chest. "Hold him. Hold his arms. I will kill him."

Someone seized him from behind, a small man whom he grabbed by the hair and flung into Kaigyet. Others were on him then. He was thrown to the beach. His arms and legs were pinned, struggle was useless. Then miraculously he was released. He got to his feet and saw that Kat's brother was there, raising his hands for silence, looking nervous and uncertain. Surely this pair of white-skinned traitors would be killed, he said. But it would be a mistake to kill them before the whole truth of the affair had come out. When Haidamasa Kat returned, he would want to know the truth. He had heard that Skyil did indeed visit the night guards and send them on an errand. What did they have to say?

One of them stepped forward, the big, toothless slave who seemed to be in charge of the others. Hesitantly, he told of the spirit tube Skyil had brought and of her request that it be sunk in deep water. Skyil screamed that the man was lying; then she whirled and ran up the beach.

The crowd parted for Kwawlang, who had brought the old chief of the village with him. The old man tottered up to Alex and looked down at him distastefully. He turned to David, raised a fist, and struck him clublike on the shoulder. He then turned to Kat's brother, speaking so feebly that David couldn't catch the words. Kat's brother raised his hands again and announced that the slaves would not be punished until Kat returned. They were Kat's property; judgment was his right. The crowd groaned disapproval. The young chief pointed out that an execution would make a fine addition to the marriage ceremonies. Now there were nods of agreement. Kaigyet waved her knife and screamed a protest, but he spoke sharply to her.

"Skyil has not told the truth. You must learn it from her."

David was taken into Kat's house, taking blows on the way from everyone who could reach him. Necoon held his arm in a traplike grip and halted every few steps to give bystanders a better shot at the target.

He collapsed in his sleeping place. Alex was dragged in and left beside him. Kat's brother came in, gave them each a perfunctory kick, and gave some instructions to Necoon. David floated in and out of groaning half sleep, cursing the pain that kept waking him, wanting nothing but oblivion. The confusion caused by Skyil's lying had saved their lives, he supposed. In the long run it would make no difference. Kat would have them killed. Kaigyet would insist on it—if she didn't find a way to do them in beforehand.

In the morning, he was desperately thirsty and asked Necoon if he could have a drink. The tough old slave shook his head slowly. Necoon had welts on his shoulders, David realized. He must have been given a beating after they escaped. Hours later Susie was allowed to come to them with a wooden water bucket and dipper. Still later she brought broth.

The next day David was clear-headed and without fever. Alex was still in bad shape, not even wanting to sit up. David told Necoon he was going to get some air. Necoon made no objection, but followed him out of the house. After that they were allowed to move about the village, always in the company of Necoon or Kwung or both. They were not permitted to move about inside the house, however, but had to stay in their sleeping places. Susie was allowed to bring them a little food, never much. She was no longer allowed to sleep beside

217

David.

They were given no work to do, no small tasks to take their minds off their wait for death. No one paid much attention to them except to hurl an occasional epithet or to spit in their direction. They were called *tlkoda huldinga*, the dead slaves.

One day when they were lounging on the bank with Necoon, Skow came up to talk to them. He had been sick with his wound, he said. Alex's hot compresses were the only thing that had done any good. He was better now but still thin and hollow-eyed. He tried to strike up a conversation with Alex without success. Finally he sat down beside David. He remarked that Alex was not himself.

"He has been beaten badly," David said.

"But he has always had spells of silence."

"That is true."

"Those with strong magic are often strange. He once told me that there is a new world that one can enter if he can escape from his body. Is this true?"

"I don't know," David said.

"He said that one must find his way to it before he dies. Only then can he reach it after death."

"Perhaps it's true. I don't know."

"He is trying to find his way there," Skow said.

Here was a warrior, a maker of slaves, a seeker of power. Yet he could sit down with slaves and speak in a friendly way. That was his nature, but now perhaps there was something more to it than that. They had a common enemy. Kat.

"Why don't you buy us?" David said. He tried to speak matter-of-factly, but a note of pleading crept into his voice. "You could save our lives."

"I have tried."

"I didn't know. Kat wouldn't sell us?"

"He takes great satisfaction in owning white slaves. When he returns, he will take satisfaction in killing you. He will kill you to honor his bride and her brother."

"You could offer him a great price. You would be repaid."

Skow smiled sadly. "That would please him, but he would not sell you. The more I offer, the greater the honor in killing you."

David sighed, grasping the truth of this. "You could help us escape."

Skow was offended by that. He got to his feet haughtily. "I am a Haida!"

"It would make Kat look a fool."

"Pah! The people would be angry. They'd say I betrayed them. I am a Haida!" He turned abruptly and walked away.

Necoon sat behind them, carving figures on a wooden bowl. He met David's glance and seemed amused. David had forgotten that he was within hearing distance. He wondered if Skow would have been so quickly angry if they had been alone.

He watched Skow stride down the busy street in front of the houses. There was feverish activity in the village now. Most of the villagers had returned from their fishing camps. They were busy making last-minute repairs on houses, repainting the grotesque figures across their fronts, touching up totems. They wanted the village at its brightest for the coming of the people from the mainland.

As it turned out, Kat arrived before the Tsimshians.

As his great canoe approached shore, he stood in the bow, dressed in ceremonial costume. His crew chanted a new song praising his wealth and power.

David watched the welcoming ceremony from a distance. The whole village turned out for it, even Skow and his family. Kat's relatives were dressed in tall wooden headdresses, fur robes, Chilkat blankets. His crew sang songs that he had bought from Tsimshian chiefs, songs that were now his property and could be sung only by his family. They were in the Tsimshian tongue. David understood not a word of them.

He expected that he and Alex would be taken before Kat soon after the ceremony was over, but that didn't happen. That night they were told by Necoon that the decision had been made. They would be killed. Kat had promised Kaigyet. Necoon didn't know exactly when the execution would take place. Kweenu and the Tsimshian party were expected the next day; it would happen after their arrival. It would happen when Kat sensed the moment was right—undoubtedly during a feast or a potlatch. There would be nothing resembling a hearing. It would just happen.

This news jolted Alex out of his detachment. Surely, he insisted, they would be allowed to plead with Kat. It was their right.

"My guilt is greater than David's," he told Necoon. "I made the plan. I talked the girl into going. David had nothing to do with that. It is not right that his punishment should be as great as mine. Kat would agree to that if he would hear me."

There was no one to listen but Necoon, who sat with his back to the wall of the house and carved his bowl, squinting in the poor interior light, making no reply.

Kwung, the other guard, was stretched out in Necoon's sleeping place. The rest of the house simmered with last-minute preparations for the Tsimshians. Mats that had been scrubbed and dried were relaid. Carved wooden dishes were polished with oil. Tidbits were arranged on huge platters and covered with leaves to keep them fresh. Two cooking fires glowed. Oolaken oil lamps flared erratically. Walls and ceiling were a maze of shifting shadows.

"You're not going to talk your way out of this one," David said. They were lying close together and he spoke very softly. "Or my way, either, thank you kindly. Let's jump the guards tonight, Alex. In the midst of all this busyness, there might be a chance."

That made little sense, and he knew it. It didn't matter. They had to make a try tonight, no matter how hopeless. It would be better to die fighting. And if they were overpowered and kept alive, it would be easier to die tomorrow knowing they had tried.

"Ah, David, I betrayed myself and damned us both." Alex sighed noisily, bringing a glance from Necoon. "You were right about the girl. I wouldn't listen."

"Well, listen now. When I see a chance, I'm going to jump Necoon. You help me. We'll get that carving knife away from him and stick it into him. Kwung will wake up and be on us; we'll have to knife him, too. Then we'll dive through the doorway and make a run for the woods. We'll have to run like deer—"

He spoke softly so Necoon wouldn't hear his name, but the big slave's suspicion was aroused. He put aside the bowl and called to Kwung, who immediately awoke and got to his feet.

"I failed," Alex said. "I was tested and I failed. The lusts of the flesh—"

Necoon was barking orders, telling them to lie on their stomachs. He had two yard-long lengths of cord in his hands. He tossed one to Kwung as the two came forward.

"Now, Alex. When I count three. One—"

"Lie down," Alex said. "I have a better plan."

Kwung had David by the hair from behind and brought him down with a kick behind the knees. It was useless to resist alone, and he rolled to his stomach.

"We have no chance to escape," Alex said, "but I think I might save our lives—yours, anyway."

Kwung lashed David's wrists together behind his back. Necoon tied Alex the same way. Kwung went over and stretched out again. Necoon went back to his carving, turning to one side to catch the light from an oolaken oil lamp that burned near the end of the house. After a time Alex spoke again.

"I have a knife, one of the sheath knives Skyil brought us. I shoved it down inside my boot and they never found it. See if you can reach in and get it."

David turned so his back was toward Alex. In a moment, he felt the boot touch his hands. He got his fingers inside, touched the knife, and withdrew it. Stripping off the sheath, he shoved it and the knife under his body.

Alex turned and writhed a bit, a natural thing for a man whose hands were painfully tied behind him. Then their hands touched. David got the knife and held it steady. Alex got cord against the blade and sawed. It didn't take long. Hands free, he took the knife and rolled away.

Puzzled, David waited for him to roll again and cut him free. It didn't happen. Finally, he turned and saw that Alex was facing him, lying with hands behind his back as if they were still tied.

"Go to sleep, David. I'm not going to cut you loose."

"Alex—"

"You must remain tied. It will work in your favor."

"Damn it, if you're going to make a break, I'm going with you."

"No break, David. Go to sleep. There isn't time to explain. Shh!"

Necoon was on the alert, getting to his feet. To distract his attention from Alex, David rolled completely over.

"I ask that the cords be loosened," he said to Necoon. "The pain is great."

Necoon came close and looked at David's hands but did not loosen the binding.

"I can't sleep," David said.

Necoon grunted. He sat down again and went back to his carving. David rolled back toward Alex. Alex rolled away from him, speaking loudly in Haida.

"The hunger of my flesh has betrayed me. I am a slave to my flesh."

Down in the center of the house a woman laughed. There was hushed chatter and she laughed again. David lay on his side in silence, trying to guess what wild scheme Alex had dreamed up and what the flaw in it would be. There was certain to be a flaw. He strained at the cords that gripped his hands, but couldn't reach the knots and it was useless.

Chatter in the house died away. Lamps were extinguished, and people went to their sleeping places for two or three hours' rest. Sickening numbness crept up David's arms and into his shoulders. At last his mind slipped into a shallow forgetfulness that was more haunted musing than sleep.

A sobbing sound roused him. Alex was sitting up, head bowed. He seemed to be gasping or sobbing.

"What is it, Alex?"

"Nothing."

"You all right?"

"All right."

David lay back and closed his eyes. Necoon was stirring. Someone lighted a lamp. People were swarming around him, over him. He was bumped roughly when he tried to sit up. A woman cried out sharply. He tried again to get up, but Necoon rolled him onto his face, inspected his bonds, and stepped away.

He was surrounded by naked legs. He tried to get his feet under him and slipped in a sticky puddle. Finally he rose and found himself in the middle of a crowd clustered around Alex. He shouldered in to where he could see. Alex sat with knees drawn up. He sat in a pool of blood, clutching his groin with bloody hands. David gaped, too stunned to feel anything but a growing nausea. No one did anything. No one moved.

Kat pushed through the crowd. For a moment he, too, merely stared, mouth twisted in revulsion. He pronounced short, stern orders. Necoon seized one of Alex's arms, Kwung the other. They pulled him to his feet.

David gagged, sank to his knees. He did it, he thought. He actually did it. He rose in time to see Alex extend his hands, clutching a bloody mass of tissue. Blood flowing down his legs, Alex staggered toward

Kat and dropped his testicles at the chief's feet.

"I am guilty. I have punished myself. If it is not enough, kill me. David had nothing to do with the girl. Question her sharply and you will learn that I alone am guilty."

Kat seemed momentarily at a loss. Then he produced a snort and turned away. One of his wives stepped into his place, clapping her hands to her face.

"The blood! We'll track it all over the house. All who have stepped in it must go outside and clean their feet. These mats must be washed. Necoon, this is your fault. You didn't watch closely. Did you fall asleep? Pah! You have a beating coming. Now get this bleeding porpoise out of my house!"

Alex raised his voice in a great mournful shout. "Kat! Hear me! Does the truth frighten you so much that you turn away from it?"

Kat reappeared, standing in the crowd, looming above it.

"Look at me," Alex demanded. "It is your duty to speak, to say that justice is done."

"Pah!"

Kat turned and was gone. Alex was suddenly weak, limp. He slumped to the floor. Commanded by Kat's wife, Necoon and Kwung dragged him outside. David followed, working awkwardly through the doorway with his hands still tied. The first somber light of day was on the world. The inlet was silent, glassy. Necoon freed David's hands so he could help carry Alex a little way up the shore. They put him down in dew-soaked grass on the bank.

"We must stop the bleeding," David said. "Unless we do, he'll rob Kat of the honor of killing him. Give me your loincloth, Necoon. You, too, Kwung."

Alex raised his gaunt face. "I am free, David. Even if I live only a little while, I am free at last."

"Sure," David said. He seized Necoon by the arm and gave him a little shake. "Give me that loincloth or I will fight you for it. You'll have to stick your knife in me to stop me. That will rob Kat of the honor of killing me, too."

"You will live!" Alex protested. "I have shown where the guilt is. Surely—" His voice trailed off weakly.

Necoon peeled off his loincloth and threw it on the ground. Kwung did the same. David picked them up, wishing for something cleaner.

"Now one of you go to Skow's house and get Kwawlang."

Kwung glanced at Necoon, who stared out over the inlet in a show of unconcern. David glared at Kwung.

"You will do as I say in this matter. If you do not, my spirit will come back after I'm dead and will get inside you and torment you."

Kwung again looked to Necoon for a cue and got none. With a shrug, he walked off toward Skow's house. David knelt over Alex, pressing one of the cloths into his crotch, binding the other tightly around it.

Kwung was quickly back, with Kwawlang right on his heels. Kwawlang was shocked, incredulous, but he knew what to do and did it quickly. He and Kwung brought clay and leaves from the creek bank, and he used these to pack Alex's wound. They would stop the bleeding, he said.

David helped as best he could, wondering why they

bothered. They were both as good as dead anyway, he thought. Alex had presumed to tell Kat what was just, what he ought to do. Vain, arrogant Kat lectured by a slave he despised? If the damn fool had made his gesture in silence, David thought, if he had let it speak for itself, there might have been some small chance of its working.

Chapter 20

Kwawlang sent for blankets to cover Alex, and they spent most of the day on the bank. Skow's slaves brought broth in a big wooden bowl with a dipper to drink it from. Alex, strangely enough, was hungry and drank a good deal of it. David, too, was grateful for it. It was strong with the flavor of cod and seaweed, and he felt that his stomach was full for the first time in days.

Villagers paused to stare at them, keeping their distance now. Kaigyet came and harangued them, hurling vile words at Alex and assuring him that making a eunuch of himself would save neither of their lives. Kat had promised her they would both die, she said. She looked forward to seeing their broken heads on poles above her hut. Alex ignored her completely. At last she stalked off.

Necoon would have tied David's hands again, but Kwawlang objected, saying he needed them free in order to tend Alex. As a compromise, Necoon bound his ankles with about two feet of cord between them so he could take only short, slow steps. Necoon gave him no chance to pick at the knots.

From time to time, canoes shoved off toward the mouth of the inlet to watch for the Tsimshian party. Toward the middle of the afternoon two of them returned, racing to be the first to alert the village, calling across the water that the party had been sighted, repeating the words, making a chant of them.

"*Wad so hunna hai dlulul.* . . . *Wad so hunna hai dlulul.* . . ."

By the time they reached shore, the whole village was on the bank, chanting.

In a few minutes the procession was in sight, just a bobbing spot of color on the water at first. As it drew closer, the escorting Haida canoes fell back to allow the five big Tsimshian craft to lead the way. They were not quite so long as the largest Haida canoes but were as brightly painted and had high bowsprits inlaid with copper that flashed in the sunlight.

They curled in toward the village in file. Four nosed onto the beach, but the occupants remained in their places until the fifth had slid up and Pahl and Kweenu had disembarked. Pahl wore a headdress carved into an eagle's head. His shoulders were covered with a yellow-and-black Chilkat blanket. He left the canoe first, followed by Kweenu, who wore a smaller headdress decorated with plumes of white fur.

Kwawlang had gone down to the beach for the welcoming ceremony. David stood beside Necoon on the bank, fifty yards away from the landing party. Kweenu caught his attention at once. There was something fascinating about her, something hypnotic. She was dressed in leggings, fur-trimmed leather skirt, and Chilkat blanket; but even under all that bulk he could see that she was straight and slender. It was her face, though, that fascinated him. Proud and delicate under the headdress, it held a promise that he could only feel, that he dared not raise to the level of articulate thought. And then he did give meaning to it and a name to it. At that same moment he told himself with absolute conviction that his mind had cracked. Beaten, naked, exhausted, he accepted his madness, rejoiced in it, and spoke the name into the wind.

With Necoon's hobbles biting his ankles, he moved in shuffling steps along the bank. Necoon followed, touched his arm to restrain him. David paid no attention and kept going, passing among slaves who fringed the crowd. Necoon touched him more firmly, and he halted. After a moment, he moved on, putting people between himself and Necoon and sliding half a dozen yards into the crowd before he was stopped again.

"Stand still," Necoon hissed into his ear.

Down on the beach the old chief was speaking his words of welcome. His voice was weak. People were straining to catch a word or two.

"A little closer," David said.

People near them turned to glare. Necoon did not reply but clung tightly to David's arm.

"We will go closer," David whispered, "or I will make a fuss. You will be in trouble."

Necoon let him go. There was a space at the back of the crowd, a little aisle along the row of house fronts. David minced along this, Necoon at his heels. When he judged they were directly in front of the ceremony, David elbowed into the crowd. In spite of glares and shoves, he worked to the front of it and found himself standing just above the principals.

Pahl was responding to the chief's welcome. He looked to be somewhere in his middle thirties. He stood erect and haughty under the heavy headdress. He spoke in Tsimshian with rhythm and resonance. Occasionally he gestured with a muscular brown arm. His sister stood behind him and a little to one side. Behind her, a female slave packed a baby on her back, Pahl's nephew and heir. Kat, also in headdress and Chilkat robe, faced them, towering above everyone.

David could look directly into the face of the princess now. I am going to die, he thought, and by some miracle I am granted this strange madness in my last hours, this delicious fantasy. She looked up and saw him, looked squarely at him and raised a knuckle to her mouth. Her blanket fell away from naked breasts and she clutched at it with her other hand, her left, a child's hand half the size it should have been.

The knuckle at her lips straightened, bringing finger perpendicular to them. She held it thus a moment. He understood that he was being shushed, that he was to give no sign of recognition. He nodded slightly, and she lowered her eyes.

Necoon edged up beside him, nervous, angry, pulling at his elbow. They had no business being at the front of the crowd. David refused to move. He continued to stare at the face of his wife. Tsil-tsil. Kweenu. A Tsimshian. A princess. She had a small bright mark on her chin, a tiny lip plug of the size you would expect to see on a girl of nine or ten who had just had her lip pierced. She should never have let them do that. She would have to get rid of it. She would probably have a scar there the rest of her life. . . .

The ceremony came to an end. The crowd parted as the old chief was carried up the bank. Kat followed, walking with Pahl. They spoke casually, pointing at the sky, laughing. Clouds were gathering in the northwest and they evidently were saying the Tsimshians were lucky; they had just missed a storm. Tsil-tsil and the slave with the cradleboard followed. David got a glimpse of a tiny sleeping face and was smothered with emotion.

Necoon pulled at him roughly. He shuffled back to where Alex lay with Kwung standing nearby. Alex was awake. He sat up and started to get to his feet, but changed his mind. He raised his face to the graying sky.

"I am free," he said distantly. "I am free at last."

David sat down beside him. "Alex, I don't know how to tell you this. Tsil-tsil is here. She is the Tsimshian princess."

Alex gave him a glance, then raised his eyes to the sky again. David shook him gently.

"Did you hear me? I swear I didn't imagine it. It's Tsil-tsil. She touched her finger to her lips. I think she has some kind of plan. We're going to be free."

"Free," Alex said. "That which frees man from slavery to the beast is good. That which binds him is evil. That is the whole of morality."

David touched Alex's forehead and judged that he was mildly feverish. He pushed him gently, making him lie flat. Alex made no objection.

"Alex, you haven't heard me."

"I heard, David. Tsil-tsil. She has come to free you. I am already free. I was weak. He was too much for me. I made one great final effort of will. I altered him, altered the beast—"

David tucked the blankets around him and stood up. Necoon glared, out of sorts because he had gone into the crowd.

"You had no right to push to the front," Necoon said. "You could get me into trouble."

David grinned at him. "I have told you. All men have the same rights."

"Pah! A great burden will be lifted from me when you are dead."

"Ah, Necoon. What if I don't die?"

"You will die very soon now. You will be shown to the Tsimshians as a great prize. Kat will tell them how valuable you are. Then he'll knock in your heads. Such contempt for wealth will be a surprise for the Tsimshians."

Surprise. The word was like a blow from a club. His mind was numb; he couldn't get things into perspective. The wind was rising, licking the surface of the inlet. Canoes plied back and forth between the village and the place down the shore where the Tsimshians were setting up camp. The canoes carried mats, blankets, food. The distance was short, but ferrying supplies was easier than toting them along the shore.

He stood on the bank, trying to get his thoughts in order. Tsil-tsil was a Tsimshian. She had somehow learned that, or had remembered it. She had gone back to her people. But her being here now in these remote islands couldn't be mere coincidence. She had been looking for him, expecting him to be here. She had recognized him at once in spite of beard and long hair. She had made that shushing gesture. It was as if she had some sort of plan. But she didn't know that he was to be executed. He and Alex could be led in front of her and killed before she could stop it. It was to be a *surprise*.

After a while, people began to come out of Kat's house a few at a time. Some walked down the shore toward the Tsimshian camp, others shoved off in canoes. Kwawlang came out and came over to join David.

"They have stuffed their bellies," he said. "Now they will go to the Tsimshian camp and stuff them again."

He had brought a whole baked salmon, which he laid on the grass and divided. He handed generous portions to David and Alex. He motioned for Necoon and Kwung to help themselves.

"Necoon says we are to be killed suddenly as a surprise for the Tsimshians," David said. "Is this true?"

Kwawlang turned to Necoon, who said nothing. "I don't know," Kwawlang said. "It could be true."

"When will this be?" David demanded of Necoon.

Necoon shook his head. "The Tsimshians will give Kat many gifts when he goes to their camp. After that they will all come back and go to the potlatch house. The killing could be at either place. Or it could be tomorrow at the wedding ceremony."

"The wedding isn't until tomorrow?"

"Tonight Pahl will be a guest at Kat's house. The bride will stay at the Tsimshian camp. Tomorrow Kat will take her to his house and it is done."

Alex had sat up to eat his salmon. Now he spoke loudly in Haida. "Man is a house filled with screaming winds. How does he hear the voice that will lead him to freedom?"

Kwawlang scowled thoughtfully. David started to speak, but Alex drowned him out.

"A man must silence the winds. One by one, he must silence them, beginning with the loudest."

"Shut up," David said. To Kwawlang, he said, "There is an important thing you can do. Go to the princess, to Kweenu. Tell her Kat plans to kill the white

235

slaves. Tell her he means to do it as a surprise.''

''What is the reason for this?'' Kwawlang demanded.

''It's impossible to tell it quickly, but the princess will not want us killed. I promise you this is true.''

Kwawlang's lips pursed under the carved bone that pierced his nose. ''Many people speak favorably of what the white slave has done to himself. They say it took a man of strong spirit. Also there are those who say the girl Skyil has not been a virgin for a long time, that she has lain with others before Alex. I will speak to Kat. I will tell him these things.''

''Speak to Kweenu,'' David said. ''Tell her we are to be killed suddenly and without warning. That is the important thing.''

''There will be no stopping it,'' Necoon said.

''Still I will speak to Kat,'' Kwawlang said. ''Skyil has made a fool of her mother. I will point this out.''

''You don't understand,'' David said. ''Kweenu will save us. You must believe me and speak to her.''

Alex raised his voice again. ''The wind voices rage, but I no longer hear them. They are drowned out by the true voice.''

''Kwawlang—''

''I will speak to Kat,'' Kwawlang persisted. He turned away, hurrying down the beach to get into a canoe that was shoving off.

Kat and some other chiefs, still in cumbersome headdress, trooped down to the beach to a war canoe that was waiting for them. Pahl and Skow came last. They had both shed ceremonial costume. Surprisingly, they walked together, laughing and making jokes.

Tsil-tsil came out of the house, along with other

women. As soon as she was through the doorway, she took her cradleboard from a slave and carried the baby on her own back. David watched in an agony of self-restraint as she went down and got into the big canoe. She threw only one quick glance in his direction.

As the canoe shoved off, a slave came up from the beach to give Necoon whispered instructions from Kat. They got Alex on his feet. Taking small, slow steps, helped by David and Kwung, he got down to the beach. Necoon pointed to a twenty-foot canoe that they launched and climbed into. Alex picked up a paddle and would have done his share of the work, but David told him to forget it. The other four manned paddles, and they quickly reached the Tsimshian camp.

A row of mat huts had been set up just above the beach. Behind these was a flat, grassy area where the people were gathered in a great circle around a fire. Necoon told the prisoners to sit down on the fringe of the crowd.

There was an air of haste because of the threatening weather, and things got started at once. There was a dramatic presentation by Tsimshian actors in masks, accompanied by singers and by drummers beating on square box drums. At the conclusion of a second skit a dancer appeared in a mask the shape of a killer whale that spurted water from a blowpipe. The other dancers and some of the onlookers were drenched, and the performance caused much laughter. Tsil-tsil laughed as heartily as anyone.

Slaves passed huge bowls and platters of food. Singers praised the families of Kat and Pahl. There was an exchange of gifts between the two chiefs—oil, blankets, ornaments. Then a special group of singers sang still another new song in praise of Kat. The words were in Haida, and the final verse lauded him as owner of white slaves.

In the east the iron people live in great numbers.
They are rich in guns. They kill many in war.
Haidamasa Kat laughs at their guns.
He makes slaves of the iron people and laughs.

Kat rose, stepping to one side of the fire. He peered out over the crowd, picked out Necoon and beckoned to him. Necoon motioned to David to rise. They helped Alex to his feet and walked forward toward the fire.

Tsil-tsil sat beside her brother. Kat stood in front of them and a little to their right. He held a war club at his side, a heavy carved shaft whose end had been split and bound around a polished egg-shaped stone. His brother, standing just beyond him, held another. Kat motioned to David and Alex to come in front of him and face the fire with their backs toward him. David didn't obey. He faced Tsil-tsil and spoke in English.

"He intends to kill us. Right now."

She reacted instantly, eyes big with fear. She laid a hand on Pahl's arm.

"It's to be a surprise for you," David said. "Right now."

Necoon had him by the shoulders, turning him toward the fire before he could say more.

It was Pahl who replied, speaking in halting English. "You are Englishman?"

David shook off Necoon's strong hands and faced the Tsimshian. "American. *Boston*. We are both *Bostons*. Kat means to kill us."

238

"Trappers? Sailors?"

"Missionaries. Men of God. We live far to the south."

Pahl seemed friendly, sympathetic. He was smiling slightly. He had put the eagle headdress back on and it was slightly askew. He turned to Kat and spoke softly and at length in Tsimshian.

Kat was visibly upset. He replied loudly in Haida, gesturing with the war club. These two white bellies were rascals, seducers of women, runaways. He would show his scorn for valuable property and for the iron people by spilling their brains.

Tsil-tsil spoke quick, low words into her brother's ear. He gave her a puzzled look and she spoke again. Then he got to his feet and spoke at length, addressing himself to the people as much as to Kat. Both Haidas and Tsimshians seemed to have some grasp of the other language, although there was no similarity that David could detect. He understood only that Pahl was his champion; he had no idea what the arguments were.

He caught Tsil-tsil's eye. She gave a sharp little shake of her head and looked away. He wanted to touch her, to embrace her, to lead her forward and shout that he was her husband and the father of Pahl's nephew. He continued to stare at her, and she spoke very softly.

"It will be all right. Pahl is my brother."

"I know," he said.

"Kat will do as he says. Turn. Don't look at me."

"That's my son on your back."

"Pahl must not know that. Turn."

Necoon had heard their low exchange of words. He looked from one to the other, forehead wrinkled in bewilderment. David turned to face the fire.

239

The two chiefs quibbled, challenged, haggled. Pahl was trying to buy the two white men. He offered blankets, oil. Kat seemed more determined than ever to kill. Then Pahl spoke crisply, angrily. He seemed to be at the end of his patience, to deliver some sort of ultimatum. He sat down.

Wind tossed the trees that surrounded the meeting place. It tore at the fire. Kat consulted in low tones with his brother. Suddenly he flung wide his arms and brought his fists together on his chest. He gestured with both hands toward David and Alex and then toward Pahl. The slaves were the property of the great Tsimshian chief. They were a gift. He, Kat, cared nothing for oil and blankets. He would accept nothing in return.

Kaigyet rose in the crowd, screaming that Kat had promised her the slaves would die. She extended a gaunt, pointing arm toward Alex and shrilled that he was full of evil spirits, that he would bring misfortune to his new owner. She barked a syllable at Skyil, who sat huddled behind her. Reluctantly, the girl rose. Prompted by her mother, she accused Alex of seducing her, carrying her away. She was embarrassed, subdued to her mother's will. Her performance lacked conviction.

Pahl made a pleasant little speech, directing it to Kaigyet. David gathered that he was offering her the blankets and oil that Kat had refused. But she clung to her anger, throwing an arm in the air in a gesture of disgust, pushing her daughter ahead of her as she stomped off toward the beach.

Pahl caught Alex by the arm and shook his hand. Alex responded with glazed detachment. Pahl turned to David.

"God damn. You belong to me. I make you free."
He tapped David on the shoulder and said some words
in Tsimshian, then he did the same for Alex.

"Thank you," David said. "My friend is not himself."

"I heard what he did to himself. God damn." Pahl
gave a shake of his head. "I make you free. Save your
lives. The people at Fort Simpson will be told of this?"

"They will be told," David said.

"I trade with Hudson's Bay people at Fort Simpson.
Mahkook. Very much trade. Good friends."

Trade. Pahl wanted the Hudson's Bay people to
think well of him. To have saved the lives of whites
would be good for business.

"I go up the rivers. Into the mountains. Trade with
mountain people for furs. Trade with Chilkats for blankets. Take 'em to Hudson's Bay people at Fort
Simpson."

"Sure," David said. "Get rich."

They laughed. David clapped Pahl on the shoulder.
Pahl seemed to expect it and to be pleased. I wish we
could be friends, David thought. I'm the husband of
your sister and the father of the heir you're counting on
to preserve the honor of your lineage. It would be good
if we could be friends.

"You can be sure the Hudson's Bay people will hear
that you saved our lives," he said.

He wanted to say more. He wanted to say don't be a
damn fool. Don't let the white man destroy you. He
won't do it so much deliberately and viciously as he
will blindly, just by being there. He'll provide the
means and then he'll say you destroyed yourself.

Darkness had come early. The sky was almost black.

Off to the west, a flash of lightning split it. Thunder rumbled angrily.

Chapter 21

People filed to the beach to get into canoes or they walked along the shore toward the village. There would be another ceremony at the potlatch house. It was whispered that Pahl would present Kat with a copper. The feasting and singing would go on for most of the night.

David walked to the beach with Alex and Necoon. Alex walked with a spraddle-legged, side-to-side motion. He was silent, unresponsive. There was no telling if he grasped what had happened or if he even knew where he was. Physically, however, he was less drained of strength than David would have expected.

The largest canoe was ready to shove off. Kat, Pahl and Skow were in it, they were waiting for Tsil-tsil. She came down the bank, passed close to David, and spoke without looking at him.

"Follow me. Walk with me."

She made her excuses to Kat and her brother and climbed back up the bank, followed by the Tsimshian slave woman. At the top of the bank she waited to watch the canoe shove off. Big waves were breaking on the beach, but the crew managed the craft skillfully and it was quickly away from shore. As David started up the bank, Necoon caught his arm.

"Ah, Necoon, I'm a free man. You have no more duty to guard me."

"Yes." He was confused, embarrassed. He gave a little shake of his head. "Yes. It is hard to believe." He went back to the small canoe.

Tsil-tsil had transferred the baby to the back of the woman who was with her. She began to walk along the path to the village. The wind was sharp. There were drops of rain in it.

"You mustn't touch me," she said as David fell in beside her. The slave woman with the baby walked a few feet behind them.

"Does she speak English?" he asked Tsil-tsil.

"Not more than a word or two."

"How did you find us?"

"For a long time it was not clear what had happened to you. Some of the Nisquallies who were with you said you had been taken by Haidas. Some said you had been killed. The people at Fort Nisqually said they would try to find out. After a long time, the *Beaver* came, the Hudson's Bay boat. The captain had talked to some Kwakiutls who spoke of Haida warriors going north with white slaves. He promised he would send word to your government at Oregon City.

"Nothing happened. No one did anything. I kept asking God what to do. The next time the *Beaver* came, it was going north. God told me to go with it. I knew where that gold was hidden in the bedroom wall. I took some of it. I gave it to the Hudson's Bay people for my passage.

"I questioned the Kwakiutls who had seen you, but I learned no more. They didn't know if the Haidas were from these islands or from far to the north. I learned nothing. Then we got to Fort Simpson and I knew I had been there before. I could understand the language of the people there, and I knew I was a Tsimshian. I had grown up near the fort. I had gone to school. The teacher was Mrs. Wing. She was still there, and I went to see her. She saw my small hand and remembered me. She took me to my brother. He had thought I was dead, but he knew me because of my hand. He was very happy. It was time for the oolaken to come, and he gave a great potlatch. Right in the middle of it my baby came.''

''Our baby, Tsil-tsil. I must look at him, hold him.''

''Not now!'' she said urgently. ''And you must not call me by that name. . . . David, the baby is barely two months old and already he is rich. He will become a great chief, as great as his uncle—''

A gust of wind stole her words. People passed on the path, heads down against the wind. Now and then they stopped to watch canoes that had got into trouble by clinging too close to shore and were in danger of being grounded by big rolling waves. Men leaped out of them, pointed them against the waves, guided them toward deeper water.

''The Haidas came to the Nass for the oolaken,'' Tsil-tsil said. ''The chiefs came to Pahl to buy the right to fish. I asked them about white slaves. I learned nothing. Then I sent slaves to ask Haida slaves if there were whites among them. I learned that you were at this village, that you belonged to Kat.''

''Did you tell the Hudson's Bay people that?''

''No. They would talk to Pahl about it. He doesn't know that the father of his nephew is a white man.''

''That would make him angry?''

She sighed as if unsure of the answer. ''When I found my people, many memories came back. I was happy. I said that God had brought me home. The people made up songs and stories. I said that my husband had been killed in a slave raid. Among my people, to be taken as a slave is the same as being killed. Such a person is considered dead."

"What about Kat? Did you really mean to marry him?"

"He was friendly with Pahl and stayed at our house. I was friendly to him because I wanted him to speak of his white slaves. He spoke of you only in anger."

They were almost to the village. They slowed their steps a bit.

"I didn't know what to do," she said. "Then Pahl came to me and said he wanted me to marry Kat. It would be a good thing for us, he said. Kat would soon be chief of his village. Our family would be more powerful than ever. We would come here for the wedding, he said. It seemed to me that God had spoken. It was a way to get here. I wanted to see Kat's slaves, to be sure they were you and Alex. I thought I would ask Kat to free you in honor of our wedding. Instead, he almost killed you. It was a good thing you spoke quickly. Pahl saved you. I didn't count on his being so eager to save you. You can go to the mainland with him when he returns. The *Beaver* must be due at Fort Simpson soon. It will take you south."

David came to a stop. "Now, just hold your horses. You're not planning to go ahead with this wedding?"

"I agreed. Pahl gave his word."

"Tsil-tsil, I'm your husband. This is my son."

"Yes, you told me how it is among white people. It's not the same with my people. A woman does what will be good for her family. And a son is not so important to a man as a nephew."

He turned to the slave who was carrying the baby. He motioned for her to turn around. The child was asleep on his cradleboard. David touched his face, and he opened curious dark eyes.

"You will cause talk!" Tsil-tsil said nervously.

"What's his name?"

"I call him Watserh. It means sea otter puppy."

"You're not going to marry Kat—that's nonsense. We'll leave tonight. You and I and Watserh."

"David, I am the sister of a chief, the mother of a chief. It is not as it was."

"Do you have people you can trust? Friends? Slaves?"

"There is no one who would help me run away."

"Then leave it to me. Go to the potlatch house now. When you see me at the back of the crowd, make some excuse and leave. Bring Watserh with you."

"David, I care nothing for Kat. But I won't run from Pahl. I won't leave my people. God has led me to my people."

"And to me, your husband. To be married is a holy thing. We were married in God's house."

"I don't know," she said.

"Go and wait."

They walked on into the village street and she turned toward the potlatch house, followed by the slave woman. He stood at the edge of the bank, watching canoes land. He saw Necoon and Kwung leading Alex up the bank, and he went to meet them.

"I'll take care of him now," David said. "Your duties are finished."

Necoon wrinkled his forehead. "It is a wonderful thing."

David led Alex to Skow's house and took him inside. It was empty except for two slaves asleep on the upper level and an old woman huddled near the fire. Alex moved to the same place near the door that had been his in Kat's house. He didn't seem to know where he was. David left him there and went to the potlatch house, waiting outside, scanning faces in the rainy darkness. Kat came up from the beach. He was followed by other chiefs, Pahl and Skow among them. David waited until Kat had gone into the house; then he called softly to Skow.

"I must speak to you," he said. He backed away from the door and Skow joined him. Skow grinned happily.

"Ho! The Tsimshian set you free. I will come to your country in the south one of these days. I'll make a slave of you all over again!"

"I ask you to come to your house. I have something serious to say."

Kwawlang was among the chiefs about to go into the potlatch house. David motioned to him, and the three of them walked in silence to Skow's house. Alex was stretched out asleep where David had left him. Skow led the way to the center of the house and sat down by the fire. The old woman huddled there got up and faded into the shadows.

"I must go to the mainland tonight," David said. "I ask for a canoe and a crew."

"Pah! Your freedom has been too much for you. It's made you stupid."

"It's a thing that must be done. I will pay a great price."

Skow got to his feet. "Perhaps in good weather I

would do you this favor. But it will be a bad night. I would lose a canoe. You're talking foolishness."

"Let me tell you the price. I will take Kat's bride with me. There will be no marriage tomorrow."

"You're making a joke?"

"I tell you she will go with me. She has agreed."

Skow turned to Kwawlang. They exchanged looks of bewilderment.

"He spoke with Kweenu in a strange tongue," Kwawlang said. "I heard them. And he walked along the shore with her."

Skow sat down again, frowning into the fire. "Pah! Even if he speaks the truth, the plan is foolishness. If he takes her to the mainland, Pahl will go after her. The marriage will still take place."

"No," David said. "She will go to the south with me."

"How can this be? It doesn't seem reasonable."

"She is my wife. That baby is my son. She came here to free me."

There was a silence. Then he found himself talking rapidly, explaining, answering questions. When Skow had got it all straight, he threw back his head and laughed.

"She came here to free you! Ho, what a fool Kat is!"

"Unless I take her away tonight, there will be a marriage."

Skow considered this, then chuckled. "I'll tell the people the truth. Kat will be humiliated. There will be no marriage."

"No," David said. "You must keep our secret. If you tell it, Pahl will also be humiliated. He will turn against me. He will have me killed, I think. Then the marriage will take place.''

Skow considered this possibility. He turned to Kwawlang.

''It seems reasonable,'' Kwawlang said.

''This is a night of angry water spirits,'' Skow said. ''It will be worse outside the inlet.''

''Give me a good canoe, a good crew.''

''I don't know,'' Skow said. ''I have four strong slaves who will keep their mouths shut. Four. That means a small canoe.''

''Give it to me.''

''The slaves might be missed,'' Kwawlang said. ''It will be said Skow had a hand in this.''

''No.'' David said. ''When it's discovered Kweenu is gone, there'll be much confusion. Many will join in a search. Surely four slaves won't be missed.''

Skow laughed again, slapping Kwawlang on the arm. ''Ho, I'll do it! I'll put Kat in his place. I'll be the next chief.''

''Put a mast and a sail in the canoe.''

''A sail? That will be useless in this weather.''

''Your crew must take us far to the south. We'll be traveling for many days. A sail will come in handy.''

Skow called a slave down out of the shadows of the house and sent him and Kwawlang off to get the crew together. David and Skow lingered by the fire, discussing details. They walked together to the potlatch house. Skow went inside. David waited a moment before he followed.

Inside the big, crowded house, he stood by the door, trying to pick out Tsil-tsil. Singers were singing. Masked dancers danced in firelight at the center of the crowd. The air was hot, smoky. Faces near the fire glistened with sweat.

He saw her near the fire. He worked his way around the crowd toward her. She was staring thoughtfully into the fire and didn't see him. He moved closer, picking his way among sitting humanity. Everyone seemed entranced, part of a fantasy of heat and song and swaying shadows. Tsil-tsil seemed a part of it, too, a vision that seeped through some crack in his mind from a reality that was not his.

He edged close to her and touched her and she was startled. Kat, a few feet to her right, was glaring at them. No one else paid any attention to them.

"Wait till I've left," David whispered. "Then follow. Bring Watserh."

Her nod was barely perceptible. Her eyes were frightened. He made his way back and was glad to be through the door and into the slashing rain. She came out promptly, the baby on her back. He took her hand and led her away from the house, angling upshore toward the sweat huts. She suddenly hung back.

"Where are you taking me, David?"

"Everything should be ready," he muttered. He clung to her wrist and kept moving.

"Wait. I want to talk."

"There'll be plenty of time for that."

They passed the sweat huts and went down to the beach. The canoe was there. Alex was already in it, sitting at its center with a blanket over his shoulders. The crew stood beside the craft, holding it straight in the lashing surf.

"David, I'm not going with you."

He looked into the canoe and saw that a mast and rolled mat sail lay in its bottom. There were rolled mats and a number of boxes stowed between the thwarts. Tsil-tsil turned her back and started toward the bank, but Kwawlang came out of the darkness to face her. She whirled on David.

"It would be dangerous to travel tonight."

"You'd stay and marry Kat?"

"If we go, we'll be drowned."

"We'll be all right. If the storm gets worse, we'll go no farther than the sandspit tonight. We won't try to cross the strait until morning."

Kwawlang handed David a charm, a flat disk of dark stone with an eye carved on it. It was threaded with a thong and David was to wear it around his neck. It would frighten away the water spirits that hid in waves. There were also eyes painted on either side of the canoe at the bow, Kwawlang pointed out, and they would serve the same purpose.

Tsil-tsil backed away and refused to get into the canoe. "God tells me not to go!" she said.

He caught her by the arm. "Get in. There's no time to argue."

"You are not God!"

Before she realized what he was doing, he seized the strap fastened to the cradleboard and pulled it over her head. With the baby in his arms, he got into the canoe. She reached for the baby and he pulled her in. He pushed her down, put the cradleboard into her arms, and motioned to the crew to shove off. They were agilely aboard, paddling skillfully, maneuvering into the waves. He waved to Kwawlang, touching the charm around his neck. Then he seized a paddle and went to work.

Keeping the craft under control took all their concentration. The world shrank to a little area of dark, churning water. The crew wasted no breath on songs; they grunted to mark the stroke, and that was all. At times the rhythm was broken by the helmsman, who barked urgent orders to pull hard to left or right.

Beatings and meager food had left David weaker than he realized, and he was quickly tired. Worse, he had eaten too much today too quickly, and his stomach was churning. Tsil-tsil climbed up beside him. She had the cradleboard on her back again. She kept glancing at David as if puzzled about him.

There was the illusion that they were going nowhere in the darkness, but the wind was with them, and they were actually moving very fast. The island that split the inlet loomed up suddenly, and David was amazed that they had reached it so soon. They were near the mouth of the inlet now. Waves were much bigger. Twice, the canoe was spun broadside to the waves and shipped water. Alex, who had been sitting crouched and motionless, came to life. He found a bailing scoop and went to work.

They were suddenly crossing the bar off the sandspit, and great curling waves threatened to swamp them. The crew seemed as surprised as David. The helmsman called frantic instructions that were unintelligible in the roaring anger of wind and water. David yelled to make for the sandspit, but even as the words came out he knew it would be madness to try to turn. The wind was behind them; their only chance was to go with it.

They were tossed, whipped, jolted. They shipped water a dozen times; it was ankle deep in the canoe. But by some miracle of skill and intuition, they rode the waves one by one, catching each at the precise angle that kept them afloat. Alex was on his knees, bailing unhurriedly, steadily. David caught a glimpse of his face and saw lips drawn back and teeth exposed in a grin of pain. Tsil-tsil sat gripping the thwart to balance herself. Her expression of stoic acceptance was an accusation more scalding than anger.

Somehow they avoided bottoming, and at last they were over the bar. But there was no moment of rest, no time even to sigh and miss a stroke, no breath to make a joke or call out a word of encouragement. They were in a dizzying sea of massive heights and sucking troughs. It took more strength than ever to manage the canoe.

The thought of trying to make the mainland was madness now. They could perhaps ride the next soaring surge successfully. The next and the next. But long before the night was out, exhaustion would betray them. Skill would fail just once, and it would be all over.

Nausea swept through him. He was dizzy and almost lost his paddle. Tsil-tsil saw and took it from him. He grasped the gunwale and vomited, sinking to the bottom of the canoe. With great effort he pulled himself back on the thwart. He was dizzy again and bent double. He felt Tsil-tsil's arm across his back, steadying him. When he straightened, he saw that Alex had taken the paddle. He was putting his back into the work. Some trick of vision made him seem huge and shining white.

David closed his eyes. He forced himself to breathe deeply and slowly. He let Alex work for perhaps ten minutes; then he called out and reached for the paddle. Alex handed it to him with a grin and collapsed into the bilge.

All sense of direction was gone. In the violence of swirling gusts and lashing rain, it was hard even to tell the direction of the wind. It seemed that they had turned and were quartering into it. They must be heading west, David thought, trying for the east coast of the great sandspit. But that made no sense; there was a chain of shallow bars there. At last he realized that the crew was merely trying to hold its own against the wind, trying to stay near the archipelago rather than commit itself to the sixty-mile strait and certain death.

The crew, he thought. They were the one small hope. They were Haidas. The best sailors among native Americans, surely. Probably the best canoeists on earth. They were Haidas, so there was hope.

He tried to think of himself as a machine, reaching with the paddle, digging with it. Keep the rhythm. Ignore fire spreading from shoulders into chest and bowels. Press eyes to slits, keeping only enough vision to do you work; open them wider and you'll be dizzy.

After a while he fell into a kind of trance of which the rhythmic motion of his body was a condition, the kind of detachment that dancers find when they dance beyond exhaustion. Thought stopped, only will remained, and numbness replaced pain.

Shouts brought him out of it, shouts that he resented at first. Then he saw shoreline to port and less than a hundred yards away. They quartered and rode breakers to a steep and dangerous beach. With Alex still in the canoe, they dragged it across a slippery accumulation of kelp and driftwood and into grass and brush.

Chapter 22

They were on a small island. The crew had known it was here. They had used the wind to take them to it. Even so, it was very small, and hitting it in the black, thrashing turbulence seemed a miracle.

Its surface was covered with grass, brush, rock, and a few small trees. The crew cut boughs and used them in combination with mats to build a shelter. Alex climbed out of the canoe and tried to help, but he fell against the shelter and collapsed a corner of it. After that, he crawled under it and was quiet.

They slept until daylight and found the storm still raging. There was tinder and a fire bow among their supplies, and they got a slow, smoky fire going. They made a cold meal of food from their supply boxes and washed it down with water from seal bladders. Alex ate stolidly and went back to sleep.

The rain stopped around noon, but the wind did not let up and the sky remained overcast. The slaves busied themselves improving the shelter. The suggestion that they were going to be here for some time annoyed David. He spent most of the afternoon near the beach, watching sea and sky. Late in the day Tsil-tsil joined him. They sat on a rock just out of reach of breaking waves and looked out across the boiling seascape.

"It will get worse before it gets better," he said emptily.

"We've lucky to be alive."

He searched her face for hint of reprimand. She stared with stoic fascination into the storm and didn't meet his eyes.

"We must leave as soon as the wind goes down," he said, "whether it's day or night. Kat will be after us."

"Pahl, too."

"We'll go home to the mission."

"David—"

"When we get there, you can decide. If you want to go to your people, I'll put you aboard the *Beaver* the first time she goes north."

"I will go to my people."

"Don't decide now."

"I have love for you in my heart. But the way of my people is very strong."

"We'll go to the chapel. Where God spoke to you. He will speak again."

"He has spoken," she said slowly. "I will go to my people."

"Did he tell you to leave me and take my son away from me? Look me in the eye and tell me God told you that."

"Among my people an uncle is more important than a father."

"Answer me. Did God tell you to take Watserh from me?"

"Yes, he tells me to do this."

"Damn it, this is claptrap about God speaking to you. You decide what you want to do, then you say God told you to do it. Before I ever made love to you, I gave you a chance to go to your people. You chose to stay with me. If that was what God wanted then, why has he changed his mind?"

"I didn't remember who my people were."

"Exactly. Now you've found they're rich. You're a princess. Watserh is the heir of a big chief. So God changed his mind."

She bowed her head, raising her dwarfed hand and studying its palm. She stroked it gently with the fingertips of her right hand. She seemed completely absorbed in this. He was exasperated.

"At least admit it. God changed his mind."

"I came after you. I set you free."

"Why?"

"I have love for you in my heart." She continued to stare at her hand. "But I will go to my people."

He got to his feet. Alex came toward them, calling, walking in a ridiculous waddle with his legs wide apart.

"David, where are we?"

"Some damned island."

"Why wasn't I consulted?"

"Consulted? Alex, we're free. We're on our way home."

"Home? Yes, I suppose so. Where's Kwawlang?"

"I see. Forgive me. I've been a bit hazy."

"You slept most of the day."

"Yes. I feel much better for it." Alex studied Tsiltsil as if recognizing her for the first time. "We're on our way home to the mission?"

"Yes, Alex."

"Ah, David, I shall not be going back there with you. The mission is a failure, you know. The people gamble after services. It's my fault. I didn't make them understand. How could I? The blind leading the blind—"

He waddled a few steps toward the sea, stopping when spray from a crashing wave hit him. Off in the distant unity of sea and sky, lightning flashed. Tsil-tsil touched David's arm and smiled shyly. They walked back to the shelter.

She seemed untroubled by the angry things he had said. She took the baby out of his cradleboard and laid him on a blanket. They played with him and she fed him. When he got sleepy, they put him back into his cradleboard and laid it in a place scooped out of the sandy earth. They ate some smoked salmon and some root cakes and drank water from a seal-bladder container. Darkness came and the rain started again. The crew stretched out and went to sleep.

Alex was restless, stalking aimlessly in the rain, coming into the shelter for a few minutes, going out again.

"You ought to be quiet," David told him when he had crawled in to sit beside them for the dozenth time. "You'll make the soreness worse by moving around so much."

"I shall live. David, I must get back."

"As soon as the weather—"

"Back to the inlet—the village. Now don't give me that patronizing look of the sane for the mad. I will just seem madder if I tell you I was never more sane."

"Get some rest." David said.

"Dorothy believed I was mad. I was—I surely was."

He got up and went into the rain again. Tsil-tsil spread two blankets and crawled between them. She touched David's hand and he crawled in with her. She snuggled into his arms with her head against his chest.

He held her like that for a time, grateful that they were alive, making himself forget everything else. She raised her lips and they kissed in the way he had taught her. They loved in warm eagerness and fell asleep.

At daylight the storm seemed to be wearing itself out. The rain had stopped and the wind slackened, although the sea still churned. David thought that it might be safe to shove off in a few hours, but the crew shook their heads. The wind had shifted to the southwest, they pointed out. When this happened after a heavy blow, it was a bad sign. It meant that the storm had bumped into the mountains on the mainland and hadn't got across. It had backed off to the south for another try.

David had his doubts about this forecast, but he put up no argument. They had not right to expect to win another gamble with the weather.

They were safe for the time being, he assured himself. No fishermen would be out in this weather. Pursuers would probably venture from the village this morning, but it seemed unlikely that they would find their way to this small island for a while.

By afternoon, however, he was uneasy. The strait had settled down to whitecapped choppiness. It was not exactly inviting, but it seemed to him to be navigable. Still the crew would not budge. They pointed to a dark line in the sky to the southwest, assuring him that it was the storm coming back. He had little choice except to trust them.

For a time, the weather continued to improve. The dark streak in the distance widened a bit but approached slowly. Overhead, clouds broke now and then and spots of blue appeared. Land was visible to the west now, a green shore not more than five or six miles away. It was the east shore of the large island that terminated in the sandspit. He kept a worrried watch in that direction. Still, when the big canoe arrived, it caught them all by surprise.

It was late in the day. They were around the fire, baking clams the slaves had managed to dig at low tide in spite of steep beach and rolling waves. The canoe came from the west, hugging the island shore. No one saw it until just before it beached.

Kat leaped out of the bow. he had twenty men with him, slaves and relatives. All were well armed. He waited till the rest had disembarked, shouting at them to hurry, scanning the sea as if someone were behind them. Then, with the others at his back, he strode into camp swinging a war club around his head. Necoon was immediately behind him. Among the others, David picked out Kat's brother and Kaigyet.

David sensed that the slightest indication of either rage or flight might bring a murderous attack. So did the slaves. They all simply sat and waited. Kat hesitated. Then he saw Alex and headed for him, threatening with the war club. Tsil-tsil rose and stepped between them.

She spoke in Tsimshian, pointing to herself, throwing back her head defiantly. She seemed to be saying that she had come willingly, that the others could not be blamed. Kat was momentarily nonplused. Again, he turned to scan the sea as if expecting pursuit. He studied the Indians seated near the fire, and he let out a roar. He pointed to the canoe lying in the grass above the beach.

"You are Skow's slaves! That's his canoe!"

He singled out one of them and ordered him to stand. The man obeyed, giving a little shrug, speaking mildly. "As you say, we are slaves. We do as we are told."

"Told by Skow? Answer me!"

"Certainly."

"He told you take take these three away from the village?"

"Certainly."

"To the mainland?"

"Yes, to the mainland and then to the south."

Kaigyet came forward. She had her *clechadarran* in her hand. She shook it at Alex, David, and then at Tsil-tsil.

"*Tiuh!*" she demanded. "Kill them. Kill the white bellies. Kill the Tsimshian slut who plotted with them. *Tiuh! Tiuh!*"

She began to dance, chanting, shaking the circle of puffin beaks. Tsil-tsil faced Kat and spoke in a controlled voice. Her quiet dignity made him angrier than ever. He seized her, raising the club. She spat words into his face, something about Pahl. He tripped her, threw her to the ground, spat on her.

"You have betrayed me," he ranted. "Pahl has betrayed me. Did you plan this from the beginning? To shame me by running away from the wedding?"

"*Tiuh!*" Kaigyet chanted. "*Tiuh! Tiuh!*"

"She planned nothing," David said. "Pahl has set me free. I wish to take her back to the south."

"I will crush your head, *huldinga*," Kat roared. "If Pahl hadn't interfered, I'd have crushed it yesterday. He was friendly with Skow. Together, they planned this."

"That's not true," David said. "If you will listen,

263

you will hear the truth."

"Pah! You're a liar. You're all liars. Who is to find truth among such liars?"

Tsil-tsil got to her feet and began to speak again. Kat interrupted her with a roar and again shook his club at her. It seemed as if he must surely stop threatening with the club and strike out with it, but his brother stepped up and said this was a matter that perhaps should be taken up directly with Pahl. Then they would get the truth.

"Pahl is against us!" Kat shouted. "Can't you see that? Last night he was to give me a copper. The white *huldinga* came to the potlatch house. He whispered to Kweenu. She followed him. Pahl made no objection. He said he would give the copper when she returned. Pah! They had it all planned."

"*Tiuh!*" Kaigyet chanted. "*Tiuh! Tiuh!*"

One of Skow's slaves leaped to his feet, pointing seaward.

"*Kloo!*"

A canoe. It was coming straight toward the island from the north, a bobbing ornament on the water. It was less than half a mile away. David saw that Skow's slaves had piled wet branches on the fire to make it smoke. The occupants of the canoe had seen the smoke and were coming straight for it.

Tsil-tsil sighed mightily. "Pahl."

"Skow will be with him," Kat snorted. "They come to protect you from my anger. Ho, they will be too late!"

"It's a big canoe," his brother said nervously. "Don't give Skow a reason to attack us."

"We will see," Kat said. "We will learn the truth now."

264

He motioned to his people, hissed orders. They formed a line perpendicular to the beach.

The canoe was one of Skow's largest. He and Pahl stood in the bow, leaping out on either side as the craft grounded. They waited until the canoe was hauled up beyond reach of the waves. Together, they walked into the camp. Their men followed in a file that halted fifty feet away from Kat's men. The new group outnumbered Kat's, but it was not nearly so well armed. Most of the men had no weapons at all except their paddles.

Pahl came forward to speak softly and briefly with Tsil-tsil. He stepped back to stand beside Skow, and the pair of them confronted Kat.

"What's this foolishness of a war line?" Skow said. "We didn't come to fight."

"You've joined together against me," Kat said. "You will make amends or we'll fight."

Kaigyet had fallen silent and backed off. Now she began to dance and shake her *clechadarran* again. Pahl spoke in Tsimshian. Kat scoffed and spat on the ground. Tsil-tsil stepped up and began to speak, more to Pahl than to Kat.

She pointed to David, to the baby who lay in his sleeping place, snug in his cradleboard. She was telling the whole truth. David was her husband, Watserh their son. Pahl listened sternly, eyes narrowed. When she had finished, they were all staring at David. Skow gave a little shrug and walked over to stand beside him. He moved almost jauntily.

There was a long discussion among the chiefs and Tsil-tsil then. Kat seemed beyond words and did much helpless gesturing. His brother stood with fists pressed against his temples and rocked from side to side.

Kaigyet stole close to listen. Warriors in the two opposing lines sat down in their places. The wind picked up. Drops of rain fell. The chiefs and Tsil-tsil moved closer to the fire. Alex waddled off toward the beach and sat on a rock to stare at the sea.

Finally, Kat spouted a few angry syllables and turned away. He motioned to his men to follow, and they moved off to set up a camp of their own. Kaigyet walked beside him. Necoon trudged behind them, carrying a war club in each hand, his own weapon and Kat's.

David crawled into the shelter and lay down beside Watserh, trying to think. After a while he got up and joined Pahl and Skow and Tsil-tsil. A new, square shelter had been built of poles and mats from Skow's canoe, and they sat around a fire in the center of it. David sat down facing Tsil-tsil over the fire. After a brief silence, Pahl spoke.

"God damn. You married my sister."

David nodded slowly and gravely.

"You didn't say nothing."

"I was a slave."

"I set you free."

"Slaves get used to keeping their mouths shut."

Pahl thought that over. "God damn. You should have said something."

Skow's slaves were putting the finishing touches on the shelter. There was an interruption while one of them moved into the circle to adjust the mats around the smoke hole in the roof. The mats were tied to a framework of poles. Some of them were flopping in the wind and needed tightening.

Tsil-tsil spoke in Tsimshian to the slave. When he

266

had finished his work, he went out and came back with Watserh in his cradleboard. Tsil-tsil reached for the baby, but Pahl took him and beamed on him proudly.

"My sister talks good about you," Pahl said to David. "You good man. You make me this little one, huh? He will be a great chief."

"He is my son."

"Trade with mountain Indians belong me. My property. Trade with Chilkats belong me. He will be rich, give many potlatches."

"I want him and his mother with me."

Pahl smiled, not understanding or not wanting to. "Oolaken belong me. My property. Haidas come, pay to fish."

"I will take him and his mother to my people." David said.

Pahl regarded him across the fire. He passed the baby to Tsil-tsil and stared thoughtfully into the fire. After a time he raised his eyes.

"You come live at Fort Simpson. Lots of whites there."

David shook his head slowly and emphatically. "No."

"You rich?"

"I own land," David said.

Pahl nodded, looking disappointed.

"There is money to be made cutting trees. I'll take good care of my wife and my son."

"Trees?" Pahl said. "Yes, I have heard that they can be sold to ships. God damn."

"They take the lumber to the south where there are many people who need houses."

"Hudson's Bay buy furs from me. Buy Chilkat

blankets. Anybody else sells blankets, he pays tax. To me.''

You have been touched by the first pale tentacle, David thought. You have been touched and you are lost.

''You saved my life,'' he said. ''You set me free. I'll write a letter to the Hudson's Bay people at Fort Simpson and tell them these things.''

Kat's brother crawled into the shelter, followed by another man from Kat's party. They took places at the fire. Faintly, David could hear chanting. It was coming from Kat's camp. The rhythm was that of Kaigyet's chant. *Tiuh! Tiuh!* . . .

Alex crawled in to join them, moving very slowly, breathing heavily. He took a place at the fire beside David.

Pahl rose, folded his arms, and began a long speech in Tsimshian. It was addressed to the whole gathering as if this were a council matter, a matter to be decided by all those present. His tone was sometimes plaintive, sometimes angry. Now and then he seemed to remember that David couldn't understand and he threw in a terse English translation. He spoke in great detail about his ancestors, naming them, their accomplishments, their possessions. He told the story of Tsil-tsil's return, as if from the dead, and of the birth of Watserh, heir to the ancient lineage. His tone made it sound mystical and mythical, a thing ordained by forces beyond the tampering touch of men.

When at last he finished, Kat's brother rose and spoke demandingly in Haida. Pahl had made a promise to Kat. If it was to be broken, there must be compensation. Kat was entitled to at least two coppers.

Pahl replied testily. He seemed to feel that Kat's brother was confusing the issue with irrelevancies. He turned to David, indicating that he should speak now.

David didn't bother to get to his feet. "I'll take my wife and my son with me. There is no more to be said."

"Speak in Haida!" Kat's brother demanded.

"Pahl understands," David said.

Pahl confirmed that he did indeed know the language of the white people. He was deeply hurt, but it was toward Kat's brother that he showed his temper. To David he was patient.

"God damn. We make a deal. *Mahkook*. You take my sister. I take the baby. I give you a little gold to boot."

"Are you a Christian?"

"Sure." Pahl spoke with eager pride. Then his face fell. "God damn."

"Then you must know that I will have my wife and son. There's no other way."

Kat's brother started to speak again, but Pahl silenced him with a monosyllable. Pahl stared into the fire, rocking slightly from side to side. Kat's brother crawled out of the hut, followed by the other man from Kat's group.

Skow, who had said nothing at all, was staring at David with a hint of sly amusement in his face. I've won, David thought, and he knows it. It's not a council matter now; it's between Pahl and me, and I've won. The only thing Pahl can do is kill me. And Pahl won't do it. He'd be afraid that word would get to Fort Simpson, for one thing. It probably would, too. Skow would see to it.

"I will do this," David said to Pahl. "I'll raise the

269

boy in the way of the white man. I'll send him to school. Sometimes in the summers I'll bring him to your village to live a month or so with you. You can teach him your ways, too."

Pahl spread his hands helplessly. "He grows up with you, he'll be white."

"He will also be with his mother."

"Yes," Pahl said. "God damn."

"When he's a man, he can do as he chooses."

"Yes." Pahl blew into the fire, causing a little explosion of sparks and ashes. "We talk some more in the morning."

"No. It's finished."

David reached out for Watserh, and Tsil-tsil passed him over. David crawled out of the shelter, taking the baby, and she followed. When they reached their sleeping place, she took Watserh out of his cradleboard and took him to bed with her, spreading her blankets a little way from David.

Alex came in and eased himself down on a blanket.

"I won," David said. "I sat there and said no to everything and I won."

"Yes," Alex said. "You won over a mainland Indian. You wouldn't have beaten a Haida. Not yet. Ten years from now perhaps, but not yet."

"Skow was with me," David said.

"For purely political reasons."

"It doesn't matter. I won."

"A great tragedy."

"I'm alive. I'm free. I have my wife and son. What's tragic about that?"

"The Hudson's Bay Company won," Alex said.

Wind bit at the shelter, hissing, flapping mats. David

tucked his blankets around him. He wished that Tsil-tsil would move closer to him. He thought about going to her and knew it was best not to, not tonight.

"The Hudson's Bay Company and the Christian missionaries," he said.

"Yes," Alex said.

Chapter 23

Morning was dark and threatening. Skow's men traipsed to the beach to relieve themselves and crawled back into shelters. Slaves gathered firewood. Others nibbled at scanty food supplies, wrapped themselves in blankets, and dozed. Tsil-tsil stayed in her sleeping place, silent and withdrawn. David brought her a bowl of pasty soup made of smoked fish and water. She ate only a few mouthfuls. She took Watserh out of his cradleboard and was nursing him when, with no warning at all, Kat's men fell upon them.

David was seized by the heels and dragged out of the shelter. He was pulled to his feet and held between two men, each pinning an arm. One of the men was Kwung. He grinned at David. His grip was like iron.

Tsil-tsil was also held by two of Kat's men. Watserh had been taken from her by Necoon, and she was kicking and screaming. Necoon carried the baby toward a line of men who stood near Kat's camp.

They were armed, ready for a fight. They stood in a half circle around a sandy mound near the shore. Kat stood in front of them, war club in his hand. Necoon carried Watserh past him and through the line of warriors to the top of the mound.

Skow had come out of his shelter. He stood with hands on hips and shouted at Kat. "What's this foolishness? You want to fight? We'll pound you into the ground!"

Pahl moved up beside him. Others gathered behind them. A few had weapons. Others snatched up firewood, stones, whatever was handy. Someone handed Pahl a halibut club, a short, heavy shaft designed for killing big fish. He strode a few paces forward.

"Stay where you are!" Kat screamed. Pahl halted. Kat pointed at him accusingly. "You've shamed me. Now you'll pay for it. I have your precious nephew. The spirits are with me."

Pahl spoke in Tsimshian, expressing bewilderment. Kat shouted him down.

"You've lied enough! Now you'll listen. I have your heir. He'll be taken to my house. His mother will be taken, too, to nurse him. When you have paid me two coppers, they'll be released.

Pahl gestured helplessly. Before he could find words, Skow shouted a challenge.

"You'll return the baby at once or we'll butcher you like seals!"

"Wait," Pahl said. He started to speak, but again Kat outshouted him.

"Two coppers. That's the price for your heir."

"Step up and fight me." Skow demanded. Someone had handed him a war club. "Just the two of us. Ho, you won't do it! You'd rather steal babies."

"I'm not so foolish as that," Kat said. "I have the baby. Why should I fight? I speak to Pahl for the last time. Agree to two coppers or I'll have your heir killed before your eyes."

"No!" Tsil-tsil screamed. "He will pay!"

Pahl was furious. He shook the halibut club. He

asked an angry question in Tsimshian.

Kat turned toward the mound where Necoon stood with the baby in his arms. Necoon was smiling down at the baby, purring to him. Kat called his name and he looked up with his wrinkled, puzzled-puppy expression.

"Raise your club," Kat commanded. "Bash the baby's head in when I give the word."

"Wait," Pahl said.

"Agree! Agree at once or you'll have no heir."

"A copper," Pahl said. "One."

Necoon hadn't obeyed the command to raise his club. He still cuddled the baby. Kat gestured to his brother, who walked quickly to Necoon's side and snatched the baby from him. He held it by the heels in one hand and raised a war club in the other.

"Wait," Pahl said. "I wish to speak to my sister."

The baby was writhing strangely. His mouth was open but he made no sound. Tsil-tsil screamed Tsimshian words, struggling with the men who held her.

"No," Kat said. "I'll give you no chance for more tricks."

Necoon reached for the child but Kat's brother elbowed him off. "He can't get his breath," Necoon said. "He's strangling."

"I'm guilty of no tricks," Pahl was saying. He was groping for words, speaking in a mixture of Haida and Tsimshian. "Strange things have happened that I don't understand. But I'll pay the coppers. Free the baby and his mother. Now. I will pay. You have my word."

"Don't speak to me of your word!" Kat said. "You will bring two coppers to my house. Then I'll free the baby and his mother."

Tsil-tsil was screaming hysterically. Pahl had not noticed that the baby was in trouble. He lunged angrily toward Kat, but Skow caught his arm. David called out desperately to Kat's brother to hold the child right side up. He responded by raising the baby above his head and waving him as if he were a hunting trophy. Necoon stepped close, protesting, reaching for the child. Kat's brother jabbed him in the ribs with his war club.

Necoon staggered backward. He got his balance and seized one of the baby's arms. For a moment it looked as if Watserh might be torn in two. Necoon chopped a swift, crushing blow at Kat's brother's head. It caught him solidly on the temple and dropped him in a lifeless heap.

Necoon clung to the baby, righted him, patted him on the back. Watserh gasped and began to breathe again, big-eyed, too frightened to cry at once.

Kat roared and raced toward Necoon. Necoon laid the baby on the ground and strode through the line of warriors to meet him. He moved woodenly, the faintest trace of a smile on his face. Kat swung his war club in a great looping blow. Necoon sidestepped, reaching out deftly to bring his weapon against Kat's arm. There was an audible snap. Kat's weapon went flying.

Necoon performed reflexively, a practiced warrior in his last battle. He swung backhanded, a flat blow that crashed the head of his club against Kat's kidneys. Kat grunted and fell on his face. Necoon put a foot on his master's back and knocked his head to pieces.

David found himself free. Tsil-tsil was running through the line of Kat's men. She reached the baby and picked him up. Necoon stood with his club ready, looking from one to another of the warriors. It seemed as if they must surge forward to beat him to a pulp, but astonishment and lack of a leader paralyzed them. Necoon put his back to them and walked toward Skow and Pahl. He tossed his bloody club at Skow's feet.

"I wanted only to save the baby. I've made you chief of the village in the bargain."

"You've done an unforgivable thing," Skow said. Necoon watched him pick up the club. "Certainly."

"The people will demand that you be killed."

"Certainly."

Skow handed the war club back to him. "Stay with my people. I'll take you back to the village. You'll be punished in front of all the people."

Pahl laid palms on Necoon's shoulders. He gave him a friendly little shake and spoke Tsimshian words. Skow spoke sadly to Pahl.

"As he said, he's made me chief, mother of the village. He saved your nephew. He saved you two coppers. But he has doomed himself."

Tsil-tsil came up to them, Watserh in her arms. She touched Necoon's arm, looked into his face, said nothing. He pointed to David.

"The white belly has given me strange thoughts. He says every man is as good as every other. Certainly that is foolishness, but I couldn't get it out of my head. There is pleasure in thinking it."

"Foolishness," Skow muttered. "Certainly."

"Who decides such things?" Necoon said whimsically. "Is there a spirit who decides what is right and what is wrong?"

Kaigyet came forward, her face ashen. She faced Skow and said, "There will be many stories told of what happened here, strange stories."

"Then you will make the truth known," Skow said. "You, Kaigyet. I will count on it."

She nodded and turned away, the passion gone from her. Her power had been all but snuffed out with Kat's life. Skow was unchallenged now, and she was afraid of him.

Necoon stared after her in wrinkled bewilderment. "I wanted only to save the baby," he muttered.

The bodies of Kat and his brother were wrapped in blankets and laid in his canoe. The wind was up again. It was clear that a new and violent thrust of the storm was on its way. The people of both camps improved their shelters. Kat's people chanted sadly as they worked. Sometimes Skow's people joined in.

Tsil-tsil and Pahl had a long talk in Skow's shelter. David joined Alex, who sat alone near the beach, watching the sweep of the storm in the early twilight.

"Necoon," Alex said. "Imagine."

"He went mad."

"Or sane."

"He tried to destroy everything he's lived by all his life. Thank God he did it, but that's madness."

"Sanity," Alex insisted.

Darkness thickened as a jet-black cloud mass slid in from the south-southwest. Great drops of rain slapped them. This lasted only a minute or so and was followed by a period of ominous calm. David found that Necoon had joined them. He was sitting slightly behind them as he always had done when it had been his responsibility to guard them.

"For a short time I was looking at myself from a distance," he said. His eyes dropped to Alex's groin. "I think you understand this."

Alex shifted his position, studying the old slave.

"I have often felt that I am part of my master," Necoon said. "He speaks, I obey. Today when I killed him, Kat was no longer my master. There was a new master, not a man. Was it a spirit?"

Alex nodded, saying nothing.

"I don't think it was a spirit," Necoon went on. "It was myself watching from a distance."

"The distant self." Alex's tone was musing, reverent.

"They will take me to the village and kill me. That's of no importance. For a moment I had a new master and it was myself."

Lightning flashed and was followed almost instantly by a deafening crack of thunder. Wind tore at them, lifting their uncut hair and pointing it to sea. This is the last of it, David thought. It has to be. Hilunga, the Thunderbird, is tired. The wind spirits are tired. Tomorrow will be a good day and we'll begin the journey south.

"Have you been north of the country of the Tsimshians?" Alex asked Necoon.

"Many times. I have raided many villages."

"I've heard of Haida villages on the mainland, far to the north of these islands."

"Kaigani Haida," Necoon said. "I have been there."

"It's a long journey?"

"A few days. But dangerous, very dangerous."

There was another blinding flash and the roar of thunder. Rain struck in wind-driven sheets. David got to his feet. He was very tired. He held out a hand to Alex, who shook his head. Necoon, too, was content to stay. David raced for shelter, leaving the pair of them in the drenching rain.

He snuggled into his blanket. After a time, Tsil-tsil came. She put the baby into his cradleboard and laid him in his sleeping place. She sat down beside David. He pulled her down beside him and they snuggled together in the blanket.

The wind drew violent. He woke several times, thinking the shelter would blow down on them. Then there were shouts in the wind, men crawling out of the shelter. Skow bent over him, yelling at him. David crawled into the angry night and stumbled after him to the shore.

The canoe was sixty yards out, angling into great breaking waves that threatened to flip it over like a toy. It was the small canoe in which they had escaped from the village. Its mast was up, crossed by the mat sail, which was unrolled a foot or two.

"Alex," Skow yelled in David's ear. "Necoon. They are both crazy."

How they had launched the craft was a mystery. David cupped hands to mouth and laid useless words on the wind. A lightning flash gave him a chalky glimpse of Necoon in the stern, Alex a bit forward, both paddling furiously. He called to strike the mast, to come back. The words were lost.

The craft was lost in surging darkness, then it appeared again, moving fast, caught by the wind. It caught a mountainous wave, was swallowed, and then another lightning flash gave him his last look at it, still afloat. It seemed to him that the sail was fully unrolled now, but he couldn't be sure. If it was, they were certain to capsize within the next minute.

He spent the next several hours walking in the storm with Skow, circling the island several times. There was no point to this, no chance that the canoe could circle back and land, no chance that, swamped, it would wash ashore here. With wind and tide as they were, it might eventually turn up on some desolate beach far to the north on the mainland. Or perhaps, given the right change of wind, it would be swept north of the Charlottes and westward into the infinity of the Pacific. think they could get to? Were they so crazy as to have hope of reaching shore somewhere?

"They had hope," David said.

They built up a fire and sat in its heat until they fell asleep. At first frail light the rain had stopped and there was less anger in the wind. A few fading stars showed in the darkness to the west.

David went to the shore and sat where he had last been with Alex and Necoon. The world lightened. The shoreline of the island to the west came into sight. Show came to say that he would go back to the village in Kat's canoe. He would leave his own and a crew to take David and Tsil-tsil home. He made his joke about coming south and taking David prisoner all over again.

"Ho!" David said. "Next time I'll blow your head off."

Skow laughed and left him. Tsil-tsil came with Watserh on her back. David took him out of his cradleboard and held him in his arms. After a while Pahl came, smiling shyly, and sat with them. No one had anything to say, and they watched the sea. It still churned, but it would calm down now. Hilunga was tired.

The Biggest, Boldest, Fastest-Selling Titles in Western Adventure!

★★★★★★★★★★★★★★★★★★

CHARTER'S MOST WANTED LIST

Frank Bonham
__07876-1 BREAK FOR THE BORDER $2.50
__77596-9 SOUND OF GUNFIRE $2.50

Giles A. Lutz
__34286-8 THE HONYOCKER $2.50
__88852-6 THE WILD QUARRY $2.50

Will C. Knott
__29758-7 THE GOLDEN MOUNTAIN $2.25
__71146-4 RED SKIES OVER WYOMING $2.25

Benjamin Capps
__74920-8 SAM CHANCE $2.50
__82139-1 THE TRAIL TO OGALLALA $2.50
__88549-7 THE WHITE MAN'S ROAD $2.50

Blazing heroic adventures
of the gunfighters of the WILD WEST
by Spur Award-winning author

LEWIS B. PATTEN

_____ **GIANT ON HORSEBACK**	0-441-28816-2/$2.50
_____ **THE GUN OF JESSE HAND**	0-441-30797-3/$2.50
_____ **THE RUTHLESS RANGE**	0-441-74181-9/$2.50
_____ **THE STAR AND THE GUN**	0-441-77955-7/$2.50

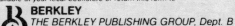